The Day of the Beast

by

Zane Grey

The Echo Library 2006

Published by

The Echo Library

Echo Library
131 High St.
Teddington
Middlesex TW11 8HH

www.echo-library.com

Please report serious faults in the text to complaints@echo-library.com

ISBN 1-40683-354-1

THE DAY OF THE BEAST

DEDICATION

Herein is embodied my tribute to the American men who gave themselves to the service in the great war, and my sleepless and eternal gratitude for what they did for me.

ZANE GREY.

THE DAY OF THE BEAST

CHAPTER I

His native land! Home!

The ship glided slowly up the Narrows; and from its deck Daren Lane saw the noble black outline of the Statue of Liberty limned against the clear gold of sunset. A familiar old pang in his breast—longing and homesickness and agony, together with the physical burn of gassed lungs—seemed to swell into a profound overwhelming emotion.

"My own—my native land!" he whispered, striving to wipe the dimness from his eyes. Was it only two years or twenty since he had left his country to go to war? A sense of strangeness dawned upon him. His home-coming, so ceaselessly dreamed of by night and longed for by day, was not going to be what his hopes had created. But at that moment his joy was too great to harbor strange misgivings. How impossible for any one to understand his feelings then, except perhaps the comrades who had survived the same ordeal!

The vessel glided on. A fresh cool spring breeze with a scent of land fanned Lane's hot brow. It bore tidings from home. Almost he thought he smelled the blossoms in the orchard, and the damp newly plowed earth, and the smoke from the wood fire his mother used to bake over. A hundred clamoring thoughts strove for dominance over his mind—to enter and flash by and fade. His sight, however, except for the blur that returned again and again, held fast to the entrancing and thrilling scene—the broad glimmering sun-track of gold in the rippling channel, leading his eye to the grand bulk of America's symbol of freedom, and to the stately expanse of the Hudson River, dotted by moving ferry-boats and tugs, and to the magnificent broken sky-line of New York City, with its huge dark structures looming and its thousands of windows reflecting the fire of the sun.

It was indeed a profound and stirring moment for Daren Lane, but not quite full, not all-satisfying. The great city seemed to frown. The low line of hills in the west shone dull gray and cold. Where were the screaming siren whistles, the gay streaming flags, the boats crowded with waving people, that should have welcomed disabled soldiers who had fought for their country? Lane hoped he had long passed by bitterness, but yet something rankled in the unhealed wound of his heart.

Some one put a hand in close clasp upon his arm. Then Lane heard the scrape of a crutch on the deck, and knew who stood beside him.

"Well, Dare, old boy, does it look good to you?" asked a husky voice.

"Yes, Blair, but somehow not just what I expected," replied Lane, turning to his comrade.

"Uhuh, I get you."

Blair Maynard stood erect with the aid of a crutch. There was even a hint of pride in the poise of his uncovered head. And for once Lane saw the thin white face softening and glowing. Maynard's big brown eyes were full of tears.

"Guess I left my nerve as well as my leg over there," he said.

"Blair, it's so good to get back that we're off color," returned Lane. "On the level, I could scream like a madman."

"I'd like to weep," replied the other, with a half laugh.

"Where's Red? He oughtn't miss this."

"Poor devil! He sneaked off from me somewhere," rejoined Maynard. "Red's in pretty bad shape again. The voyage has been hard on him. I hope he'll be well enough to get his discharge when we land. I'll take him home to Middleville."

"Middleville!" echoed Lane, musingly. "Home!... Blair, does it hit you—kind of queer? Do you long, yet dread to get home?"

Maynard had no reply for that query, but his look was expressive.

"I've not heard from Helen for over a year," went on Lane, more as if speaking to himself.

"My God, Dare!" exclaimed his companion, with sudden fire. "Are you still thinking of her?"

"We—we are engaged," returned Lane, slowly. "At least we *were*. But I've had no word that she——"

"Dare, your childlike faith is due for a jar," interrupted his comrade, with bitter scorn. "Come down to earth. You're a crippled soldier—coming home—and damn lucky at that."

"Blair, what do you know—that I do not know? For long I've suspected you're wise to—to things at home. You know I haven't heard much in all these long months. My mother wrote but seldom. Lorna, my kid sister, forgot me, I guess.... Helen always was a poor correspondent. Dal answered my letters, but she never *told* me anything about home. When we first got to France I heard often from Margie Henderson and Mel Iden—crazy kind of letters—love-sick over soldiers.... But nothing for a long time now."

"At first they wrote! Ha! Ha!" burst out Maynard. "Sure, they wrote love-sick letters. They sent socks and cigarettes and candy and books. And they all wanted us to hurry back to marry them.... Then—when the months had gone by and the novelty had worn off—when we went against the hell of real war—sick or worn out, sleepless and miserable, crippled or half demented with terror and dread and longing for home—then, by God, they quit!"

"Oh, no, Blair—not all of them," remonstrated Lane, unsteadily.

"Well, old man, I'm sore, and you're about the only guy I can let out on," explained Maynard, heavily. "One thing I'm glad of—we'll face it together. Daren, we were kids together—do you remember?—playing on the commons—straddling the old water-gates over the brooks—stealing cider from the country presses—barefoot boys going to school together. We played Post-Office with the girls and Indians with the boys. We made puppy love to Dal and Mel and Helen and Margie—all of them.... Then, somehow the happy thoughtless years of youth passed.... It seems strange and sudden now—but the war came. We enlisted. We had the same ideal—you and I.—We went to France—and you know what we did there together.... Now we're on this ship—getting into port of the good old U.S.—good as bad as she is!—going home together. Thank God for that. I want to be buried in Woodlawn.... Home! Home?... We feel its meaning. But, Dare, we'll have no home—no place.... We are old—we are through—we have served—we are done.... What we dreamed of as glory will be cold ashes to our lips, bitter as gall.... You always were a dreamer, an idealist, a believer in God, truth, hope and womanhood. In spite of the war these somehow survive in you.... But Dare, old friend, steel yourself now against disappointment and disillusion."

Used as Lane was to his comrade's outbursts, this one struck singularly home to Lane's heart and made him mute. The chill of his earlier misgiving returned, augmented by a strange uneasiness, a premonition of the unknown and dreadful future. But he threw it off. Faith would not die in Lane. It could not die utterly because of what he felt in himself. Yet—what was in store for him? Why was his hope so unquenchable? There could be no *resurgam* for Daren Lane. Resignation should have brought him peace—peace—when every nerve in his shell-shocked body racked him—when he could not subdue a mounting hope that all would be well at home—when he quivered at thought of mother, sister, sweetheart!

The ship glided on under the shadow of America's emblem—a bronze woman of noble proportions, holding out a light to ships that came in the night—a welcome to all the world. Daren Lane held to his maimed comrade while they stood bare-headed and erect for that moment when the, ship passed the statue. Lane knew what Blair felt. But nothing of what that feeling was could ever be spoken. The deck of the ship was now crowded with passengers, yet they were seemingly dead to anything more than a safe arrival at their destination. They were not crippled American soldiers. Except these two there were none in service uniforms. There across the windy space of water loomed the many-eyed buildings, suggestive of the great city. A low roar of traffic came on the breeze. Passengers and crew of the liner were glad to dock before dark. They took no notice of the rigid, erect soldiers. Lane, arm in arm with Blair, face to the front, stood absorbed in his sense of a nameless sublimity for them while passing the Statue of Liberty. The spirit of the first man who ever breathed of freedom for the human race burned as a white flame in the heart of Lane and his comrade. But it was not so much that spirit which held them erect, aloof, proud. It was a supreme consciousness of immeasurable sacrifice for an ideal that existed only in the breasts of men and women kindred to them—an unutterable and never-to-be-spoken glory of the duty done for others, but that they owed themselves. They had sustained immense loss of health and happiness; the future seemed like the gray, cold, gloomy expanse of the river; and there could never be any reward except this white fire of their souls. Nameless! But it was the increasing purpose that ran through the ages.

The ship docked at dark. Lane left Blair at the rail, gloomily gazing down at the confusion and bustle on the wharf, and went below to search for their comrade, Red Payson. He found him in his stateroom, half crouched on the berth, apparently oblivious to the important moment. It required a little effort to rouse Payson. He was a slight boy, not over twenty-two, sallow-faced and freckled, with hair that gave him the only name his comrades knew him by. Lane packed the boy's few possessions and talked vehemently all the time. Red braced up, ready to go, but he had little to say and that with the weary nonchalance habitual with him. Lane helped him up on deck, and the exertion, slight as it was, brought home to Lane that he needed help himself. They found Maynard waiting.

"Well, here we are—the Three Musketeers," said Lane, in a voice he tried to make cheerful.

"Where's the band?" inquired Maynard, sardonically.

"Gay old New York—and me broke!" exclaimed Red Payson, as if to himself.

Then the three stood by the rail, at the gangplank, waiting for the hurried stream of passengers to disembark. Down on the wharf under the glaring white lights, swarmed a crowd from which rose a babel of voices. A whistle blew sharply at intervals. The whirr and honk of taxicabs, and the jangle of trolley cars, sounded beyond the wide dark portal of the dock-house. The murky water below splashed between ship and pier. Deep voices rang out, and merry laughs, and shrill glad cries of welcome. The bright light shone down upon a motley, dark-garbed mass, moving slowly. The spirit of the occasion was manifest.

When the three disabled soldiers, the last passengers to disembark, slowly and laboriously descended to the wharf, no one offered to help them, no one waited with a smile and hand-clasp of welcome. No one saw them, except a burly policeman, who evidently had charge of the traffic at the door. He poked his club into the ribs of the one-legged, slowly shuffling Maynard and said with cheerful gruffness: "Step lively, Buddy, step lively!"

Lane, with his two comrades, spent three days at a barracks-hospital for soldiers in Bedford Park. It was a long flimsy structure, bare except for rows of cots along each wall, and stoves at middle, and each end. The place was overcrowded with disabled service men, all worse off than Lane and his comrades. Lane felt that he really was keeping a sicker man than himself from what attention the hospital afforded. So he was glad, at the end of the third day, to find they could be discharged from the army.

This enforced stay, when he knew he was on his way home, had seemed almost unbearable to Lane. He felt that he had the strength to get home, and that was about all. He began to expectorate blood—no unusual thing for him—but this time to such extent that he feared the return of hemorrhage. The nights seemed sleepless, burning, black voids; and the days were hideous with noise and distraction. He wanted to think about the fact that he was home—an astounding and unbelievable thing. Once he went down to the city and walked on Broadway and Fifth Avenue, taxing his endurance to the limit. But he had become used to pain and exhaustion. So long as he could keep up he did not mind.

That day three powerful impressions were forced upon Lane, never to be effaced. First he found that the change in him was vast and incalculable and vague. He could divine but not understand. Secondly, the men of the service, disabled or not, were old stories to New Yorkers. Lane saw soldiers begging from pedestrians. He muttered to himself: "By God, I'll starve to death before I ever do that!" He could not detect any aloofness on the part of passers-by. They were just inattentive. Lane remembered with sudden shock how differently soldiers had been regarded two or three years ago. He had read lengthy newspaper accounts of the wild and magnificent welcome accorded to the first soldiers to return to New York. How strange the contrast! But that was long ago—past history—buried under the immense and hurried and inscrutable changes of a nation. Lane divined that, as he felt the mighty resistless throb of the great city. His third and strongest impression concerned the women he met and passed on the streets. Their lips and cheeks were rouged. Their dresses were cut too low at the neck. But even this fashion was not nearly so striking as the short skirts, cut off at the knees, and in many cases above. At first this roused a strange amaze in Lane. "What's the idea, I wonder?" he mused. But in the end it disgusted him. He reflected that for two swift years he had been out of the track of events, away from centers of population. Paris itself had held no attraction for him. Dreamer and brooder, he had failed to see the material things. But this third impression troubled him more than the other two and stirred thoughts he tried to dispel. Returning to the barracks he learned that he and his friends would be free on the morrow; and long into the night he rejoiced in the knowledge. Free! The grinding, incomprehensible Juggernaut and himself were at the parting of the ways. Before he went to sleep he remembered a forgotten prayer his mother had taught him. His ordeal was over. What had happened did not matter. The Hell was past and he must bury memory. Whether or not he had a month or a year to live it must be lived without memories of his ordeal.

Next day, at the railroad station, even at the moment of departure, Lane and Blair Maynard had their problem with Red Payson. He did not want to go to Blair's home.

"But hell, Red, you haven't any home—any place to go," blurted out Maynard.

So they argued with him, and implored him, and reasoned with him. Since his discharge from the hospital in France Payson had always been cool, weary, abstracted, difficult to reach. And here at the last he grew strangely aloof and stubborn. Every word that bore relation to his own welfare seemed only to alienate him the more. Lane sensed this.

"See here, Red," he said, "hasn't it occurred to you that Blair and I need you?"

"Need me? What!" he exclaimed, with perceptible change of tone, though it was incredulous.

"Sure," interposed Blair.

"Red—listen," continued Lane, speaking low and with difficulty. "Blair and I have been through the—the whole show together.... And we've been in the hospitals with you for months.... We've all got—sort of to rely on each other.... Let's stick it out to the end. I guess—you know—we may not have a long time...."

Lane's voice trailed off. Then the stony face of the listener changed for a fleeting second.

"Boys, I'll go over with you," he said.

And then the maimed Blair, awkward with his crutch and bag, insisted on helping Lane get Red aboard the train. Red could just about walk. Sombrely they clambered up the steps into the Pullman.

Middleville was a prosperous and thriving inland town of twenty thousand inhabitants, identical with many towns of about the same size in the middle and eastern United States.

Lane had been born there and had lived there all his life, seldom having been away up to the advent of the war. So that the memories of home and town and place, which he carried away from America with him, had never had any chance, up to the time of his departure, to change from the vivid, exaggerated image of boyhood. Since he had left Middleville he had seen great cities, palaces, castles, edifices, he had crossed great rivers, he had traveled thousands of miles, he had looked down some of the famous thoroughfares of the world.

Was this then the reason that Middleville, upon his arrival, seemed so strange, sordid, shrunken, so vastly changed? He stared, even while he helped Payson off the train—stared at the little brick station at once so familiar and yet so strange, that had held a place of dignity in the picture of his memory. The moment was one of shock.

Then he was distracted from his pondering by tearful and joyful cries, and deeper voices of men. He looked up to recognize Blair's mother, father, sister; and men and women whose faces appeared familiar, but whose names he could not recall. His acute faculty of perception took quick note of a change in Blair's mother. Lane turned his gaze away. The agony of joy and sorrow—the light of her face—was more than Lane could stand. He looked at the sister Margaret—a tall, fair girl. She had paint on her cheeks. She did not see Lane. Her strained gaze held a beautiful and piercing intentness. Then her eyes opened wide, her hand went to cover her mouth, and she cried out: "Oh Blair!— poor boy! Brother!"

Only Lane heard her. The others were crying out themselves as Blair's gray-haired mother received him into her arms. She seemed a proud woman, broken and unsteady. Red Payson's grip on Lane's arm told what that scene meant to him. How pitiful the vain effort of Blair's people to hide their horror! Presently mother and sister and women relatives fell aside to let the soldier boy meet his father. This was something that rang the bells in Lane's heart. Men were different, and Blair faced his father differently. The wild boy had come home—the scapegoat of many Middleville escapades had returned—the ne'er-do-well sought his father's house. He had come home to die. It was there in Blair's white face—the dreadful truth. He wore a ribbon on his breast and he leaned on a crutch. For the instant, as father and son faced each other, there was something in Blair's poise, his look of an eagle, that carried home a poignant sense of his greatness. Lane thrilled with it and a lump constricted his throat. Then with Blair's ringing "Dad!" and the father's deep and broken: "My son! My son!" the two embraced.

In a stifling moment more it seemed, attention turned on Red Payson, who stood nearest. Blair's folk were eager, kind, soft-spoken and warm in their welcome.

Then it came Lane's turn, and what they said or did he scarcely knew, until Margaret kissed him. "Oh, Dare! I'm *so* glad to see you home." Tears were standing in her clear blue eyes. "You're changed, but—not—not so much as Blair."

Lane responded as best he could, and presently he found himself standing at the curb, watching the car move away.

"Come out to-morrow," called back Blair.

The Maynard's car was carrying his comrades away. His first feeling was one of gladness—the next of relief. He could be alone now—alone to find out what had happened to him, and to this strange Middleville. An old negro wearing a blue uniform accosted Lane, shook hands with him, asked him if he had any baggage. "Yas sir, I sho knowed you, Mistah Dare Lane. But you looks powerful bad."

Lane crossed the station platform, and the railroad yard and tracks, to make a short cut in the direction of his home. He shrank from meeting any one. He had not sent word just when he would arrive, though he had written his mother from New York that it would be soon, He was glad that no one belonging to him had been at the station. He wanted to see his mother in his home. Walking fast exhausted him, and he had to rest. How dead his legs felt! In fact he felt queer all over. The old burn and gnaw in his breast had expanded to a heavy, full, suffocating sensation. Yet his blood seemed to race. Suddenly an overwhelming emotion of rapture flooded over him. Home at last! He did not think of any one. He was walking across the railroad yards where as a boy he had been wont to steal rides on freight trains. Soon he reached the bridge. In the gathering twilight he halted to clutch at the railing and look out across where the waters met— where Sycamore Creek flowed into Middleville River. The roar of water falling over the dam came melodiously and stirringly to his ears. And as he looked again he was assailed by that strange sense of littleness, of shrunkenness, which had struck him so forcibly at the station. He listened to the murmur of running water. Then, while the sweetness of joy pervaded him, there seemed to rise from below or across the river or from somewhere the same strange misgiving, a keener dread, a chill that was not in the air, a fatal portent of the future. Why should this come to mock him at such a sacred and beautiful moment?

Passers-by stared at Lane, and some of them whispered, and one hesitated, as if impelled to speak. Wheeling away Lane crossed the bridge, turned up River Street, soon turned off again into a darker street, and reaching High School Park he sat down to rest again. He was almost spent. The park was quiet and lonely. The bare trees showed their skeleton outlines against the cold sky. It was March and the air was raw and chilly. This park that had once been a wonderful place now appeared so small. Everything he saw was familiar yet grotesque in the way it had become dwarfed. Across the street from where he sat lights shone in the windows of a house. He knew the place. Who lived there? One of the girls—he had forgotten which. From somewhere the discordance of a Victrola jarred on Lane's sensitive ears.

Lifting his bag he proceeded on his way, halting every little while to catch his breath. When he turned a corner into a side street, recognizing every tree and gate and house, there came a gathering and swelling of his emotions and he began to weaken and shake. He was afraid he could not make it half way up the street. But he kept on. The torture now was more a mingled rapture and grief than the physical protest of his racked body. At last he saw the modest little house—and then he stood at the gate, quivering. Home! A light in the window of his old room! A terrible and tremendous storm of feeling forced him to lean on the gate. How many endless hours had the pictured memory of that house haunted him? There was the beloved room where he had lived and slept and read, and cherished over his books and over his compositions a secret hope and ambition to make of himself an author. How strange to remember that! But it was true. His day labor at Manton's office, for all the years since he had graduated from High School, had been only a means to an end. No one had dreamed of his dream. Then the war had come and now his hope, if not his faith, was dead. Never before had the realization been so galling, so bitter. Endlessly and eternally he must be concerned with himself. He had driven that habit of thought away a million times, but it would return. All he had prayed for was to get home—only to reach home alive—to see his mother, and his sister Lorna—and Helen—and then.... But he was here now and all that prayer was falsehood. Just to get home was not enough.. He had been cheated of career, love, happiness.

It required extreme effort to cross the little yard, to mount the porch. In a moment more he would see his mother. He heard her within, somewhere at the back of the house. Wherefore he tip-toed round to the kitchen door. Here he paused, quaking. A cold sweat broke out all over him. Why was this return so dreadful? He pressed a shaking hand over his heart. How surely he knew he could not deceive his mother! The moment she saw him, after the first flash of joy, she would see the wreck of the boy she had let go to war. Lane choked over his emotion, but he could not spare her. Opening the door he entered.

There she stood at the stove and she looked up at the sound he made. Yes! but stranger than all other changes was the change in her. She was not the mother of his boyhood. Nor was the change alone age or grief or wasted cheek. The moment tore cruelly at Lane's heart. She did not recognize him swiftly. But when she did....

"Oh God!... Daren! My boy!" she whispered.

"Mother!"

CHAPTER II

His mother divined what he knew. And her embrace was so close, almost fierce in its tenderness, her voice so broken, that Lane could only hide his face over her, and shut his eyes, and shudder in an ecstasy. God alone had omniscience to tell what his soul needed, but something of it was embodied in home and mother.

That first acute moment past, he released her, and she clung to his hands, her face upturned, her eyes full of pain and joy, and woman's searching power, while she broke into almost incoherent speech; and he responded in feeling, though he caught little of the content of her words, and scarcely knew what he was saying.

Then he reeled a little and the kitchen dimmed in his sight. Sinking into a chair and leaning on the table he fought his weakness. He came close to fainting. But he held on to his sense, aware of his mother fluttering over him. Gradually the spell passed.

"Mother—maybe I'm starved," he said, smiling at her.

That practical speech released the strain and inspired his mother to action. She began to bustle round the kitchen, talking all the while. Lane watched her and listened, and spoke occasionally. Once he asked about his sister Lorna, but his mother either did not hear or chose not to reply. All she said was music to his ears, yet not quite what his heart longed for. He began to distrust this strange longing. There was something wrong with his mind. His faculties seemed too sensitive. Every word his mother uttered was news, surprising, unusual, as if it emanated from a home-world that had changed. And presently she dropped into complaint at the hard times and the cost of everything.

"Mother," he interrupted, "I didn't blow my money. I've saved nearly a year's pay. It's yours."

"But, Daren, you'll need money," she protested.

"Not much. And maybe—I'll be strong enough to go to work—presently," he said, hopefully. "Do you think Manton will take me back—half days at first?"

"I have my doubts, Daren," she replied, soberly. "Hattie Wilson has your old job. And I hear they're pleased with her. Few of the boys got their places back."

"Hattie Wilson!" exclaimed Lane. "Why, she was a kid in the eighth grade when I left home."

"Yes, my son. But that was nearly three years ago. And the children have sprung up like weeds. Wild weeds!"

"Well! That tousle-headed Wilson kid!" mused Lane. An uneasy conviction of having been forgotten dawned upon Lane. He remembered Blair Maynard's bitter prophecy, which he had been unable to accept.

"Anyway, Daren, are you able to work?" asked his mother.

"Sure," he replied, lying cheerfully, with a smile on his face. "Not hard work, just yet, but I can do something."

His mother did not share his enthusiasm. She went on preparing the supper.

"How do you manage to get along?" inquired Lane.

"Lord only knows," she replied, sombrely. "It has been very hard. When you left home I had only the interest on your father's life insurance. I sold the farm—"

"Oh, no!" exclaimed Lane, with a rush of boyhood memories.

"I had to," she went on. "I made that money help out for a long time. Then I—I mortgaged this place.... Things cost so terribly. And Lorna had to have so much more.... But she's just left school and gone to work. That helps."

"Lorna left school!" ejaculated Lane, incredulously. "Why, mother, she was only a child. Thirteen years old when I left! She'll miss her education. I'll send her back."

"Well, son, I doubt if you can make Lorna do anything she doesn't want to do," returned his mother. "She wanted to quit school—to earn money. Whatever she was when you left home she's grown up now. You'll not know her."

"Know Lorna! Why, mother dear, I carried Lorna's picture all through the war."

"You won't know her," returned Mrs. Lane, positively. "My boy, these years so short to you have been ages here at home. You will find your sister—different from the little girl you left. You'll find all the girls you knew changed—changed. I have given up trying to understand what's come over the world."

"How—about Helen?" inquired Lane, with strange reluctance and shyness.

"Helen who?" asked his mother.

"Helen Wrapp, of course," replied Lane, quickly in his surprise. "The girl I was engaged to when I left."

"Oh!—I had forgotten," she sighed.

"Hasn't Helen been here to see you?"

"Let me see—well, now you tax me—I think she did come once—right after you left."

"Do you—ever see her?" he asked, with slow heave of breast.

"Yes, now and then, as she rides by in an automobile. But she never sees me.... Daren, I don't know what your—your—that engagement means to you, but I must tell you—Helen Wrapp doesn't conduct herself as if she were engaged. Still, I don't know what's in the heads of girls to-day. I can only compare the present with the past."

Lane did not inquire further and his mother did not offer more comment. At the moment he heard a motor car out in front of the house, a girl's shrill voice in laughter, the slamming of a car-door—then light, quick footsteps on the porch. Lane could look from where he sat to the front door—only a few yards down the short hall. The door opened. A girl entered.

"That's Lorna," said Lane's mother. He grew aware that she bent a curious gaze upon his face.

Lane rose to his feet with his heart pounding, and a strange sense of expectancy. His little sister! Never during the endless months of drudgery, strife and conflict, and agony, had he forgotten Lorna. Not duty, nor patriotism, had forced him to enlist in the army before the draft. It had been an ideal which he imagined he shared with the millions of American boys who entered the service. Too deep ever to be spoken of! The barbarous and simian Hun, with his black record against Belgian, and French women, should never set foot on American soil.

In the lamplight Lane saw this sister throw coat and hat on the banister, come down the hall and enter the kitchen. She seemed tall, but her short skirt counteracted that effect. Her bobbed hair, curly and rebellious, of a rich brown-red color, framed a pretty face Lane surely remembered. But yet not the same! He had carried away memory of a child's face and this was a woman's. It was bright, piquant, with darkly glancing eyes, and vivid cheeks, and carmine lips.

"Oh, *hot dog!* if it isn't Dare!" she squealed, and with radiant look she ran into his arms.

The moment, or moments, of that meeting between brother and sister passed, leaving Lane conscious of hearty welcome and a sense of unreality. He could not at once adjust his mental faculties to an incomprehensible difference affecting everything.

They sat down to supper, and Lane, sick, dazed, weak, found eating his first meal at home as different as everything else from what he had expected. There had been no lack of warmth or love in Lorna's welcome, but he suffered disappointment. Again for the hundredth time he put it aside and blamed his morbid condition. Nothing must inhibit his gladness.

Lorna gave Lane no chance to question her. She was eager, voluble, curious, and most disconcertingly oblivious of a possible sensitiveness in Lane.

"Dare, you look like a dead one," she said. "Did you get shot, bayoneted, gassed, shell-shocked and all the rest? Did you go over the top? Did you kill any Germans? Gee! did you get to ride in a war-plane? Come across, now, and tell me."

"I guess about—everything happened to me—except going west," returned Lane. "But I don't want to talk about that. I'm too glad to be home."

"What's that on your breast?" she queried, suddenly, pointing at the *Croix de Guerre* he wore.

"That? Lorna, that's my medal."

"Gee! Let me see." She got up and came round to peer down closely, to finger the decoration. "French! I never saw one before.... Daren, haven't you an American medal too?"

"No."

"Why not?"

"My dear sister, that's hard to say. Because I didn't deserve it, most likely."

She leaned back to gaze more thoughtfully at him.

"What did you get this for?"

"It's a long story. Some day I'll tell you."

"Are you proud of it?"

For answer he only smiled at her.

"It's so long since the war I've forgotten so many things," she said, wonderingly. Then she smiled sweetly. "Dare, I'm proud of you."

That was a moment in which his former emotion seemed to stir for her. Evidently she had lost track of something once memorable. She was groping back for childish impressions. It was the only indication of softness he had felt in her. How impossible to believe Lorna was only fifteen! He could form no permanent conception of her. But in that moment he sensed something akin to a sister's sympathy, some vague and indefinable thought in her, too big for her to grasp. He never felt it again. The serious sweet mood vanished.

"Hot dog! I've a brother with the *Croix de Guerre*. I'll swell up over that. I'll crow over some of these Janes."

Thus she talked on while eating her supper. And Lane tried to eat while he watched her. Presently he moved his chair near to the stove. Lorna did not wait upon her mother. It was the mother who did the waiting, as silently she moved from table to stove.

Lorna's waist was cut so low that it showed the swell of her breast. The red color of her cheeks, high up near her temples, was not altogether the rosy line of health and youth. Her eyebrows were only faint, thin, curved lines, oriental in effect. She appeared to be unusually well-developed in body for so young a girl. And the air of sophistication, of experience that seemed a part of her manner completely mystified Lane. If it had not been for the slangy speech, and the false color in her face, he would have been amused at what he might have termed his little sister's posing as a woman of the world. But in the light of these he grew doubtful of his impression. Lastly, he saw that she wore her stockings rolled below her knees and that the edge of her short skirt permitted several inches of her bare legs to be seen. And at that he did not know what to think. He was stunned.

"Daren, you served a while under Captain Thesel in the war," she said.

"Yes, I guess I did," replied Lane, with sombre memory resurging.

"Do you know he lives here?"

"I knew him here in Middleville several years before the war."

"He's danced with me at the Armory. Some swell dancer! He and Dick Swann and Hardy MacLean sometimes drop in at the Armory on Saturday nights. Captain Thesel is chasing Mrs. Clemhorn now. They're always together.... Daren, did he ever have it in for you?"

"He never liked me. We never got along here in Middleville. And naturally in the service when he was a captain and I only a private—we didn't get along any better."

"Well, I've heard Captain Thesel was to blame for—for what was said about you last summer when he came home."

"And what was that, Lorna?" queried Lane, curiously puzzled at her, and darkly conscious of the ill omen that had preceded him home.

"You'll not hear it from me," declared Lorna, spiritedly. "But that *Croix de Guerre* doesn't agree with it, I'll tell the world."

A little frown puckered her smooth brow and there was a gleam in her eye.

"Seems to me I heard some of the kids talking last summer," she mused, ponderingly. "Vane Thesel was stuck on Mel Iden and Dot Dalrymple both before the war. Dot handed him a lemon. He's still trying to rush Dot, and the gossip is he'd go after Mel even now on the sly, if she'd stand for it."

"Why on the sly?" inquired Lane. "Before I left home Mel Iden was about the prettiest and most popular girl in Middleville. Her people were poor, and ordinary, perhaps, but she was the equal of any one."

"Thesel couldn't rush Mel now and get away with it, unless on the q-t," replied Lorna. "Haven't you heard about Mel?"

"No, you see the fact is, my few correspondents rather neglected to send me news," said Lane.

The significance of this was lost upon his sister. She giggled. "Hot dog! You've got some kicks coming, I'll say!"

"Is that so," returned Lane, with irritation. "A few more or less won't matter.... Lorna, do you know Helen Wrapp?"

"That red-headed dame!" burst out Lorna, with heat. "I should smile I do. She's one who doesn't shake a shimmy on tea, believe me."

Lane was somewhat at a loss to understand his sister's intimation, but as it was vulgarly inimical, and seemed to hold some subtle personal scorn or jealousy, he shrank from questioning her. This talk with his sister was the most unreal happening he had ever experienced. He could not adjust himself to its verity.

"Helen Wrapp is nutty about Dick Swann," went on Lorna. "She drives down to the office after——"

"Lorna, do you know Helen and I are engaged?" interrupted Lane.

"Hot dog!" was that young lady's exposition of utter amaze. She stared at her brother.

"We were engaged," continued Lane. "She wore my ring. When I enlisted she wanted me to marry her before I left. But I wouldn't do that."

Lorna promptly recovered from her amaze. "Well, it's a damn lucky thing you didn't take her up on that marriage stuff."

There was a glint of dark youthful passion in Lorna's face. Lane felt rise in him a desire to bid her sharply to omit slang and profanity from the conversation. But the desire faded before his bewilderment. All had suffered change. What had he come home to? There was no clear answer. But whatever it was, he felt it to be enormous and staggering. And he meant to find out. Weary as was his mind, it grasped peculiar significances and deep portents.

"Lorna, where do you work?" he began, shifting his interest.

"At Swann's," she replied.

"In the office—at the foundry?" he asked.

"No. Mr. Swann's at the head of the leather works."

"What do you do?"

"I type letters," she answered, and rose to make him a little bow that held the movement and the suggestion of a dancer.

"You've learned stenography?" he asked, in surprise.

"I'm learning shorthand," replied Lorna. "You see I had only a few weeks in business school before Dick got me the job."

"Dick Swann? Do you work for him?"

"No. For the superintendent, Mr. Fryer. But I go to Dick's office to do letters for him some of the time."

She appeared frank and nonchalant, evidently a little proud of her important position. She posed before Lane and pirouetted with fancy little steps.

"Say, Dare, won't you teach me a new dance—right from Paris?" she interposed. "Something that will put the shimmy and toddle out of biz?"

"Lorna, I don't know what the shimmy and toddle are. I've only heard of them."

"Buried alive, I'll say," she retorted.

Lane bit his tongue to keep back a hot reprimand. He looked at his mother, who was clearing off the supper table. She looked sad. The light had left her worn face. Lane did not feel sure of his ground here. So he controlled his feelings and directed his interest toward more news.

"Of course Dick Swann was in the service?" he asked.

"No. He didn't go," replied Lorna.

The information struck Lane singularly. Dick Swann had always been a prominent figure in the Middleville battery, in those seemingly long past years since before the war.

"Why didn't Dick go into the service? Why didn't the draft get him?"

"He had poor eyesight, and his father needed him at the iron works."

"Poor eyesight!" ejaculated Lane. "He was the best shot in the battery—the best hunter among the boys. Well, that's funny."

"Daren, there are people who called Dick Swann a slacker," returned Lorna, as if forced to give this information. "But I never saw that it hurt him. He's rich now. His uncle left him a million, and his father will leave him another. And I'll say it's the money people want these days."

The materialism so pregnant in Lorna's half bitter reply checked Lane's further questioning. He edged closer to the stove, feeling a little cold. A shadow drifted across the warmth and glow of his mind. At home now he was to be confronted with a monstrous and insupportable truth—the craven cowardice of the man who had been eligible to service in army or navy, and who had evaded it. In camp and trench and dug-out he had heard of the army of slackers. And of all the vile and stark profanity which the war gave birth to on the lips of miserable and maimed soldiers, that flung on the slackers was the worst.

"I've got a date to go to the movies," said Lorna, and she bounced out of the kitchen into the hall singing:

"Oh by heck
You never saw a wreck
Like the wreck she made of me."

She went upstairs, while Lane sat there trying to adapt himself to a new and unintelligible environment. His mother began washing the dishes. Lane felt her gaze upon his face, and he struggled against all the weaknesses that beset him.

"Mother, doesn't Lorna help you with the house work?" he asked.

"She used to. But not any more."

"Do you let her go out at night to the movies—dances, and all that?"

Mrs. Lane made a gesture of helplessness. "Lorna goes out all the time. She's never here. She stays out until midnight—one o'clock—later. She's popular with the boys. I couldn't stop her even if I wanted to. Girls can't be stopped these days. I do all I can for her—make her dresses—slave for her—hoping she'll find a good husband. But the young men are not marrying."

"Good Heavens, are you already looking for a husband for Lorna?" broke out Lane.

"You don't understand, Dare. You've been away so long. Wait till you've seen what girls—are nowadays. Then you'll not wonder that I'd like to see Lorna settled."

"Mother, you're right," he said, gravely. "I've been away so—long. But I'm back home now. I'll soon get on to things. And I'll help you. I'll take Lorna in hand. I'll relieve you of a whole lot."

"You were always a good boy, Daren, to me and Lorna," murmured Mrs. Lane, almost in tears. "It's cheered me to get you home, yet.... Oh, if you were well and strong!"

"Never mind, mother. I'll get better," he replied, rising to take up his bag. "I guess now I'd better go to bed. I'm just about all in.... Wonder how Blair and Red are."

His mother followed him up the narrow stairway, talking, trying to pretend she did not see his dragging steps, his clutch on the banisters.

"Your room's just as you left it," she said, opening the door. Then on the threshold she kissed him. "My son, I thank God you have come home alive. You give me hope in—in spite of all.... If you need me, call. Good night."

Lane was alone in the little room that had lived in waking and dreaming thought. Except to appear strangely smaller, it had not changed. His bed and desk—the old bureau—the few pictures—the bookcase he had built himself—these were identical with images in his memory.

A sweet and wonderful emotion of peace pervaded his soul—fulfilment at last of the soldier's endless longing for home, bed, quiet, rest.

"If I have to die—I can do it *now* without hate of all around me," he whispered, in the passion of his spirit.

But as he sat upon his bed, trying with shaking and clumsy hands to undress himself, that exalted mood flashed by. Some of the dearest memories of his life were associated with this little room. Here he had dreamed; here he had read and studied; here he had fought out some of the poignant battles of youth. So much of life seemed behind him. At last he got undressed, and extinguishing the light, he crawled into bed.

The darkness was welcome, and the quiet was exquisitely soothing. He lay there, staring into the blackness, feeling his body sink slowly as if weighted. How cool and soft the touch of sheets! Then, the river of throbbing fire that was his blood, seemed to move again. And the dull ache, deep in the bones, possessed his nerves. In his breast there began a vibrating, as if thousands of tiny bubbles were being pricked to bursting in his lungs. And the itch to cough came back to his throat. And all his flesh seemed in contention with a slowly ebbing force. Sleep might come perhaps after pain had lulled. His heart beat unsteadily and weakly, sometimes with a strange little flutter. How many weary interminable hours had he endured! But to-night he was too far spent, too far gone for long wakefulness. He drifted away and sank as if into black oblivion where there sounded the dreadful roll of drums, and images moved under gray clouds, and men were running like phantoms. He awoke from nightmares, wet with cold sweat, and lay staring again at the blackness, once more alive to recurrent pain. Pain that was an old, old story, yet ever acute and insistent and merciless.

The night wore on, hour by hour. The courthouse clock rang out one single deep mellow clang. One o'clock! Lane thrilled to the sound. It brought back the school days, the vacation days, the Indian summer days when the hills were golden and the purple haze hung over the land—the days that were to be no more for Daren Lane.

In the distance somewhere a motor-car hummed, and came closer, louder down the street, to slow its sound with sliding creak and jar outside in front of the house. Lane heard laughter and voices of a party of young people. Footsteps, heavy and light, came up the walk, and on to the porch. Lorna was returning rather late from the motion-picture, thought Lane, and he raised his head from the pillow, to lean toward the open window, listening.

"Come across, kiddo," said a boy's voice, husky and low.

Lane heard a kiss—then another.

"Cheese it, you boob!"

"Gee, your gettin' snippy. Say, will you ride out to Flesher's to-morrow night?"

"Nothing doing, I've got a date. Good night."

The hall door below opened and shut. Footsteps thumped off the porch and out to the street. Lane heard the giggle of girls, the snap of a car-door, the creaking of wheels, and then a low hum, dying away.

Lorna came slowly up stairs to enter her room, moving quietly. And Lane lay on his bed, wide-eyed, staring into the blackness. "My little sister," he whispered to himself. And the words that had meant so much seemed a mockery.

CHAPTER III

Lane saw the casement of his window grow gray with the glimmering light of dawn. After that he slept several hours. When he awoke it was nine o'clock. The long night with its morbid dreams and thoughts had passed, and in the sunshine of day he saw things differently.

To move, to get up was not an easy task. It took stern will, and all the strength of muscle he had left, and when he finally achieved it there was a clammy dew of pain upon his face. With slow guarded movements he began to dress himself. Any sudden or violent action might burst the delicate gassed spots in his lungs or throw out of place one of the lower vertebrae of his spine. The former meant death, and the latter bent his body like a letter S and caused such excruciating agony that it was worse than death. These were his two ever-present perils. The other aches and pains he could endure.

He shaved and put on clean things, and his best coat, and surveyed himself in the little mirror. He saw a thin face, white as marble, but he was not ashamed of it. His story was there to read, if any one had kind enough eyes to see. What would Helen think of him—and Margaret Maynard—and Dal—and Mel Iden? Bitter curiosity seemed his strongest feeling concerning his fiancee. He would hold her as engaged to him until she informed him she was not. As for the others, thought of them quickened his interest, especially in Mel. What had happened to her.

It was going to be wonderful to meet them—and to meet everybody he had once known. Wonderful because he would see what the war had done to them and they would see what it had done to him. A peculiar significance lay between his sister and Helen—all these girls, and the fact of his having gone to war.

"They may not think of it, but *I know*," he muttered to himself. And he sat down upon his bed to plan how best to meet them, and others. He did not know what he was going to encounter, but he fortified himself against calamity. Strange portent of this had crossed the sea to haunt him. As soon as he was sure of what had happened in Middleville, of the attitude people would have toward a crippled soldier, and of what he could do with the month or year that might be left him to live, then he would know his own mind. All he sensed now was that there had been some monstrous inexplicable alteration in hope, love, life. His ordeal of physical strife, loneliness, longing was now over, for he was back home. But he divined that his greater ordeal lay before him, here in this little house, and out there in Middleville. All the subtlety, intelligence, and bitter vision developed by the war sharpened here to confront him with terrible possibilities. Had his countrymen, his people, his friends, his sweetheart, all failed him? Was there justice in Blair Maynard's scorn? Lane's faith cried out in revolt. He augmented all possible catastrophe, and then could not believe that he had sacrificed himself in vain. He knew himself. In him was embodied all the potentiality for hope of the future. And it was with the front and stride of a soldier, facing the mystery, the ingratitude, the ignorance and hell of war, that he left his room and went down stairs to meet the evils in store.

His mother was not in the kitchen. The door stood open. He heard her outside talking to a neighbor woman, over the fence.

"—Daren looks dreadful," his mother was saying in low voice. "He could hardly walk.... It breaks my heart. I'm glad to have him along—but to see him waste away, day by day, like Mary Dean's boy—" she broke off.

"Too bad! It's a pity," replied the neighbor. "Sad—now it comes home to us. My son Ted came in last night and said he'd talked with a boy who'd seen young Maynard and the strange soldier who was with him. They must be worse off than Daren—Blair Maynard with only one leg and—"

"Mother, where are you? I'm hungry," called Lane, interrupting that conversation.

She came hurriedly in, at once fearful he might have heard, and solicitous for his welfare.

"Daren, you look better in daylight—not so white," she said. "You sit down now, and let me get your breakfast."

Lane managed to eat a little this morning, which fact delighted his mother.

"I'm going to see Dr. Bronson," said Lane, presently. "Then I'll go to Manton's, and round town a little. And if I don't tire out I'll call on Helen. Of course Lorna has gone to work?"

"Oh yes, she leaves at half after eight."

"Mother, I was awake last night when she got home," went on Lane, seriously. "It was one o'clock. She came in a car. I heard girls tittering. And some boy came up on the porch with Lorna and kissed her. Well, that might not mean much—but something about their talk, the way it was done—makes me pretty sick. Did you know this sort of thing was going on?"

"Yes. And I've talked with mothers who have girls Lorna's age. They've all run wild the last year or so. Dances and rides! Last summer I was worried half to death. But we mothers don't think the girls are really *bad*. They're just crazy for fun, excitement, boys. Times and pleasures have changed. The girls say the mothers don't understand. Maybe we don't. I try to be patient. I trust Lorna. I can't see through it all."

"Don't worry, mother," said Lane, patting her hand. "I'll see through it for you. And if Lorna is—well, running too much—wild as you said—I'll stop her."

His mother shook her head.

"One thing we mothers all agree on. These girls, of this generation, say fourteen to sixteen, *can't* be stopped."

"Then that is a serious matter. It must be a peculiarity of the day. Maybe the war left this condition."

"The war changed all things, my son," replied his mother, sadly.

Lane walked thoughtfully down the street toward Doctor Bronson's office. As long as he walked slowly he managed not to give any hint of his weakness. The sun was shining with steely brightness and the March wind was living up to its fame. He longed for summer and hot days in quiet woods or fields where daisies bloomed. Would he live to see the Indian summer days, the smoky haze, the purple asters?

Lane was admitted at once into the office of Doctor Bronson, a little, gray, slight man with shrewd, kind eyes and a thoughtful brow. For years he had been a friend as well as physician to the Lanes, and he had always liked Daren. His surprise was great and his welcome warm. But a moment later he gazed at Lane with piercing eyes.

"Look here, boy, did you go to the bad over there?" he demanded.

"How do you mean, Doctor?"

"Did you let down—debase yourself morally?"

"No. But I went to the bad physically and spiritually."

"I see that. I don't like the color of your face.... Well, well, Daren. It was hell, wasn't it? Did you kill a couple of Huns for me?"

Questions like this latter one always alienated Lane in some unaccountable way. It must have been revealed in his face.

"Never mind, Daren. I see that you *did*.... I'm glad you're back alive. Now what can I do for you?"

"I've been discharged from three hospitals in the last two months—not because I was well, but because I was in better shape than some other poor devil. Those doctors in the service grew hard—they had to be hard—but they saw the worst, the agony of the war. I always felt sorry for them. They never seemed to eat or sleep or rest. They had no time to save a man. It was cut him up or tie him up—then on to the next.... Now, Doc, I want you to look me over and—well—tell me what to expect."

"All right," replied Doctor Bronson, gruffly.

"And I want you to promise not to tell mother or any one. Will you?"

"Yes, I promise. Now come in here and get off some of your clothes."

"Doctor, it's pretty tough on me to get in and out of my clothes."

"I'll help you. Now tell me what the Germans did to you."

Lane laughed grimly. "Doctor, do you remember I was in your Sunday School class?"

"Yes, I remember that. What's it got to do with Germans?"

"Nothing. It struck me funny, that's all.... Well, to get it over. I was injured several times at the training camp."

"Anything serious?"

"No, I guess not. Anyway I forgot about *them*. Doctor, I was shot four times, once clear through. I'll show you. Got a bad bayonet jab that doesn't seem to heal well. Then I had a dose of both gases—chlorine and mustard—and both all but killed me. Last I've a weak place in my spine. There's a vertebra that slips out of place occasionally. The least movement may do it. I *can't* guard against it. The last time it slipped out I was washing my teeth. I'm in mortal dread of this. For it twists me out of shape and hurts horribly. I'm afraid it'll give me paralysis."

"Humph! It would. But it can be fixed.... So that's all they did to you?"

Underneath the dry humor of the little doctor, Lane thought he detected something akin to anger.

"Yes, that's all they did to my body," replied Lane.

Doctor Bronson, during a careful and thorough examination of Lane's heart, lungs, blood pressure, and abdominal region, did not speak once. But when he turned him over, to see and feel the hole in Lane's back, he exclaimed: "My God, boy, what made this—a shell? I can put my fist in it."

"That's the bayonet jab."

Doctor Bronson cursed in a most undignified and unprofessional manner. Then without further comment he went on and completed the examination.

"That'll do," he said, and lent a hand while Lane put on his clothes. It was then he noticed Lane's medal.

"Ha! The *Croix de Guerre!*... Daren, I was a friend of your father's. I *know* how that medal would have made him feel. Tell me what you did to get it?"

"Nothing much," replied Lane, stirred. "It was in the Argonne, when we took to open fighting. In fact I got most of my hurts there.... I carried a badly wounded French officer back off the field. He was a heavy man. That's where I injured my spine. I had to run with him. And worse luck, he was dead when I got him back. But I didn't know that."

"So the French decorated you, hey?" asked the doctor, leaning back with hands on hips, and keenly eyeing Lane.

"Yes."

"Why did not the American Army give you equal honor?"

"Well, for one thing it was never reported. And besides, it wasn't anything any other fellow wouldn't do."

Doctor Bronson dropped his head and paced to and fro. Then the door-bell rang in the reception room.

"Daren Lane," began the doctor, suddenly stopping before Lane, "I'd hesitate to ask most men if they wanted the truth. To many men I'd lie. But I know a few words from me can't faze you."

"No, Doctor, one way or another it is all the same to me."

"Well, boy, I can fix up that vertebra so it won't slip out again.... But, if there's anything in the world to save your life, I don't know what it is."

"Thank you, Doctor. It's—something to know—what to expect," returned Lane, with a smile.

"You might live a year—and you might not.... You might improve. God only knows. Miracles *do* happen. Anyway, come back to see me."

Lane shook hands with him and went out, passing another patient in the reception room. Then as Lane opened the door and stepped out upon the porch he almost collided with a girl who evidently had been about to come in.

"I beg your——" he began, and stopped. He knew this girl, but the strained tragic shadow of her eyes was strikingly unfamiliar. The transparent white skin let the blue tracery of veins show. On the instant her lips trembled and parted.

"Oh, Daren—don't you know me?" she asked.

"Mel Iden!" he burst out. "Know you? I should smile I do. But it—it was so sudden. And you're older—different somehow. Mel, you're sweeter—why you're beautiful."

He clasped her hands and held on to them, until he felt her rather nervously trying to withdraw them.

"Oh, Daren, I'm glad to see you home—alive—whole," she said, almost in a whisper. "Are you—well?"

"No, Mel. I'm in pretty bad shape," he replied. "Lucky to get home alive—to see you all."

"I'm sorry. You're so white. You're wonderfully changed, Daren."

"So are you. But I'll say I'm happy it's not painted face and plucked eyebrows.... Mel, what's happened to you?"

She suddenly espied the decoration on his coat. The blood rose and stained her clear cheek. With a gesture of exquisite grace and sensibility that thrilled Lane she touched the medal. "Oh! The *Croix de Guerre*.... Daren, you were a hero."

"No, Mel, just a soldier."

She looked up into his face with eyes that fascinated Lane, so beautiful were they— the blue of corn-flowers—and lighted then with strange rapt glow.

"Just a soldier!" she murmured. But Lane heard in that all the sweetness and understanding possible for any woman's heart. She amazed him—held him spellbound. Here was the sympathy—and something else—a nameless need—for which he yearned. The moment was fraught with incomprehensible forces. Lane's sore heart responded to her rapt look, to the sudden strange passion of her pale face. Swiftly he divined that Mel Iden gloried in the presence of a maimed and proven soldier.

"Mel, I'll come to see you," he said, breaking the spell. "Do you still live out on the Hill road? I remember the four big white oaks."

"No, Daren, I've left home," she said, with slow change, as if his words recalled something she had forgotten. All the radiance vanished, leaving her singularly white.

"Left home! What for?" he asked, bluntly.

"Father turned me out," she replied, with face averted. The soft roundness of her throat swelled. Lane saw her full breast heave under her coat.

"What're you saying, Mel Iden?" he demanded, as quickly as he could find his voice.

Then she turned bravely to meet his gaze, and Lane had never seen as sad eyes as looked into his.

"Daren, haven't you heard—about me?" she asked, with tremulous lips.

"No. What's wrong?"

"I—I can't let you call on me."

"Why not? Are you married—jealous husband?"

"No, I'm not married—but I—I have a baby," she whispered.

"Mel!" gasped Lane. "A war baby?"

"Yes."

Lane was so shocked he could not collect his scattered wits, let alone think of the right thing to say, if there were any right thing. "Mel, this is a—a terrible surprise. Oh, I'm sorry.... How the war played hell with all of us! But for you—Mel Iden—I can't believe it."

"Daren, so terribly true," she said. "Don't I look it?"

"Mel, you look—oh—heartbroken."

"Yes, I am broken-hearted," she replied, and drooped her head.

"Forgive me, Mel. I hardly know what I'm saying.... But listen—I'm coming to see you."

"No," she said.

That trenchant word was thought-provoking. A glimmer of understanding began to dawn in Lane. Already an immense pity had flooded his soul, and a profound sense of the mystery and tragedy of Mel Iden. She had always been unusual, aloof, proud, unattainable, a girl with a heart of golden fire. And now she had a nameless child and was an outcast from her father's house. The fact, the fatality of it, stunned Lane.

"Daren, I must go in to see Dr. Bronson," she said. "I'm glad you're home. I'm proud of you. I'm happy for your mother and Lorna. You must watch Lorna—try to restrain her. She's going wrong. All the young girls are going wrong. Oh, it's a more dreadful time *now* than before or during the war. The let-down has been terrible.... Good-bye, Daren."

In other days Manton's building on Main Street had appeared a pretentious one to Lane's untraveled eyes. It was an old three-story red-brick-front edifice, squatted between higher and more modern structures. When he climbed the dirty dark stairway up to the second floor a throng of memories returned with the sensations of creaky steps, musty smell, and dim light. When he pushed open a door on which MANTON & CO. showed in black letters he caught his breath. Long—long past! Was it possible that he had been penned up for three years in this stifling place?

Manton carried on various lines of business, and for Middleville, he was held to be something of a merchant and broker. Lane was wholly familiar with the halls, the several lettered doors, the large unpartitioned office at the back of the building. Here his slow progress was intercepted by a slip of a girl who asked him what he wanted. Before answering, Lane took stock of the girl. She might have been all of fifteen—no older. She had curly bobbed hair, and a face that would have been comely but for the powder and rouge. She was chewing gum, and she ogled Lane.

"I want to see Mr. Manton," Lane said.

"What name, please."

"Daren Lane."

She tripped off toward the door leading to Manton's private offices, and Lane's gaze, curiously following her, found her costume to be startling even to his expectant eyes. Then she disappeared. Lane's gaze sought the corner and desk that once upon a time had been his. A blond young lady, also with bobbed hair, was operating a typewriter at his desk. She glanced up, and espying Lane, she suddenly stopped her work. She recognized him. But, if she were Hattie Wilson, it was certain that Lane did not recognize her. Then the office girl returned.

"Step this way, please. Mr. Smith will see you."

How singularly it struck Lane that not once in three years had he thought of Smith. But when he saw him, the intervening months were as nothing. Lean, spare, pallid, with baggy eyes, and the nose of a drinker, Smith had not changed.

"How do, Lane. So you're back? Welcome to our city," he said, extending a nerveless hand that felt to Lane like a dead fish.

"Hello, Mr. Smith. Yes, I'm back," returned Lane, taking the chair Smith indicated. And then he met the inevitable questions as best he could in order not to appear curt or uncivil.

"I'd like to see Mr. Manton to ask for my old job," interposed Lane, presently.

"He's busy now, Lane, but maybe he'll see you. I'll find out."

Smith got up and went out. Lane sat there with a vague sense of absurdity in the situation. The click of a typewriter sounded from behind him. He wanted to hurry out. He wanted to think of other things, and twice he drove away memory of the girl he had just left at Doctor Bronson's office. Presently Smith returned, slipping along in his shiny black suit, flat-footed and slightly bowed, with his set dull expression.

"Lane, Mr. Manton asks you to please excuse him. He's extremely busy," said Smith. "I told him that you wanted your old job back. And he instructed me to tell you he had been put to the trouble of breaking in a girl to take your place. She now does the work you used to have—very satisfactorily, Mr. Manton thinks, and at less pay. So, of course, a change is impossible."

"I see," returned Lane, slowly, as he rose to go. "I had an idea that might be the case. I'm finding things—a little different."

"No doubt, Lane. You fellows who went away left us to make the best of it."

"Yes, Smith, we fellows 'went away,'" replied Lane, with satire, "and I'm finding out the fact wasn't greatly appreciated. Good day."

On the way out the little office girl opened the door for him and ogled him again, and stood a moment on the threshold. Ponderingly, Lane made his way down to the street. A rush of cool spring air seemed to refresh him, and with it came a realization that he never would have been able to stay cooped up in Manton's place. Even if his services had been greatly desired he could not have given them for long. He could not have stood that place. This was a new phase of his mental condition. Work almost anywhere in Middleville would be like that in Manton's. Could he stand work at all, not only in a physical sense, but in application of mind? He began to worry about that.

Some one hailed Lane, and he turned to recognize an old acquaintance—Matt Jones. They walked along the street together, meeting other men who knew Lane, some of whom greeted him heartily. Then, during an ensuing hour, he went into familiar stores and the postoffice, the hotel and finally the Bradford Inn, meeting many people whom he had known well. The sum of all their greetings left him in cold amaze. At length Lane grasped the subtle import—that people were tired of any one or anything which reminded them of the war. He tried to drive that thought from lodgment in his mind. But it stuck. And slowly he gathered the forces of his spirit to make good the resolve with which he had faced this day—to withstand an appalling truth.

At the inn he sat before an open fire and pondered between brief conversations of men who accosted him. On the one hand it was extremely trying, and on the other a fascinating and grim study—to meet people, and find that he could read their minds. Had the war given him some magic sixth sense, some clairvoyant power, some gift of vision? He could not tell yet what had come to him, but there was something.

Business men, halting to chat with Lane a few moments, helped along his readjustment to the truth of the strange present. Almost all kinds of business were booming. Most people had money to spend. And there was a multitude, made rich by the war, who were throwing money to the four winds. Prices of every commodity were at their highest peak, and supply could not equal demand. An orgy of spending was in full swing, and all men in business, especially the profiteers, were making the most of the unprecedented opportunity.

After he had rested, Lane boarded a street car and rode out to the suburbs of Middleville where the Maynards lived. Although they had lost their money they still lived in the substantial mansion that was all which was left them of prosperous days. House and grounds now appeared sadly run down.

A maid answered Lane's ring, and let him in. Lane found himself rather nervously expecting to see Mrs. Maynard. The old house brought back to him the fact that he had never liked her. But he wanted to see Margaret. It turned out, however, that mother and daughter were out.

"Come up, old top," called Blair's voice from the hall above.

So Lane went up to Blair's room, which he remembered almost as well as his own, though now it was in disorder. Blair was in his shirt sleeves. He looked both gay and spent. Red Payson was in bed, and his face bore the hectic flush of fever.

"Aw, he's only had too much to eat," declared Blair, in answer to Lane's solicitation.

"How's that, Red?" asked Lane, sitting down on the bed beside Payson.

"It's nothing, Dare.... I'm just all in," replied Red, with a weary smile.

"I telephoned Doc Bronson to come out," said Blair, "and look us over. That made Red as sore as a pup. Isn't he the limit? By thunder, you can't do anything for some people."

Blair's tone and words of apparent vexation were at variance with the kindness of his eyes as they rested upon his sick comrade.

"I just came from Bronson's," observed Lane. "He's been our doctor for as long as I can remember."

Both Lane's comrades searched his face with questioning eyes, and while Lane returned that gaze there was a little constrained silence.

"Bronson examined me—and said I'd live to be eighty," added Lane, with dry humor.

"You're a liar!" burst out Blair.

On Red Payson's worn face a faint smile appeared. "Carry on, Dare."

Then Blair fell to questioning Lane as to all the news he had heard, and people he had met.

"So Manton turned you down cold," said Blair, ponderingly.

"I didn't get to see him," replied Lane. "He sent out word that my old job was held by a girl who did my work better and at less pay."

The blood leaped to Blair's white cheek.

"What'd you say?" he queried.

"Nothing much. I just trailed out.... But the truth is, Blair—I couldn't have stood that place—not for a day."

"I get you," rejoined Blair. "That isn't the point, though. I always wondered if we'd find our old jobs open to us. Of course, I couldn't fill mine now. It was an outside job—lots of walking."

So the conversation see-sawed back and forth, with Red Payson listening in languid interest.

"Have you seen any of the girls?" asked Blair.

"I met Mel Iden," replied Lane.

"You did? What did she—"

"Mel told me what explained some of your hints."

"Ahuh! Poor Mel! How'd she look?"

"Greatly changed," replied Lane, thoughtfully. "How do you remember Mel?"

"Well, she was pretty—soulful face—wonderful smile—that sort of thing."

"She's beautiful now, and sad."

"I shouldn't wonder. And she told you right out about the baby?"

"No. That came out when she said I couldn't call on her, and I wanted to know why."

"But you'll go anyhow?"

"Yes."

"So will I," returned Blair, with spirit. "Dare, I've known for over a year about Mel's disgrace. You used to like her, and I hated to tell you. If it had been Helen I'd have told you in a minute. But Mel.... Well, I suppose we must expect queer things. I got a jolt this morning. I was pumping my sister Margie about everybody, and, of course, Mel's name came up. You remember Margie and Mel were as thick as two peas in a pod. Looks like Mel's fall has hurt Margie. But I don't just *get* Margie yet. She might be another fellow's sister—for all the strangeness of her."

"I hardly knew *my* kid sister," responded Lane.

"Ahuh! The plot thickens.... Well, I couldn't get much out of Marg. She used to babble everything. But what little she told me made up in—in shock for what it lacked in volume."

"Tell me," said Lane, as his friend paused.

"Nothing doing." ... And turning to the sick boy on the bed, he remarked, "Red, you needn't let this—this gab of ours bother you. This is home talk between a couple of boobs who're burying their illusions in the grave. You didn't leave a sister or a lot of old schoolgirl sweethearts behind to———"

"What the hell do you know about whom I left behind?" retorted Red, with a swift blaze of strange passion.

"Oh, say, Red—I—I beg your pardon, I was only kidding," responded Blair, in surprise and contrition. "You never told me a word about yourself."

For answer Red Payson rolled over wearily and turned his back.

"Blair, I'll beat it, and let Red go to sleep," said Lane, taking up his hat. "Red, good-bye this time. I hope you'll be better soon."

"I'm—sorry, Lane," came in muffled tones from Payson.

"Cut that out, boy. You've nothing to be sorry for. Forget it and cheer up."

Blair hobbled downstairs after Lane. "Don't go just yet, Dare."

They found seats in the parlor that appeared to be the same shabby genteel place where Lane had used to call upon Blair's sister.

"What ails Red?" queried Lane, bluntly.

"Lord only knows. He's a queer duck. Once in a while he lets out a crack like that. There's a lot to Red."

"Blair, his heart is broken," said Lane, tragically.

"Well!" exclaimed Blair, with quick almost haughty uplift of head. He seemed to resent Lane's surprise and intimation. It was a rebuke that made Lane shrink.

"I never thought of Red's being hurt—you know—or as having lost.... Oh, he just seemed like so many other boys ruined in health. I——"

"All right. Cut the sentiment," interrupted Blair. "The fact is Red is more of a problem than we had any idea he'd be.... And Dare, listen to this—I'm ashamed to have to tell you. Mother raised old Harry with me this morning for fetching Red home. She couldn't see it my way. She said there were hospitals for sick soldiers who hadn't homes. I lost my temper and I said: 'The hell of it, mother, is that there's nothing of the kind.' ... She said we couldn't keep him here. I tried to coax her.... Margie helped, but nothing doing."

Blair had spoken hurriedly with again a stain of red in his white cheek, and a break in his voice.

"That's—tough," replied Lane, haltingly. He could choke back speech, but not the something in his voice he would rather not have heard. "I'll tell you what. As soon as Red is well enough we'll move him over to my house. I'm sure mother will let him share my room. There's only Lorna—and I'll pay Red's board.... You have quite a family—"

"Hell, Dare—don't apologize to me for my mother," burst out Blair, bitterly.

"Blair, I believe you realize what we are up against—and I don't," rejoined Lane, with level gaze upon his friend.

"Dare, can't you see we're up against worse than the Argonne?—worse, because back here at home—that beautiful, glorious thought—idea—spirit we had is gone. Dead!"

"No, I can't see," returned Lane, stubbornly.

"Well, I guess that's one reason we all loved you, Dare—you couldn't see.... But I'll bet you my crutch Helen makes you see. Her father made a pile out of the war. She's a war-rich snob now. And going the pace!"

"Blair, she may make me see her faithlessness—and perhaps some strange unrest—some change that's seemed to come over everything. But she can't prove to me the death of anything outside of herself. She can't prove that any more than Mel Iden's confession proved her a wanton. It didn't. Not to me. Why, when Mel put her hand on my breast—on this medal—and looked at me—I had such a thrill as I never had before in all my life. Never!... Blair, it's *not* dead. That beautiful thing you mentioned—that spirit—that fire which burned so gloriously—it is *not* dead."

"Not in you—old pard," replied Blair, unsteadily. "I'm always ashamed before your faith. And, by God, I'll say you're my only anchor."

"Blair, let's play the game out to the end," said Lane.

"I get you, Dare.... For Margie, for Lorna, for Mel—even if they have—"

"Yes," answered Lane, as Blair faltered.

CHAPTER IV

As Lane sped out Elm Street in a taxicab he remembered that his last ride in such a conveyance had been with Helen when he took her home from a party. She was then about seventeen years old. And that night she had coaxed him to marry her before he left to go to war. Had her feminine instinct been infallibly right? Would marrying her have saved her from what Blair had so forcibly suggested?

Elm Street was a newly developed part of Middleville, high on one of its hills, and manifestly a restricted section. Lane had found the number of Helen's home in the telephone book. When the chauffeur stopped before a new and imposing pile of red brick, Lane understood an acquaintance's reference to the war rich. It was a mansion, but somehow not a home. It flaunted something indefinable.

Lane instructed the driver to wait a few moments, and, if he did not come out, to go back to town and return in about an hour. The house stood rather far from the street, and as Lane mounted the terrace he observed four motor cars parked in the driveway. Also his sensitive ears caught the sound of a phonograph.

A maid answered his ring. Lane asked for both Mrs. Wrapp and Helen. They were at home, the maid informed him, and ushered Lane into a gray and silver reception room. Lane had no card, but gave his name. As he gazed around the room he tried to fit the delicate decorative scheme to Mrs. Wrapp. He smiled at the idea. But he remembered that she had always liked him in spite of the fact that she did not favor his attention to Helen. Like many mothers of girls, she wanted a rich marriage for her daughter. Manifestly now she had money. But had happiness come with prosperity?

Then Mrs. Wrapp came down. Rising, he turned to see a large woman, elaborately gowned. She had a heavy, rather good-natured face on which was a smile of greeting.

"Daren Lane!" she exclaimed, with fervor, and to his surprise, she kissed him. There was no doubt of her pleasure. Lane's thin armor melted. He had not anticipated such welcome. "Oh, I'm glad to see you, soldier boy. But you're a man now. Daren, you're white and thin. Handsomer, though!... Sit down and talk to me a little."

Her kindness made his task easy.

"I've called to pay my respects to you—and to see Helen," he said.

"Of course. But talk to me first," she returned, with a smile. "You'll find me better company than that crowd upstairs. Tell me about yourself.... Oh, I know soldiers hate to talk about themselves and the war. Never mind the war. Are you well? Did you get hurt? You look so—so frail, Daren."

There was something simple and motherly about her, that became her, and warmed Lane's cold heart. He remembered that she had always preferred boys to girls, and regretted she had not been the mother of boys. So Lane talked to her, glad to find that the most ordinary news of the service and his comrades interested her very much. The instant she espied his *Croix de Guerre* he seemed lifted higher in her estimation. Yet she had the delicacy not to question him about that. In fact, after ten minutes with her, Lane had to reproach himself for the hostility with which he had come. At length she rose with evident reluctance.

"You want to see Helen. Shall I send her down here or will you go up to her studio?"

"I think I'd like to go up," replied Lane.

"If I were you, I would," advised Mrs. Wrapp. "I'd like your opinion—of, well, what you'll see. Since you left home, Daren, we've been turned topsy-turvy. I'm old-fashioned.

I can't get used to these goings-on. These young people 'get my goat,' as Helen expresses it."

"I'm hopelessly behind the times, I've seen that already," rejoined Lane.

"Daren, I respect you for it. There was a time when I objected to your courting Helen. But I couldn't see into the future. I'm sorry now she broke her engagement to you."

"I—thank you, Mrs. Wrapp," said Lane, with agitation. "But of course Helen was right. She was too young.... And even if she had been—been true to me—I would have freed her upon my return."

"Indeed. And why, Daren?"

"Because I'll never be well again," he replied sadly.

"Boy, don't say that!" she appealed, with a hand going to his shoulder.

In the poignancy of the moment Lane lost his reserve and told her the truth of his condition, even going so far as to place her hand so she felt the great bayonet hole in his back. Her silence then was more expressive than any speech. She had the look of a woman in whom conscience was a reality. And Lane divined that she felt she and her daughter, and all other women of this distraught land, owed him and his comrades a debt which could never be paid. For once she expressed dignity and sweetness and genuine sorrow.

"You shock me, Daren. But words are useless. I hope and pray you're wrong. But right or wrong—you're a real American—like our splendid forefathers. Thank God *that* spirit still survives. It is our only hope."

Lane crossed to the window and looked out, slowly conscious of resurging self-control. It was well that he had met Mrs. Wrapp first, for she gave him what he needed. His bleeding vanity, his pride trampled in the dirt, his betrayed faith, his unquenchable spirit of hope for some far-future good—these were not secrets he could hide from every one.

"Daren," said Mrs. Wrapp, as he again turned to her, "if I were in my daughter's place I'd beg you to take me back. And if you would, I'd never leave your side for an hour until you were well or—or gone.... But girls now are possessed of some infernal frenzy.... God only knows how *far* they go, but I'm one mother who is no fool. I see little sign of real love in Helen or any of her friends.... And the men who lounge around after her! Walk upstairs—back to the end of the long hall—open the door and go in. You'll find Helen and some of her associates. You'll find the men, young, sleek, soft, well-fed—without any of the scars or ravages of war. They didn't go to war!... They *live* for their bodies. And I hate these slackers. So does Helen's father. And for three years our house has been a rendezvous for them. We've prospered, but *that* has been bitter fruit."

Strong elemental passions Lane had seen and felt in people during the short twenty-four hours since his return home. All of them had stung and astounded him, flung into his face the hard brutal facts of the materialism of the present. Surely it was an abnormal condition. And yet from the last quarter where he might have expected to find uplift, and the crystallizing of his attitude toward the world, and the sharpening of his intelligence—from the hard, grim mother of the girl who had jilted him, these had come. It was in keeping with all the other mystery.

"On second thought, I'll go up with you," continued Mrs. Wrapp, as he moved in the direction she had indicated. "Come."

The wide hall, the winding stairway with its soft carpet, the narrower hallway above—these made a long journey for Lane. But at the end, when Mrs. Wrapp stopped with hand on the farthest door, Lane felt knit like cold steel.

The discordant music and the soft shuffling of feet ceased. Laughter and murmur of voices began.

"Come, Daren," whispered Mrs. Wrapp, as if thrilled. Certainly her eyes gleamed. Then quickly she threw the door open wide and called out:

"Helen, here's Daren Lane home from the war, wearing the *Croix de Guerre*."

Mrs. Wrapp pushed Lane forward, and stood there a moment in the sudden silence, then stepping back, she went out and closed the door.

Lane saw a large well-lighted room, with colorful bizarre decorations and a bare shiny floor. The first person his glance encountered was a young girl, strikingly beautiful, facing him with red lips parted. She had violet eyes that seemed to have a startled expression as they met Lane's. Next Lane saw a slim young man standing close to this girl, in the act of withdrawing his arm from around her waist. Apparently with his free hand he had either been lowering a smoking cigarette from her lips or had been raising it there. This hand, too, dropped down. Lane did not recognize the fellow's smooth, smug face, with its tiny curled mustache and its heated swollen lines.

"Look who's here," shouted a gay, vibrant voice. "If it isn't old Dare Lane!"

That voice drew Lane's fixed gaze, and he saw a group in the far corner of the room. One man was standing, another was sitting beside a lounge, upon which lay a young woman amid a pile of pillows. She rose lazily, and as she slid off the lounge Lane saw her skirt come down and cover her bare knees. Her red hair, bobbed and curly, marked her for recognition. It was Helen. But Lane doubted if he would have at once recognized any other feature. The handsome insolence of her face was belied by a singularly eager and curious expression. Her eyes, almost green in line, swept Lane up and down, and came back to his face, while she extended her hands in greeting.

"Helen, how are you?" said Lane, with a cool intent mastery of himself, bowing over her hands. "Surprised to see me?"

"Well, I'll say so! Daren, you've changed," she replied, and the latter part of her speech flashed swiftly.

"Rather," he said, laconically. "What would you expect? So have you changed."

There came a moment's pause. Helen was not embarrassed or agitated, but something about Lane or the situation apparently made her slow or stiff.

"Daren, you—of course you remember Hardy Mackay and Dick Swann," she said.

Lane turned to greet one-time schoolmates and rivals of his. Mackay was tall, homely, with a face that lacked force, light blue eyes and thick sandy hair, brushed high. Swann was slight, elegant, faultlessly groomed and he had a dark, sallow face, heavy lips, heavy eyelids, eyes rather prominent and of a wine-dark hue. To Lane he did not have a clean, virile look.

In their greetings Lane sensed some indefinable quality of surprise or suspense. Swann rather awkwardly put out his hand, but Lane ignored it. The blood stained Swann's sallow face and he drew himself up.

"And Daren, here are other friends of mine," said Helen, and she turned him round. "Bessy, this is Daren Lane.... Miss Bessy Bell." As Lane acknowledged the introduction he felt that he was looking at the prettiest girl he had ever seen—the girl whose violet eyes had met his when he entered the room.

"Mr. Daren Lane, I'm very happy to meet some one from 'over there,'" she said, with the ease and self-possession of a woman of the world. But when she smiled a beautiful, wonderful light seemed to shine from eyes and face and lips—a smile of youth.

Helen introduced her companion as Roy Vancey. Then she led Lane to the far corner, to another couple, manifestly disturbed from their rather close and familiar position in a window seat. These also were strangers to Lane. They did not get up, and they were not interested. In fact, Lane was quick to catch an impression from all, possibly excepting Miss Bell, that the courtesy of drawing rooms, such as he had been familiar with as a young man, was wanting in this atmosphere. Lane wondered if it was antagonism toward him. Helen drew Lane back toward her other friends, to the lounge where she seated herself. If the situation had disturbed her equilibrium in the least, the moment had passed. She did not care what Lane thought of her guests or what they thought of him. But she seemed curious about him. Bessy Bell came and sat beside her, watching Lane.

"Daren, do you dance?" queried Helen. "You used to be good. But dancing is not the same. It's all fox-trot, toddle, shimmy nowadays."

"I'm afraid my dancing days are over," replied Lane.

"How so? I see you came back with two legs and arms."

"Yes. But I was shot twice through one leg—it's about all I can do to walk now."

Following his easy laugh, a little silence ensued. Helen's green eyes seemed to narrow and concentrate on Lane. Dick Swann inhaled a deep draught of his cigarette, then let the smoke curl up from his lips to enter his nostrils. Mackay rather uneasily shifted his feet. And Bessy Bell gazed with wonderful violet eyes at Lane.

"Oh! You were *shot*!" she whispered.

"Yes," replied Lane, and looked directly at her, prompted by her singular tone. A glance was enough to show Lane that this very young girl was an entirely new type to him. She seemed to vibrate with intensity. All the graceful lines of her body seemed strangely instinct with pulsing life. She was bottled lightning. In a flash Lane sensed what made her different from the fifteen-year-olds he remembered before the war. It was what made his sister Lorna different. He felt it in Helen's scrutiny of him, in the speculation of her eyes. Then Bessy Bell leaned toward Lane, and softly, reverently touched the medal upon his breast.

"The *Croix de Guerre*," she said, in awe. "That's the French badge of honor.... It means you must have done something great.... You must have—*killed* Germans!"

Bessy sank back upon the lounge, clasping her hands, and her eyes appeared to darken, to turn purple with quickening thought and emotion. Her exclamation brought the third girl of the party over to the lounge. She was all eyes. Her apathy had vanished. She did not see the sulky young fellow who had followed her.

Lane could have laughed aloud. He read the shallow souls of these older girls. They could not help their instincts and he had learned that it was instinctive with women to become emotional over soldiers. Bessy Bell was a child. Hero-worship shone from her speaking eyes. Whatever other young men might be to her, no one of them could compare with a soldier.

The situation had its pathos, its tragedy, and its gratification for Lane. He saw clearly, and felt with the acuteness of a woman. Helen had jilted him for such young men as these. So in the feeling of the moment it cost him nothing to thrill and fascinate these girls with the story of how he had been shot through the leg. It pleased him to see Helen's green eyes dilate, to see Bessy Bell shudder. Presently Lane turned to speak to the supercilious Swann.

"I didn't have the luck to run across you in France!" he queried.

"No. I didn't go," replied Swann.

"How was that? Didn't the draft get you?"

"Yes. But my eyes were bad. And my father needed me at the works. We had a big army contract in steel."

"Oh, I see," returned Lane, with a subtle alteration of manner he could not, did not want to control. But it was unmistakable in its detachment. Next his gaze on Mackay did not require the accompaniment of a query.

"I was under weight. They wouldn't accept me," he explained.

Bessy Bell looked at Mackay disdainfully. "Why didn't you drink a bucketful of water—same as Billy Means did? He got in."

Helen laughed gayly. "What! Mac drink water? He'd be ill.... Come, let's dance. Dick put on that new one. Daren, you can watch us dance."

Swann did as he was bidden, and as a loud, violent discordance blared out of the machine he threw away his cigarette, and turned to Helen. She seemed to leap at him. She had a pantherish grace. Swann drew her closely to him, with his arm all the way round her, while her arm encircled his neck. They began a fast swaying walk, in which Swann appeared to be forcing the girl over backwards. They swayed, and turned, and glided; they made strange abrupt movements in accordance with the jerky tune; they halted at the end of a walk to make little steps forward and back; then they began to bounce and sway together in a motion that Lane instantly recognized as a toddle. Lane remembered the one-step, the fox-trot and other new dances of an earlier day, when the craze for new dancing had become general, but this sort of gyration was vastly something else. It disgusted Lane. He felt the blood surge to his face. He watched Helen Wrapp in the arms of Swann, and he realized, whatever had been the state of his heart on his return home, he did not love her now. Even if the war had not disrupted his mind in an unaccountable way, even if he had loved Helen Wrapp right up to that moment, such singular abandonment to a distorted strange music, to the close and unmistakably sensual embrace of a man—that spectacle would have killed his love.

Lane turned his gaze away. The young fellow Vancey was pulling at Bessy Bell, and she shook his hand off. "No, Roy, I don't want to dance." Lane heard above the jarring, stringing notes. Mackay was smoking, and looked on as if bored. In a moment more the Victrola rasped out its last note.

Helen's face was flushed and moist. Her bosom heaved. Her gown hung closely to her lissom and rather full form. A singular expression of excitement, of titillation, almost wild, a softer expression almost dreamy, died out of her face. Lane saw Swann lead Helen up to a small table beside the Victrola. Here stood a large pitcher of lemonade, and a number of glasses. Swann filled a glass half full, from the pitcher, and then, deliberately pulling a silver flask from his hip pocket he poured some of its dark red contents into the glass. Helen took it from him, and turned to Lane with a half-mocking glance.

"Daren, I remember you never drank," she said. "Maybe the war made a man of you!... Will you have a sip of lemonade with a shot in it?"

"No, thank you," replied Lane.

"Didn't you drink over there?" she queried.

"Only when I had to," he rejoined, shortly.

All of the four dancers partook of a drink of lemonade, strengthened by something from Swann's flask. Lane was quick to observe that when it was pressed upon Bessy Bell she refused to take it: "I hate booze," she said, with a grimace. His further impression of Bessy Bell, then, was that she had just fallen in with this older crowd, and sophisticated though she was, had not yet been corrupted. The divination of this heightened his interest.

"Well, Daren, you old prune, what'd you think of the toddle?" asked Helen, as she took a cigarette offered by Swann and tipped it between her red lips.

"Is that what you danced?"

"I'll say so. And Dick and I are considered pretty spiffy."

"I don't think much of it, Helen," replied Lane, deliberately. "If you care to—to do that sort of thing I'd imagine you'd rather do it alone."

"Oh Lord, you talk like mother," she exclaimed.

"Lane, you're out of date," said Swann, with a little sneer.

Lane took a long, steady glance at Swann, but did not reply.

"Daren, everybody has been dancing jazz. It's the rage. The old dances were slow. The new ones have pep and snap."

"So I see. They have more than that," returned Lane. "But pray, never mind me. I'm out of date. Go ahead and dance.... If you'd rather, I'll leave and call on you some other time."

"No, you stay," she replied. "I'll chase this bunch pretty soon."

"Well, you won't chase me. I'll go," spoke up Swann, sullenly, with a fling of his cigarette.

"You needn't hurt yourself," returned Helen, sarcastically.

"So long, people," said Swann to the others. But it was perfectly obvious that he did not include Lane. It was also obvious, at least to Lane, that Swann showed something of intolerance and mastery in the dark, sullen glance he bestowed upon Helen. She followed him across the room and out into the hall, from whence her guarded voice sounded unintelligibly. But Lane's keen ear, despite the starting of the Victrola, caught Swann's equally low, yet clearer reply. "You can't kid me. I'm on. You'll vamp Lane if he lets you. Go to it!"

As Helen came back into the room Mackay ran for her, and locking her in the same embrace—even a tighter one than Swann's—he fell into the strange steps that had so shocked Lane. Moreover, he was manifestly a skilful dancer, and showed the thin, lithe, supple body of one trained down by this or some other violent exercise.

Lane did not watch the dancers this time. Again Bessy Bell refused to get up from the lounge. The youth was insistent. He pawed at her. And manifestly she did not like that, for her face flamed, and she snapped: "Stop it—you bonehead! Can't you see I want to sit here by Mr. Lane?"

The youth slouched away fuming to himself.

Whereupon Lane got up, and seated himself beside Bessy so that he need not shout to be heard.

"That was nice of you, Miss Bell—but rather hard on the youngster," said Lane.

"He makes me sick. All he wants to do is lolly-gag.... Besides, after what you said to Helen about the jazz I wouldn't dance in front of you on a bet."

She was forceful, frank, naive. She was impressed by his nearness; but Lane saw that it was the fact of his being a soldier with a record, not his mere physical propinquity that affected her. She seemed both bold and shy. But she did not show any modesty. Her short skirt came above her bare knees, and she did not try to hide them from Lane's sight. At fifteen, like his sister Lorna, this girl had the development of a young woman. She breathed health, and something elusive that Lane could not catch. If it had not been for her apparent lack of shame, and her rouged lips and cheeks, and her plucked eyebrows, she would have been exceedingly alluring. But no beauty, however striking, could under these circumstances, stir Lane's heart. He was fascinated, puzzled, intensely curious.

"Why wouldn't you dance jazz in front of me?" he inquired, with a smile.

"Well, for one thing I'm not stuck on it, and for another I'll say you said a mouthful."

"Is that all?" he asked, as if disappointed.

"No. I'd respect what you said—because of where you've been and what you've done."

It was a reply that surprised Lane.

"I'm out of date, you know."

She put a finger on the medal on his breast and said: "You could never be out of date."

The music and the sliding shuffle ceased.

"Now beat it," said Helen. "I want to talk to Daren." She gayly shoved the young people ahead of her in a mass, and called to Bessy: "Here, you kid vamp, lay off Daren."

Bessy leaned to whisper in his ear: "Make a date with me, quick!"

"Surely, I'll hunt you up. Good-bye."

She was the only one who made any pretension of saying good-bye to Lane. They all crowded out before Helen, with Mackay in the rear. From the hall Lane heard him say to Helen: "Dick'll sure go to the mat with you for this."

Presently Helen returned to shut the door behind her; and her walk toward Lane had a suggestion of the oriental dancer. For Lane her face was a study. This seemed a woman beyond his comprehension. She was the Helen Wrapp he had known and loved, plus an age of change, a measureless experience. With that swaying, sinuous, pantherish grace, with her green eyes narrowed and gleaming, half mocking, half serious, she glided up to him, close, closer until she pressed against him, and her face was uplifted under his. Then she waited with her eyes gazing into his. Slumberous green depths, slowly lighting, they seemed to Lane. Her presence thus, her brazen challenge, affected him powerfully, but he had no thrill.

"Aren't you going to kiss me?" she asked.

"Helen, why didn't you write me you had broken our engagement?" he counter-queried.

The question disconcerted her somewhat. Drawing back from close contact with him she took hold of his sleeves, and assumed a naive air of groping in memory. She used her eyes in a way that Lane could not associate with the past he knew. She was a flirt—not above trying her arts on the man she had jilted.

"Why, didn't I write you? Of course I did."

"Well, if you did I never got the letter. And if you were on the level you'd admit you never wrote."

"How'd you find out then?" she inquired curiously.

"I never knew for sure until your mother verified it."

"Are you curious to know why I did break it off?"

"Not in the least."

This reply shot the fire into her face, yet she still persisted in the expression of her sentimental motive. She began to finger the medal on his breast.

"So, Mr. Soldier Hero, you didn't care?"

"No—not after I had been here ten minutes," he replied, bluntly.

She whirled from him, swiftly, her body instinct with passion, her expression one of surprise and fury.

"What do you mean by that?"

"Nothing I care to explain, except I discovered my love for you was dead—perhaps had been dead for a long time."

"But you never discovered it until you *saw* me—here—with Swann—dancing, drinking, smoking?"

"No. To be honest, the shock of that enlightened me."

"Daren Lane, I'm just what *you* men have made me," she burst out, passionately.

"You are mistaken. I beg to be excluded from any complicity in the—in whatever you've been made," he said, bitterly. "I have been true to you in deed and in thought all this time."

"You must be a queer soldier!" she exclaimed, incredulously.

"I figure there were a couple of million soldiers like me, queer or not," he retorted.

She gazed at him with something akin to hate in her eyes. Then putting her hands to her full hips she began that swaying, dancing walk to and fro before the window. She was deeply hurt. Lane had meant to get under her skin with a few just words of scorn, and he had imagined his insinuation as to the change in her had hurt her feelings. Suddenly he divined it was not that at all—he had only wounded her vanity.

"Helen, let's not talk of the past," he said. "It's over. Even if you had been true to me, and I loved you still—I would have been compelled to break our engagement."

"You would! And why?"

"I am a physical wreck—and a mental one, too, I fear.... Helen, I've come home to die."

"Daren!" she cried, poignantly.

Then he told her in brief, brutal words of the wounds and ravages war had dealt him, and what Doctor Bronson's verdict had been. Lane felt shame in being so little as to want to shock and hurt her, if that were possible.

"Oh, I'm sorry," she burst out. "Your mother—your sister.... Oh, that damned horrible war! *What* has it not done to us?... Daren, you looked white and weak, but I never thought you were—going to die.... How dreadful!"

Something of her girlishness returned to her in this moment of sincerity. The past was not wholly dead. Memories lingered. She looked at Lane, wide-eyed, in distress, caught between strange long-forgotten emotions.

"Helen, it's not dreadful to have to die," replied Lane. "*That* is not the dreadful part in coming home."

"What *is* dreadful, then?" she asked, very low.

Lane felt a great heave of his breast—the irrepressible reaction of a profound and terrible emotion, always held in abeyance until now. And a fierce pang, that was physical as well as emotional, tore through him. His throat constricted and ached to a familiar sensation—the welling up of blood from his lungs. The handkerchief he put to his lips came away stained red. Helen saw it, and with dilated eyes, moved instinctively as if to touch him, hold him in her pity.

"Never mind, Helen," he said, huskily. "That's nothing....·Well, I was about to tell you what is so dreadful—for me.... It's to reach home grateful to God I was spared to get home—resigned to the ruin of my life—content to die for whom I fought—my mother, my sister, *you*, and all our women (for I fought for nothing else)—and find my mother aged and bewildered and sad, my sister a painted little hussy—and *you*—a strange creature I despise.... And all, everybody, everything changed—changed in some horrible way which proves my sacrifice in vain.... It is not death that is dreadful, but the uselessness, the hopelessness of the ideal I cherished."

Helen fell on the couch, and burying her face in the pillows she began to sob. Lane looked down at her, at her glistening auburn hair, and slender, white, ringed hand clutching the cushions, at her lissom shaking form, at the shapely legs in the rolled-down silk stockings—and he felt a melancholy happiness in the proof that he had reached her shallow heart, and in the fact that this was the moment of loss.

"Good-bye—Helen," he said.

"Daren—don't—go," she begged.

But he had to go, for other reasons beside the one that this was the end of all intimate relation between him and Helen. He had overtaxed his strength, and the burning pang in his breast was one he must heed. On the hall stairway a dizzy spell came over him. He held on to the banister until the weakness passed. Fortunately there was no one to observe him. Somehow the sumptuous spacious hall seemed drearily empty. Was this a home for that twenty-year-old girl upstairs? Lane opened the door and went out. He was relieved to find the taxi waiting. To the driver he gave the address of his home and said: "Go slow and don't give me a jar!"

But Lane reached home, and got into the house, where he sat at the table with his mother and Lorna, making a pretense of eating, and went upstairs and into his bed without any recurrence of the symptoms that had alarmed him. In the darkness of his room he gradually relaxed to rest. And rest was the only medicine for him. It had put off hour by hour and day by day the inevitable.

"If it comes—all right—I'm ready," he whispered to himself. "But in spite of all I've been through—and have come home to—I don't *want* to die."

There was no use in trying to sleep. But in this hour he did not want oblivion. He wanted endless time to think. And slowly, with infinite care and infallible memory, he went over every detail of what he had seen and heard since his arrival home. In the headlong stream of consciousness of the past hours he met with circumstances that he lingered over, and tried to understand, to no avail. Yet when all lay clearly before his mental gaze he felt a sad and tremendous fascination in the spectacle.

For many weeks he had lived on the fancy of getting home, of being honored and loved, of being given some little meed of praise and gratitude in the short while he had to live. Alas! this fancy had been a dream of his egotism. His old world was gone. There was nothing left. The day of the soldier had passed—until some future need of him stirred the emotions of a selfish people. This new world moved on unmindful, through its travail and incalculable change, to unknown ends. He, Daren Lane, had been left alone on the vast and naked shores of Lethe.

Lane made not one passionate protest at the injustice of his fate. Labor, agony, war had taught him wisdom and vision. He began to realize that no greater change could there be than this of his mind, his soul. But in the darkness there an irresistible grief assailed him. He wept as never before in all his life. And he tasted the bitter salt of his own tears. He wept for his mother, aged and bowed by trouble, bewildered, ready to give up the struggle—his little sister now forced into erotic girlhood, blind, wilful, bold, on the wrong path, doomed beyond his power or any earthly power—the men he had met, warped by the war, materialistic, lost in the maze of self-preservation and self-aggrandizement, dead to chivalry and the honor of women—Mel Iden, strangest and saddest of mysteries—a girl who had been noble, aloof, proud, with a heart of golden fire, now disgraced, ruined, the mother of a war-baby, and yet, strangest of all, not vile, not bad, not lost, but groping like he was down those vast and naked shores of life. He wept for the hard-faced Mrs. Wrapp, whose ideal had been wealth and who had found prosperity bitter ashes at her lips, yet who preserved in this modern maelstrom some sense of its falseness, its baseness. He wept for Helen, playmate of the years never to return, sweetheart of his youth, betrayer of his manhood, the young woman of the present, blase, unsexed, seeking, provocative, all perhaps, as she had said, that men had made her—a travesty on splendid girlhood. He wept for her friends, embodying in them all of their class—for little Bessy Bell, with her exquisite golden beauty, her wonderful smile that was a light of joy—a child of fifteen with character and mind, not yet sullied, not yet wholly victim to the unstable spirit of the day.

And traveling in this army that seemed to march before Lane's eyes were the slackers, like Mackay and Swann, representative of that horde of cowards who in one way or another had avoided the service—the young men who put comfort, ease, safety, pleasure before all else—who had no ideal of womanhood—who could not have protected women—who would not fight to save women from the apish Huns—who remained behind to fall in the wreck of the war's degeneration, and to dance, to drink, to smoke, to ride the women to their debasement.

And for the first and the last time Lane wept for himself, pitifully as a child lost and helpless, as a strong man facing irreparable loss, as a boy who had dreamed beautiful dreams, who had loved and given and trusted, who had suffered insupportable agonies of body and soul, who had fought like a lion for what he represented to himself, who had killed and killed—and whose reward was change, indifference, betrayal and death.

That dark hour passed. Lane lay spent in the blackness of his room. His heart had broken. But his spirit was as unquenchable as the fire of the sun. If he had a year, a month, a week, a day longer to live he could never live it untrue to himself. Life had marked him to be a sufferer, a victim. But nothing could kill his soul. And his soul was his faith—something he understood as faith in God or nature or life—in the reason for his being—in his vision of the future.

How then to spend this last remnant of his life! No one would guess what passed through his lonely soul. No one would care. But out of the suffering that now seemed to give him spirit and wisdom and charity there dawned a longing to help, to save. He would return good for evil. All had failed him, but he would fail no one.

Then he had a strange intense desire to understand the present. Only a day home—and what colossal enigma! The war had been chaos. Was this its aftermath? Had people been rocked on their foundations? What were they doing—how living—how changing? He would see, and be grateful for a little time to prove his faith. He knew he would find the same thing in others that existed in himself.

He would help his mother, and cheer her, and try to revive something of hope in her. He would bend a keen and patient eye upon Lorna, and take the place of her father, and be kind, loving, yet blunt to her, and show her the inevitable end of this dancing, dallying road. Perhaps he could influence Helen. He would see the little soldier-worshiping Bessy Bell, and if by talking hours and hours, by telling the whole of his awful experience of war, he could take up some of the time so fraught with peril for her, he would welcome the ordeal of memory. And Mel Iden—how thought of her seemed tinged with strange regret! Once she and he had been dear friends, and because of a falsehood told by Helen that friendship had not been what it might have been. Suppose Mel, instead of Helen, had loved him and been engaged to him! Would he have been jilted and would Mel have been lost? No! It was a subtle thing—that answer of his spirit. It did not agree with Mel Iden's frank confession.

It might be difficult, he reflected, to approach Mel. But he would find a way. He would rest a few days—then find where she lived and go to see her. Could he help her? And he had an infinite exaltation in his power to help any one who had suffered. Lane recalled Mel's pale sweet face, the shadowed eyes, the sad tremulous lips. And this image of her seemed the most lasting of the impressions of the day.

CHAPTER V

The arbiters of social fate in Middleville assembled at Mrs. Maynard's on a Monday afternoon, presumably to partake of tea. Seldom, however, did they meet without adding zest to the occasion by a pricking down of names.

Mrs. Wrapp was the leading spirit of this self-appointed tribunal—a circumstance of expanding, resentment to Mrs. Maynard, who had once held the reins with aristocratic hands. Mrs. Kingsley, the third member of the great triangle, claimed an ancestor on the Mayflower, which was in her estimation a guerdon of blue blood. Her elaborate and exclusive entertainments could never be rivalled by those of Mrs. Wrapp. She was a widow with one child, the daughter Elinor, a girl of nineteen.

Mrs. Maynard was tall, pale, and worldly. Traces of lost beauty flashed in her rare smiles. When Frank Maynard had failed in business she had shrouded her soul in bitterness; and she saw the slow cruel years whiten his head and bend his shoulders with the cold eye of a woman who had no forgiveness for failure. After Mr. Maynard's reverse, all that kept the pair together were the son Blair, and the sweet, fair-haired, delicate Margaret, a girl of eighteen, whom the father loved, and for whom the mother had large ambitions. They still managed, in ways mysterious to the curious, to keep their fine residence in the River Park suburb of Middleville.

On this April afternoon the tea was neglected in the cups, and there was nothing of the usual mild gossip. The discussion involved Daren Lane, and when two of those social arbiters settled back in their chairs the open sesame of Middleville's select affairs had been denied to him.

"Why did he do it?" asked Mrs. Kingsley.

"He must have been under the influence of liquor," replied Mrs. Maynard, who had her own reasons for being relieved at the disgrace of Daren Lane.

"No, Jane, you're wrong," spoke up Mrs. Wrapp, who, whatever else she might be, was blunt and fair-minded. "Lane wasn't drunk. He never drank before the war. I knew him well. He and Helen had a puppy-love affair—they were engaged before Lane went to war. Well, the day after his return he called on us. And if I never liked him before I liked him then. He's come back to die! He was ill for two weeks—and then he crawled out of bed again. I met him down town one day. He really looked better, and told me with a sad smile that he had 'his ups and downs'.... No, Lane wasn't drunk at Fanchon Smith's dance the other night. I was there, and I was with Mrs. Smith when Lane came up to us. If ever I saw a cool, smooth, handsome devil it was Lane.... Well, he said what he said. I thought Mrs. Smith would faint. It is my idea Lane had a deep motive back of his remark about Fanchon's dress and her dancing. The fact is Lane was *sick* at what he saw—sick and angry. And he wanted Fanchon's mother and me to know what he thought."

"It was an insult," declared Mrs. Maynard, vehemently.

"It made Mrs. Smith ill," added Mrs. Kingsley. "She told me Fanchon tormented the life out of her, trying to learn what Lane said. Mrs. Smith would not tell. But Fanchon came to me and *I* told her. Such a perfectly furious girl! She'll not wear *that* dress or dance *that* dance very soon again. The story is all over town."

"Friends, there are two sides to every question," interposed the forceful Mrs. Wrapp. "If Lane cared to be popular he would have used more tact. But I don't think his remark was an insult. It was pretty raw, I admit. But the dress was indecent and the dance was rotten. Helen told me Fanchon was half shot. So how could she be insulted?"

Mrs. Maynard and Mrs. Kingsley, as usual, received Mrs. Wrapp's caustic and rather crude opinions with as good grace as they could muster. Plain it was that they felt themselves a shade removed from this younger and newer member of society. But they could not show direct antagonism to her influence any more than they could understand the common sense and justice of her arguments.

"No one will ever invite him again," declared Mrs. Maynard.

"He's done in Middleville," echoed Mrs. Kingsley. And that perhaps was a gauntlet thrown.

"Rot!" exclaimed Mrs. Wrapp, with more force than elegance. "I'll invite Daren Lane to my house.... You women don't get the point. Daren Lane is a soldier come home to die. He gave himself. And he returns to find all—all this sickening—oh, what shall I call it? What does he care whether or not we invite him? Can't you see that?"

"There's a good deal in what you say," returned Mrs. Kingsley, influenced by the stronger spirit. "Maybe Lane hated the new styles. I don't blame him much. There's something wrong with our young people. The girls are crazy. The boys are wild. Few of them are marrying—or even getting engaged. They'll do *anything*. The times are different. And we mothers don't know our daughters."

"Well, I know *mine*" returned Mrs. Maynard, loftily. "What you say may be true generally, but there are exceptions. My daughter has been too well brought up."

"Yes, Margie is well-bred," retorted Mrs. Wrapp. "We'll admit she hasn't gone to extremes, as most of our girls have. But I want to observe to you that she has been a wall-flower for a year."

"It certainly *is* a problem," sighed Mrs. Kingsley. "I feel helpless—out of it. Elinor does precisely what she wants to do. She wears outlandish clothes. She smokes and—I'm afraid drinks. And dances—*dreadfully*. Just like the other girls—no better, no worse. But with all that I think she's good. I feel the same as Jane feels about that. In spite of this—this modern stuff I believe all the girls are fundamentally the same as ten years ago."

"Well, that's where you mothers get in wrong," declared Mrs. Wrapp with her vigorous bluntness. "It's your pride. Just because they're *your* daughters they are above reproach.... What have you to say about the war babies in town? Did you ever hear of *that* ten years ago? You bet you didn't. These girls are a speedy set. Some of them are just wild for the sake of wildness. Most of them *have* to stand for things, or be left out altogether."

"What in the world can we do?" queried Mrs. Maynard, divided between distress and chagrin.

"The good Lord only knows," responded Mrs. Wrapp, herein losing her assurance. "Marriage would save most of them. But Helen doesn't want to marry. She wants to paint pictures and be free."

"Perhaps marriage is a solution," rejoined Mrs. Maynard thoughtfully.

"Whom on earth can we marry them to?" asked Mrs. Kingsley. "Most of the older men, the bachelors who're eligible haven't any use for these girls except to *play* with them. True, these young boys only think of little but dances, car-rides, and sneaking off alone to spoon—they get engaged to this girl and that one. But nothing comes of it."

"You're wrong. Never in my time have I seen girls find lovers and husbands as easily as now," declared Mrs. Wrapp. "Nor get rid of them so quickly.... Jane, you can marry Margaret. She's pretty and sweet even if you have spoiled her. The years are slipping by. Margaret ought to marry. She's not strong enough to work. Marriage for her would make things so much easier for you."

With that parting dig Mrs. Wrapp rose to go. Whereupon she and Mrs. Kingsley, with gracious words of invitation and farewell, took themselves off leaving Mrs. Maynard contending with an outraged spirit. Certain terse remarks of the crude and practical Mrs. Wrapp had forced to her mind a question that of late had assumed cardinal importance, and now had been brought to an issue by a proposal for Margaret's hand. Her daughter was a great expense, really more than could longer be borne in these times of enormous prices and shrunken income. A husband had been found for Margaret, and the matter could be adjusted easily enough, if the girl did not meet it with the incomprehensible obstinacy peculiar to her of late.

Mrs. Maynard found the fair object of her hopes seated in the middle of her room with the bright contents of numerous boxes and drawers strewn in glittering heaps around her.

"Margaret, what on earth are you doing there?" she demanded.

"I'm looking for a little picture Holt Dalrymple gave me when we went to school together," responded Margaret.

"Aren't you ever going to grow up? You'll be hunting for your dolls next."

"I will if I like," said the daughter, in a tone that did not manifest a seraphic mood.

"Don't you feel well?" inquired the mother, solicitously. Margaret was frail and subject to headaches that made her violent.

"Oh, I'm well enough."

"My dear," rejoined Mrs. Maynard, changing the topic. "I'm sorry to tell you Daren Lane has lost his standing in Middleville."

The hum and the honk of a motor-car sounded in the street.

"Poor Daren! What's he done?... Any old day he'll care!"

Mrs. Maynard was looking out of the window. "Here comes a crowd of girls.... Helen Wrapp has a new suit. Well, I'll go down. And after they leave I want a serious talk with you."

"Not if I see you first!" muttered Margaret, under her breath, as her mother walked out.

Presently, following gay talk and laughter down stairs, a bevy of Margaret's friends entered her boudoir.

"Hello, old socks!" was Helen's greeting. "You look punk."

"Marg, where's the doll? Your mother tipped us off," was Elinor's greeting.

"Where's the eats?" was Flossie Dickerson's greeting. She was a bright-eyed girl, with freckles on her smiling face, and the expression of a daring, vivacious and happy spirit—and acknowledged to be the best dancer and most popular girl in Middleville. Her dress, while not to be compared with her friends' costumes in costliness, yet was extreme in the prevailing style.

"Glad to see you, old dear," was dark-eyed, dark-haired Dorothy Dalrymple's greeting. Her rich color bore no hint of the artificial. She sank down on her knees beside Margaret.

The other girls draped themselves comfortably round the room; and Flossie with a 'Yum Yum' began to dig into a box of candy on Margaret's couch. They all talked at once. "Hear the latest, Marg?"

"Look at Helen's spiffy suit!"

"Oh, money, money, what it will buy!"

"Money'll never buy *me*, I'll say."

"Marg, who's been fermentin' round lately? Girls, get wise to the flowers."

"Hot dog! See Marg blush! That comes from being so pale. What are rouge and lip-stick and powder for but to hide truth from our masculine pursuers?"

"Floss, you haven't blushed for a million years."

It was Dorothy Dalrymple who silenced the idle badinage.

"Marg, you rummaging in the past?" she cried.

"Yes, and I love it," replied Margaret. "I haven't looked over this stuff for years. Just to remember the things I did!... Here, Dal, is a picture you once drew of our old teacher, Miss Hill."

Dorothy, whom the girls nicknamed "Dal," gazed at the drawing with amaze and regret.

"She was a terror," continued Margaret. "But Dal, you never had any reason to draw such a horrible picture of her. You were her pet."

"I wasn't," declared Dorothy.

"Maybe you never knew Miss Hill adored you, Dal," interposed Elinor. "She was always holding you up as a paragon. Not in your lessons—for you were a bonehead—but for deportment you were the class!"

"Dal, you were too good for this earth *then*, let alone these days," said Margaret.

"Miss Hill," mused Elinor, gazing at the caricature. "That's not a bad drawing. I remember Miss Hill never had any use for me. Small wonder. She was an honest-to-God teacher. I think she wanted us to be good.... Wonder how she got along with the kids that came after us."

"I saw Amanda Hill the other day," spoke up Flossie. "She looked worn out. She was nice to me. I'll bet my shirt she'd like to have us back, bad as we were.... These kids of to-day! My Gawd! they're the limit. They paralyze *me*. I thought I was pretty fast. But compared to these youngsters I'm tied to a post. My kid sister Joyce—Rose Clymer—Bessy Bell!... Some kids, believe me. And take it from me, girls, these dimple-kneed chickens are vamping the older boys."

"They're all stuck on Bessy," said Helen.

Margaret squealed in delight. "Girls, look here. Valentines! Did you ever?... Look at them.... And what's this?... 'Wonders of Nature—composition by Margaret Maynard.' Heavens! Did I write that? And what's this sear and yellow document?"

A slivery peal of laughter burst from Margaret.

"Dal, here's one of your masterpieces, composed when you were thirteen, and mooney over Daren Lane."

"I? Never! I didn't write it," denied Dorothy, with color in her dark cheeks.

"Yes you did. It's signed—'Yours forever Dot Dalrymple.' ... Besides I remember now Daren gave it to me. Said he wanted to prove he could have other girls if he couldn't have me."

"How chivalrous!" exclaimed Dorothy, joining in the laugh.

"Ah! here's what I've been hunting," declared Margaret, waving aloft a small picture. "It's a photograph of Holt, taken five years ago. Only the other evening he swore I hadn't kept it—dared me to produce it. He'll want it now—for some other girl. But nix, it's mine.... Dal, isn't he a handsome boy here?"

With sisterly impartiality Dorothy declared she could not in the wildest flight of her imagination see her brother as handsome.

"Holt used to be good-looking," said she. "But he outgrew it. That South Carolina training camp and the flu changed his looks as well as his disposition."

"Holt *is* changed," mused Margaret, gazing down at the picture, and the glow faded from her face.

"Dare Lane is handsome, even if he is a wreck," said Elinor, with sudden enthusiasm. "Friday night when he beat it from Fanchon's party he sure looked splendid."

Elinor was a staunch admirer of Lane's and she was the inveterate torment of her girl friends. She gave Helen a sly glance. Helen's green eyes narrowed and gleamed.

"Yes, Dare's handsomer than ever," she said. "And to give the devil his due he's *finer* than ever. Too damn fine for this crowd!... But what's the use—" she broke off.

"Yes, poor Dare Lane!" sighed Elinor. "Dare deserves much from all of us, not to mention *you*. He has made me think. Thank Heaven, I found I hadn't forgotten how."

"El, no one would notice it," returned Helen, sarcastically.

"It's easy to see where you get off," retorted Elinor.

Then a silence ensued, strange in view of the late banter and quick sallies; a silence breathing of restraint. The color died wholly from Margaret's face, and a subtle, indefinable, almost imperceptible change came over Dorothy.

"You bet Dare is handsome," spoke up Flossie, as if to break the embarrassment. "He's so *white* since he came home. His eyes are so dark and flashing. Then the way he holds his head—the look of him.... No wonder these damned slackers seem cheap compared to him.... I'd fall for Dare Lane in a minute, even if he is half dead."

The restraint passed, and when Floss Dickerson came out with eulogy for any man his status was settled for good and all. Margaret plunged once more into her treasures of early schooldays. Floss and Elinor made merry over some verses Margaret had handed up with a blush. Helen apparently lapsed into a brooding abstraction. And presently Dorothy excused herself, and kissing Margaret good-bye, left for home.

The instant she had gone Margaret's gay and reminiscent mood underwent a change.

"Girls, I want to know what Daren Lane did or said on Friday night at Fanchon's," spoke up Margaret. "You know mother dragged me home. Said I was tired. But I wasn't. It was only because I'm a wall-flower.... So I missed what happened. But I've heard talk enough to make me crazy to know about this scandal. Kit Benson was here and she hinted things. I met Bessy Bell. She asked me if I knew. She's wild about Daren. That yellow-legged broiler! He doesn't even know her.... My brother Blair would not tell me anything. He's strong for Daren. But mother told me Daren had lost his standing in Middleville. She always hated Daren. Afraid I'd fall in love with him. The idea! I liked him, and I like him better now—poor fellow!... And last, when El mentioned Daren, did you see Dal's face? I never saw Dal look like that."

"Neither did I," replied Elinor.

"Well, I have," spoke up Helen, with all of her mother's bluntness. "Dal always was love-sick over Daren, when she was a mere kid. She never got over it and never will."

"Still water runs deep," sapiently remarked Elinor. "There's a good deal in Dal. She's fine as silk. Of course we all remember how jealous she was of other girls when Daren went with her. But I think now it's because she's sorry for Daren. So am I. He was such a fool. Fanchon swears no nice girl in Middleville will ever dance that new camel-walk dance in public again."

"What did Daren say?" demanded Margaret, with eyes lighting.

"I was standing with Helen, and Fanchon when Daren came up. He looked—I don't know how—just wonderful. We all knew something was doing. Daren bowed to Fanchon and said to her in a perfectly clear voice that everybody heard: 'I'd like to try your camel-walk. I'm out of practice and not strong, but I can go once around, I'm sure. Will you?'"

'You're on, Dare,' replied Fanchon.

Then he asked. 'Do you like it?'

'I'll say so, Dare—crazy about it.'

'Of course you know why it's danced—and how it's interpreted by men,' said Daren.

'What do you mean?' asked Fanchon, growing red and flustered.

"Then Daren said: 'I'll tell your mother. If she lets you dance with that understanding—all right.' He bent over Mrs. Smith and said something. Mrs. Wrapp heard it. And so did Mrs. Mackay, who looked pretty sick. Mrs. Smith nearly *fainted*.... but she recovered enough to order Daren to leave."

"Do you know what Daren said?" demanded Margaret, in a frenzy of excitement.

"No. None of the girls know. We can only imagine. That makes it worse. If Fanchon knows she won't tell. But it is gossip all over town. We'll hear it soon. All the girls in town are imagining. It's spread like wildfire. And what *do* you think, Margie? In church—on Sunday—Doctor Wallace spoke of it. He mentioned no names. But he said that as the indecent dress and obscene dance of the young women could no longer be influenced by the home or the church it was well that one young man had the daring to fling the truth into the faces of their mothers."

"Oh, it was rotten of Daren," replied Margaret, with tears in her eyes. She was ashamed, indignant, incredulous. "For him to do a thing like that! He's always been the very prince of gentlemen. What on earth possessed him? Heaven knows the dances are vile, but that doesn't excuse Daren Lane. What do I care what Doctor Wallace said? Never in a thousand years will Mrs. Smith or mother or any one forgive him. Fanchon Smith is a little snob. I always hated her. She's spiteful and catty. She's a flirt all the way. She would dance any old thing. But that's not the point. Daren's disgraced himself. It was rotten—of him. And—I'll never—forgive—him, either."

"Don't cry, Margie," said Elinor. "It always makes your eyes red and gives you a headache. Poor Daren made a blunder. But some of us will stick to him. Don't take it so badly."

"Margie, it was rotten of Daren, one way you look at it—our way," added Flossie. "But you have to hand it to him for that stunt."

Helen Wrapp preserved her sombre mood, silent and brooding.

"Margie," went on Elinor, "there's a lot back of this. If Dare Lane could do that there must be some reason for it. Maybe we all needed a jolt. Well, we've got it. Let's stand by Daren. I will. Helen will. Floss will. You will. And surely Dal will."

"If you ask *me* I'll say Dare Lane ought to hand something to the men!" burst out Floss Dickerson, with fire in her eyes.

"You said a mouthful, kiddo," responded Helen, with her narrow contracted gaze upon Margaret. "Daren gave me the once over—and then the icepick!"

"Wonder what he gave poor Mel—when he heard about her," murmured Elinor, thoughtfully.

"Mel Iden ought to be roasted," retorted Helen. "She was always so darned superior. And all the time...."

"Helen, don't you say a word against Mel Iden," burst out Margaret, hotly. "She was my dearest friend. She was lovely. Her ruin was a horrible shock. But it wasn't because she was bad.... Mel had some fanatical notion about soldiers giving all—going away to be slaughtered. She said to me, 'A woman's body is so little to give,'"

"Yes, I know Mel was cracked," replied Helen. "But she needn't have been a damn fool. She didn't need to have had that baby!"

"Helen, your idea of sin is to be found out," said Elinor, with satire.

Again Floss Dickerson dropped her trenchant personality into the breach.

"Aw, come off!" she ejaculated. "Let somebody roast the men once, will you? I'm the little Jane that *knows*, believe me. All this talk about the girls going to hell makes me sick. We may be going—and going in limousines—but it's the men who're stepping on the gas."

"Floss, I love to hear you elocute," drawled Helen. "Go to it! For God's sake, roast the men."

"You always have to horn in," retorted Floss. "Let me get this off my chest, will you?... We girls are getting talked about. There's no use denying it. Any but a blind girl could see it. And it's because we do what the men want. Every girl wants to go out—to be attractive—to have fellows. But the price is getting high. They say in Middleville that I'm rushed more than any other girl. Well, if I am I know what it costs.... If I didn't 'pet'—if I didn't mush, if I didn't park my corsets at dances—if I didn't drink and smoke, and wiggle like a jelly-fish, I'd be a dead one—an egg, and don't you overlook that. If any one says I *want* to do these things he's a fool. But I do love to have good times, and little by little I've been drawn on and on.... I've had my troubles staving off these fellows. Most of them get half drunk. Some of the girls do, too. I never went that far. I always kept my head. I never went the limit. But you can bet your sweet life it wasn't their fault I didn't fall for them.... I'll say I've had to walk home from more than one auto ride. There's something in the gag, 'I know she's a good girl because I met her walking home from an auto ride.' That's one thing I intend to cut out this summer—the auto rides. Nothing doing for little Flossie!"

"Oh, can't we talk of something else!" complained Margaret, wearily, with her hands pressing against her temples.

CHAPTER VI

Mrs. Maynard slowly went upstairs and along the hall to her daughter's room. Margaret sat listlessly by a window. The girls had gone.

"You were going for a long walk," said Mrs. Maynard.

"I'm tired," replied Margaret. There was a shadow in her eyes.

The mother had never understood her daughter. And of late a subtle change in Margaret had made her more of a puzzle.

"Margaret, I want to talk seriously with you," she began.

"Well?"

"Didn't I tell you I wanted you to break off your—your friendship with Holt Dalrymple?"

"Yes," replied Margaret, with a flush. "I did not—want to."

"Well, the thing which concerns you now is—he can't be regarded as a possibility for you."

"Possibility?" echoed Margaret.

"Just that, exactly. I'm not sure of your thoughts on the matter, but it's time I knew them. Holt is a ne'er-do-well. He's gone to the bad, like so many of these army boys. No nice girl will ever associate with him again."

"Then I'm not nice, for I will," declared Margaret, spiritedly.

"You will persist in your friendship for him in the face of my objection?"

"Certainly I will if I have any say about it. But I know Holt. I—I guess he has taken to drink—and carrying on. So you needn't worry much about our friendship."

Mrs. Maynard hesitated. She had become accustomed to Margaret's little bursts of fury and she expected one here. But none came; Margaret appeared unnaturally calm; she sat still with her face turned to the window. Mrs. Maynard was a little afraid of this cold, quiet girl.

"Margaret, you can't help seeing now that your mother's judgment was right. Holt Dalrymple once may have been very interesting and attractive for a friend, but as a prospective husband he was impossible. The worst I hear of him is that he drinks and gambles. I know you liked him and I don't want to be unjust. But he has kept other and better young men away from you."

Margaret's hand clenched and her face sank against the window-pane.

"We need say no more about him," went on Mrs. Maynard. "Margaret, you've been brought up in luxury. If your father happened to die now—he's far from well—we'd be left penniless. We've lived up every dollar.... We have our poor crippled Blair to care for. You know you must marry well. I've brought you up with that end in view. And it's imperative you marry soon."

"Why must a girl marry?" murmured Margaret, wistfulness in her voice. "I'd rather go to work." "Margaret, you are a Maynard," replied her mother, haughtily. "Pray spare me any of this new woman talk about liberty—equal rights—careers and all that. Life hasn't changed for the conservative families of blood.... Try to understand, Margaret, that you must marry and marry well. You're nobody without money. In society there are hundreds of girls like you, though few so attractive. That's all the more reason you should take the best chance you have, before it's lost. If you don't marry people will say you can't. They'll say you're fading, growing old, even if you grow prettier every day of your life, and in the end they'll make you a miserable old maid. Then you'll be glad to marry anybody. If you marry now you can help your father, who needs help badly enough. You can help poor Blair.... You can be a leader in society; you can have a house here, a cottage at the seashore and one in the mountains; everything a girl's heart yearns for—servants, horses, autos, gowns, diamonds————"

"Everything except love," interrupted Margaret, bitterly.

Mrs. Maynard actually flushed, but she kept her temper.

"It's desirable that you love your husband. Any sensible woman can learn to care for a man. Love, as you dream about it is merely a—a dream. If women waited for that they would never get married."

"Which would be preferable to living without love."

"But Margaret, what would become of the world? If there were fewer marriages—Heaven knows they're few enough nowadays—there would be fewer families—and in the end fewer children—less and less————"

"They'd be better children," said Margaret, calmly.

"Eventually the race would die out."

"And that'd be a good thing—if the people can't love each other."

"How silly—exasperating!" ejaculated Mrs. Maynard. "You don't mean such nonsense. What any girl wants is a home of her own, a man to fuss over. I didn't marry for love, as you dream it. My husband attended to his business and I've looked after his household. You've had every advantage. I flatter myself our marriage has been a success."

Margaret's eyes gleamed like pointed flames.

"I differ with you. Your married life hasn't been successful any more than it's been happy. You never cared for father. You haven't been kind to him since his failure."

Mrs. Maynard waved her hand imperiously in angry amaze.

"I won't stop. I'm not a baby or a doll," went on Margaret, passionately. "If I'm old enough to marry I'm old enough to talk. I can think, can't I? You never told me anything, but I could see. Ever since I can remember you and father have had one continual wrangle about money—bills—expenses. Perhaps I'd have been better off without all the advantages and luxury. It's because of these things you want to throw me at some man. I'd far rather go to work the same as Blaid did, instead of college."

"Whatever on earth has come over you?" gasped Mrs. Maynard, bewildered by the revolt of this once meek daughter.

"Maybe I'm learning a little sense. Maybe I got some of it from Daren Lane," flashed back Margaret.

"Mother, whatever I've learned lately has been learned away from home. You've no more idea what's going on in the world to-day than if you were actually dead. I never was bright like Mel Iden, but I'm no fool. I see and hear and I read. Girls aren't pieces of furniture to be handed out to some rich men. Girls are waking up. They can do things. They can be independent. And being independent doesn't mean a girl's not going to marry. For she can wait—wait for the right man—for love.... You say I dream. Well, why didn't you wake me up long ago—with the truth? I had my dreams about love and marriage. And I've learned that love and marriage are vastly different from what most mothers make them out to be, or let a girl think."

"Margaret, I'll not have you talk in this strange way. You owe me respect if not obedience," said Mrs. Maynard, her voice trembling.

"Oh, well, I won't say any more," replied Margaret, "But can't you spare me? Couldn't we live within our means?"

"After all these years—to skimp along! I couldn't endure it."

"Whom have you in mind for me to—to marry?" asked the girl, coldly curious.

"Mr. Swann has asked your hand in marriage for his son Richard. He wants Richard to settle down. Richard is wild, like all these young men. And I have—well, I encouraged the plan."

"*Mother!*" cried Margaret, springing up.

"Margaret, you will see"

"I despise Dick Swann."

"Why?" asked her mother.

"I just do. I never liked him in school. He used to do such mean things. He's selfish. He let Holt and Daren suffer for his tricks."

"Margaret, you talk like a child."

"Listen, mother." She threw her arms round Mrs. Maynard and kissed her and spoke pleadingly. "Oh, don't make me hate myself. It seems I've grown so much older in the last year or so—and lately since this marriage talk came up. I've thought of things as never before because I've—I've learned about them. I see so differently. I can't—can't love Dick Swann. I can't bear to have him touch me. He's rude. He takes liberties.... He's too free with his hands! Why, it'd be wrong to marry him. What difference can a marriage service make in a girl's feelings.... Mother, let me say no."

"Lord spare me from bringing up another girl!" exclaimed Mrs. Maynard. "Margaret, I can't make you marry Richard Swann. I'm simply trying to tell you what any sensible girl would see she had to do. You think it over—both sides of the question—before you absolutely decide."

Mrs. Maynard was glad to end the discussion and to get away. In Margaret's appeal she heard a yielding, a final obedience to her wish. And she thought she had better let well enough alone. The look in Margaret's clear blue eyes made her shrink; it would haunt her. But she felt no remorse. Any mother would have done the same. There was always the danger of that old love affair; there was new danger in these strange wild fancies of modern girls; there was never any telling what Margaret might do. But once married she would be safe and her position assured.

CHAPTER VII

Daren Lane left Riverside Park, and walked in the meadows until he came to a boulder under a huge chestnut tree. Here he sat down. He could not walk far these days. Many a time in the Indian summers long past he had gathered chestnuts there with Dal, with Mel Iden, with Helen. He would never do it again.

The April day had been warm and fresh with the opening of a late spring. The sun was now gold—rimming the low hills in the west; the sky was pale blue; the spring flowers whitened the meadow. Twilight began to deepen; the evening star twinkled out of the sky; the hush of the gloaming hour stole over the land.

"Four weeks home—and nothing done. So little time left!" he muttered.

Two weeks of that period he had been unable to leave his bed. The rest of the time he had dragged himself around, trying to live up to his resolve, to get at the meaning of the present, to turn his sister Lorna from the path of dalliance. And he had failed in all.

His sister presented the problem that most distressed Lane. She had her good qualities, and through them could be reached. But she was thoughtless, vacillating, and wilful. She had made him promises only to break them. Lane had caught her in falsehoods. And upon being called to account she had told him that if he didn't like it he could "lump" it. Of late she had grown away from what affection she had shown at first. She could not bear interference with her pleasures, and seemed uncontrollable. Lane felt baffled. This thing was a Juggernaut impossible to stop.

Lane had scraped acquaintance with Harry Hale, one of Lorna's admirers, a boy of eighteen, who lived with his widowed mother on the edge of the town. He appeared to be an industrious, intelligent, quiet fellow, not much given to the prevailing habits of the young people. In his humble worship of Lorna he was like a dog. Lorna went to the motion pictures with him occasionally, when she had no other opportunity for excitement. Lane gathered that Lorna really liked this boy, and when with him seemed more natural, more what a fifteen-year-old girl used to be. And somehow it was upon this boy that Lane placed a forlorn hope.

No more automobiles honked in front of the home to call Lorna out. She met her friends away from the house, and returning at night she walked the last few blocks. It was this fact that awoke Lane's serious suspicions.

Another problem lay upon Lane's heart; if not so distressing as Lorna's, still one that added to his sorrow and his perplexity. He had gone once to call on Mel Iden. Mel Iden was all soul. Whatever had been the facts of her downfall—and reflection on that hurt Lane so strangely he could not bear it—it had not been on her part a matter of sex. She was far above wantonness.

Through long hours in the dark of night, when Lane's pain kept him sleepless, he had pondered over the mystery of Mel Iden until it cleared. She typified the mother of the race. In all periods of the progress of the race, war had brought out this instinct in women—to give themselves for the future. It was a provision of nature, inscrutable and terrible. How immeasurable the distance between Mel Iden and those women who practised birth control! As the war had brought out hideous greed and baseness, so had it propelled forward and upward the noblest attributes of life. Mel Iden was a builder, not a destroyer. She had been sexless and selfless. Unconsciously during the fever and emotion of the training of American men for service abroad, and the poignancy of their departure, to fight, and perhaps never return, Mel Iden had answered to this mysterious instinct of nature. Then, with the emotion past, and face to face with staggering consequences, she had reacted to conscious instincts. She had proved the purity of her surrender. She was all mother. And Lane began to see her moving in a crystal, beautiful light.

For what seemed a long time Lane remained motionless there in the silence of the meadow. Then at length he arose and retraced his slow steps back to town. Darkness overtook him on the bridge that spanned Middleville River. He leaned over the railing and peered down into the shadows. A soft murmur of rushing water came up. How like strange distant voices calling him to go back or go on, or warning him, or giving mystic portent of something that would happen to him there! A cold chill crept over him and he seemed enveloped in a sombre menace of the future. But he shook it off. He had many battles to fight, not the least of which was with morbid imagination.

When he reached the center of town he entered the lobby of the Bradford Inn. He hoped to meet Blair Maynard there. A company of well-dressed youths and men filled the place, most of whom appeared to be making a merry uproar.

Lane observed two men who evidently were the focus of attention. One was a stranger, very likely a traveling man, and at the moment he presented a picture of mingled consternation and anger. He was brushing off his clothes while glaring at a little, stout, red-faced man who appeared about to be stricken by apoplexy. This latter was a Colonel Pepper, whose acquaintance Lane had recently made. He was fond of cards and sport, and appeared to be a favorite with the young men about town. Moreover he had made himself particularly agreeable to Lane, in fact to the extent of Lane's embarrassment. At this moment the stranger lost his consternation wholly in wrath, and made a threatening movement toward Pepper. Lane stepped between them just in time to save Pepper a blow.

"I know what he's done. I apologize for him," said Lane, to the stranger. "He's made a good many people victims of the same indignity. It's a weakness—a disease. He can't help himself. Pray overlook it."

The stranger appeared impressed with Lane's presence, probably with his uniform, and slowly shook himself and fell back, to glower at Pepper, and curse under his breath, still uncertain of himself.

Lane grasped Colonel Pepper and led him out of the lobby.

"Pepper, you're going to get in an awful mess with that stunt of yours," he declared, severely. "If you can't help it you ought at least pick on your friends, or the town people—not strangers."

"Have—a—drink," sputtered Pepper, with his hand at his hip.

"No, thanks."

"Have—a—cigar."

Lane laughed. He had been informed that Colonel Pepper's failing always took this form of remorse, and certainly he would have tried it upon his latest victim had not Lane interfered.

"Colonel, you're hopeless," said Lane, as they walked out. "I hope somebody will always be around to protect you. I'd carry a body guard.... Say, have you seen Blair Maynard or Holt Dalrymple to-night?"

"Not Blair, but Holt was here early with the boys," replied Pepper. "They've gone to the club rooms to have a little game. I'm going to sit in. Lately I had to put up a holler. If the boys quit cards how'm I to make a living?"

"Had Holt been drinking?"

"Not to-night. But he's been hitting the bottle pretty hard of late."

Suddenly Lane buttonholed the little man and peered down earnestly at him. "Pepper, I've been trying to straighten Holt up. He's going to the bad. But he's a good kid. It's only the company.... The fact is—this's strictly confidential, mind you—Holt's sister begged me to try to stop his drinking and gambling. I think I can do it, too, with a little help. Now, Pepper, I'm asking you to help me."

"Ahuh! Well, let's go in the writing room, where we can talk," said the other, and he took hold of Lane's arm. When they were seated in a secluded corner he lighted a cigar, and faced Lane with shrewd, kindly eyes. "Son, I like you and Blair as well as I hate these slackers Swann and Mackay, and their crowd. I could tell you a heap, and maybe help you, though I think young Holt is not a bad egg.... Is his sister the dark one who steps so straight and holds herself so well?"

"Yes, that sounds like Dorothy," replied Lane.

"She's about the only one I know who doesn't paint her face and I never saw her at—well, never mind where. But the fact I mean makes her stand out in this Middleville crowd like a light in the dark.... Lane, have you got on yet to the speed of the young people of this old burg?"

"I'm getting on, to my sorrow," said Lane.

"Ahuh! You mean you're getting wise to your kid sister?"

"Yes, I'm sorry to say. What do you know, Pepper?"

"Now, son, wait. I'm coming to that, maybe. But I want to know some things first. Is it true—what I hear about your health, bad shape, you know—all cut up in the war? Worse than young Maynard?"

Pepper's hand was close on Lane's. He had forgotten his cigar. His eyes were earnest.

"True?" laughed Lane, grimly. "Yes, it's true.... I won't last long, Pepper, according to Doctor Bronson. That's why I want to make hay while the sun shines."

"Ahuh!" Pepper cleared his throat. "Forgive this, boy.... Is it also true you were engaged to marry that Helen Wrapp—and she threw you down, while you were over there?"

"Yes, that's perfectly true," replied Lane, soberly.

"God, I guess maybe the soldier wasn't up against it!" ejaculated Pepper, with a gesture of mingled awe and wonder and scorn.

"What was the soldier up against, Pepper?" queried Lane. "Frankly, I don't know."

"Lane, the government jollied and forced the boys into the army," replied Pepper. "The country went wild with patriotism. The soldiers were heroes. The women threw themselves away on anything inside a uniform. Make the world safe for democracy—down the Hun—save France and England—ideals, freedom, God's country, and all that! Well, the first few soldiers to return from France got a grand reception, were made heroes of. They were lucky to get back while the sentiment was hot. But that didn't last.... Now, a year and more after the war, where does the soldier get off? Lane, there're over six hundred thousand of you disabled veterans, and for all I can read and find out the government has done next to nothing. New York is full of begging soldiers—on the streets. Think of it! And the poor devils are dying everywhere. My God! think of what's in the mind of one crippled soldier, let alone over half a million. I just have a dim idea of what I'd felt. You must know, or you will know, Lane, for you seem a thoughtful, lofty sort of chap. Just the kind to make a good soldier, because you had ideals and nerve!... Well, a selfish and weak administration could hardly be expected to keep extravagant promises to patriots. But that the American public, as a body, should now be sick of the sight of a crippled soldier—and that his sweetheart should turn him down!—this is the hideous blot, the ineradicable shame, the stinking truth, the damned mystery!"

When Pepper ended his speech, which grew more vehement toward the close, Lane could only stare at him in amaze.

"See here, Lane," added the other hastily, "pardon me for blowing up. I just couldn't help it. I took a shine to you—and to see you like this—brings back the resentment I've had all along. I'm blunt, but it's just as well for you to be put wise quick. You'll find friends, like me, who will stand by you, if you let them. But you'll also find that most of this rotten world has gone back on you...."

Then Pepper made a sharp, passionate gesture that broke his cigar against the arm of his chair, and he cursed low and deep. Presently he addressed Lane again. "Whatever comes of any disclosures I make—whatever you *do*—you'll not give me away?"

"Certainly not. You can trust me, Pepper," returned Lane.

"Son, I'm a wise old guy. There's not much that goes on in Middleville I don't get on to. And I'll make your hair curl. But I'll confine myself to what comes closest home to you. I *get* you, Lane. You're game. You're through. You have come back from war to find a hell of a mess. Your own sister—your sweetheart—your friend's brother and your soldier pard's sister—on the primrose path! And you with your last breath trying to turn them back! I'll say it's a damn fine stunt. I'm an old gambler, Lane. I've lived in many towns and mixed in tough crowds of crooked men and rotten women. But I'm here to confess that this after-the-war stuff of Middleville's better class has knocked out about all the faith I had left in human nature.... Then you came along to teach me a lesson."

"Well, Pepper, that's strong talk," returned Lane. "But cut it, and hurry to—to what comes home to me. What's the matter with these Middleville girls?"

"Lane, any intelligent man, who *knows* things, and who can think for himself, will tell you this—that to judge from the dress, dance, talk, conduct of these young girls—most of them have *apparently* gone wrong."

"You include our nice girls—from what we used to call Middleville's best families?"

"I don't only include them. I throw the emphasis on them. The girls you know best."

Lane straightened up, to look at his companion. Pepper certainly was not drunk.

"Do you know—anything about Lorna?"

"Nothing specifically to prove anything. She's in the thick of this thing in Middleville. Only a few nights ago I saw her at a roadhouse, out on the State Road, with a crowd of youngsters. They were having a high old time, I'll say. They danced jazz, and I saw Lorna drink lemonade into which liquor had been poured from a hip-pocket flask."

Lane put his head on his hands, as if to rest it, or still the throbbing there.

"Who took Lorna to this place?" he asked, presently, breathing heavily.

"I don't know. But it was Dick Swann who poured the drink out of the flask. Between you and me, Lane, that young millionaire is going a pace hereabouts. Listen," he went on, lowering his voice, and glancing round to see there was no one to overhear him, "there's a gambling club in Middleville. I go there. My rooms are in the same building. I've made a peep-hole through the attic floor next to my room. Do I see more things than cards and bottles? Do I! If the fathers of Middleville could see what I've seen they'd go out to the asylum.... I'm not supposed to know it's more than a place to gamble. And nobody knows I know. Dick Swann and Hardy Mackay are at the head of this club. Swann is the genius and the support of it. He's rich, and a high roller if I ever saw one.... Among themselves these young gentlemen call it the Strong Arm Club. Study over that, Lane. Do you *get* it? I know you do, and that saves me talking until I see red."

"Pepper, have you seen my sister—there?" queried Lane, tensely.

"Yes."

"With whom?"

"I'll not say, Lane. There's no need for that. I'll give you a key to my rooms, and you can go there—in the afternoons—and paste yourself to my peep-hole, and watch.... Honest to God, I believe it means bloodshed. But I can't help that. Something must be done. I'm not much good, but I can see that."

Colonel Pepper wiped his moist face. He was now quite pale and his hands shook.

"I never had a wife, or a sweetheart," he went on. "But once I had a little sister. Thank Heaven she didn't live her girlhood in times like these."

Lane again bowed his head on his hands, and wrestled with the might of reality.

"I'm going to take you to these club-rooms to-night," went on Pepper. "It'll cause a hell of a row. But once you get in, there'll be no help for them. Swann and his chums will have to stand for it."

"Did you ever take an outsider in?" asked Lane.

"Several times. Traveling men I met here. Good fellows that liked a game of cards. Swann made no kick at that. He's keen to gamble. And when he's drinking the sky's the limit."

"Wouldn't it be wiser just to show me these rooms, and let me watch from your place—until I find my sister there?" queried Lane.

"I don't know," replied Pepper, thoughtfully. "I think if I were you I'd butt in to-night with me. You can drag young Dalrymple home before he gets drunk."

"Pepper, I'll break up this—this club," declared Lane.

"I'll say you will. And I'm for you strong. If it was only the booze and cards I'd not have squealed. That's my living. But by God, I can't stand for the—the other stuff any longer!... Come on now. And I'll put you on to a slick stunt that'll take your breath away."

He led the way out of the hotel, in his excitement walking rather fast.

"Go slow, Pepper," said Lane. "We're not going over the top."

Pepper gave him a quick, comprehending look.

"Good Lord, Lane, you're not as—as bad as all that!"

Lane nodded. Then at slower pace they went out and down the bright Main Street for two blocks, and then to the right on West Street, which was quite comparable to the other thoroughfare as a business district. At the end of the street the buildings were the oldest in Middleville, and entirely familiar to Lane.

"Give White's the once over," said Pepper, indicating a brightly lighted store across the street. "That place is new to you, isn't it?"

"Yes, I don't remember White, or that there was a confectionery den along here."

"Den is right. It's some den, believe me.... White's a newcomer—a young sport, thick with Swann. For all I know Swann is backing him. Anyway he has a swell joint and a good trade. People kick about his high prices. Ice cream, candy, soda, soft drinks, and all that rot. But if he knows who you are you can get a shot. It'll strike you funny later to see he waits on the customers himself. But when you get wise it'll not be so funny. He's got a tea parlor upstairs—and they say it's some swell place, with a rest room or ladies' dressing room back. Now from this back room the girls can get into the club-rooms of the boys, and go out on the other side of the block. In one way and out the other—at night. Not necessary in the afternoon.... Come on now, well go round the block."

A short walk round the block brought them into a shaded, wide street with one of Middleville's parks on the left. A row of luxuriant elm trees helped the effect of gloom. The nearest electric light was across on the far corner, with trees obscuring it to some extent. At the corner where Pepper halted there was an outside stairway running up the old-fashioned building. The ground floor shops bore the signs of a florist and a milliner; above was a photograph gallery; and the two upper stories were apparently unoccupied. To the left of the two stores another stairway led up into the center of the building. Pepper led Lane up this stairway, a long, dark climb of three stories that taxed Lane's endurance.

"Sure is a junk heap, this old block," observed Pepper, as he fumbled in the dim light with his keys. At length he opened a door, turned on a light and led Lane into his apartment. "I have three rooms here, and the back one opens into a kind of areaway from which I get into an abandoned storeroom, or I guess it's an attic. To-morrow afternoon about three you meet me here and I'll take you in there and let you have a look through the peep-hole I made. It's no use to-night, because there'll be only boys at the club, and I'm going to take you right in."

He switched off the light, drew Lane out and locked the door. "I'm the only person who lives on this floor. There're three holes to this burrow and one of them is at the end of this hall. The exit where the girls slip out is on the floor below, through a hallway to that outside stairs. Oh, I'll say it's a Coney Island maze, this building! But just what these young rakes want.... Come on, and be careful. It'll be dark and the stairs are steep."

At the end of the short hall Pepper opened a door, and led Lane down steep steps in thick darkness, to another hall, dimly lighted by a window opening upon the street.

"You'll have to make a bluff at playing poker, unless my butting in with you causes a row," said Pepper, as he walked along. Presently he came to a door upon which he knocked several times. But before it was opened footsteps and voices sounded down the hall in the opposite direction from which Pepper had escorted Lane.

"Guess they're just coming. Hard luck," said Pepper. "'Fraid you'll not get in now."

Lane counted five dark forms against the background of dim light. He saw the red glow of a cigarette. Then the door upon which Pepper had knocked opened to let out a flare. Pepper gave Lane a shove across the threshold and followed him. Lane did not recognize the young man who had opened the door. The room was large, with old walls and high ceiling, a round table with chairs and a sideboard. It had no windows. The door on the other side was closed.

"Pepper, who's this you're ringin' in on me?" demanded the young fellow.

"A pard of mine. Now don't be peeved, Sammy," replied Pepper. "If there's any kick I'll take the blame. What's got into you that you can gamble and drink' with *slackers*?"

Dalrymple jammed his hat on and stepped toward the door. "Dare, you said a lot. I'll beat it with you—and I'll never come back."

"You bet your sweet life you won't," shouted Swann.

"Hold on there, Dalrymple," interposed Mackay, stepping out. "Come across with that eighty-six bucks you owe me."

"I—I haven't got it, Mackay," rejoined the boy, flushing deeply.

Lane ripped open his coat and jerked out his pocket-book and tore bills out of it. "There, Hardy Mackay," he said, with deliberate scorn, throwing the money on the table. "There are your eighty-six dollars—*earned* in France.... I should think it'd burn your fingers."

He drew Holt out into the hall, where Pepper waited. Some one slammed the door and began to curse.

"That ends that," said Colonel Pepper, as the three moved down the dim hall.

"It ends us, Pepper, but you couldn't stop those guys with a crowbar," retorted Dalrymple.

Lane linked arms with the boy and changed the conversation while they walked back to the inn. Here Colonel Pepper left them, and Lane talked to Holt for an hour. The more he questioned Holt the better he liked him, and yet the more surprised was he at the sordid fact of the boy's inclination toward loose living. There was something perhaps that Holt would not confess. His health had been impaired in the rich coloring, but his face wore a shade of sullen depression. The other two young men Lane had seen in Middleville, but they were unknown to him.

"Pepper, you beat it with your new pard," snarled Swann. "And you'll not get in here again, take that from me."

The mandate nettled Pepper, who evidently felt more deeply over this situation than had appeared on the surface.

"Sure, I'll beat it," returned he, resentfully. "But see here, Swann. Be careful how you shoot off your dirty mouth. It's not beyond me to hand a little tip to my friend Chief of Police Bell."

"You damned squealer!" shouted Swann. "Go ahead—do your worst. You'll find I pull a stroke.... Now get out of here."

With a violent action he shoved the little man out into the hall. Then turning to Lane he pointed with shaking hand to the door.

"Lane, you couldn't be a guest of mine."

"Swann, I certainly wouldn't be," retorted Lane, in tones that rang. "Pepper didn't tell me you were the proprietor of this—this joint."

"Get out of here or I'll throw you out!" yelled Swann, now beside himself with rage. And he made a threatening move toward Lane.

"Don't lay a hand on me," replied Lane. "I don't want my uniform soiled."

With that Lane turned to Dalrymple, and said quietly: "Holt, I came here to find you, not to play cards. That was a stall. Come away with me. You were not cut out for a card sharp or a booze fighter. What's got into you that you can gamble and drink' with *slackers*?"

Dalrymple jammed his hat on and stepped toward the door. "Dare, you said a lot. I'll beat it with you—and I'll never come back."

"You bet your sweet life you won't," shouted Swann.

"Hold on there, Dalrymple," interposed Mackay, stepping out. "Come across with that eighty-six bucks you owe me."

"I—I haven't got it, Mackay," rejoined the boy, flushing deeply.

Lane ripped open his coat and jerked out his pocket-book and tore bills out of it. "There, Hardy Mackay," he said, with deliberate scorn, throwing the money on the table. "There are your eighty-six dollars—*earned* in France.... I should think it'd burn your fingers."

He drew Holt out into the hall, where Pepper waited. Some one slammed the door and began to curse.

"That ends that," said Colonel Pepper, as the three moved down the dim hall.

"It ends us, Pepper, but you couldn't stop those guys with a crowbar," retorted Dalrymple.

Lane linked arms with the boy and changed the conversation while they walked back to the inn. Here Colonel Pepper left them, and Lane talked to Holt for an hour. The more he questioned Holt the better he liked him, and yet the more surprised was he at the sordid fact of the boy's inclination toward loose living. There was something perhaps that Holt would not confess. His health had been impaired in the service, but not seriously. He was getting stronger all the time. His old job was waiting for him. His mother and sister had enough to live on, but if he had been working he could have helped them in a way to afford him great satisfaction.

"Holt, listen," finally said Lane, with more earnestness. "We're friends—all boys of the service are friends. We might even become great pards, if we had time."

"What's time got to do with it?" queried the younger man. "I'm sure I'd like it—and know it'd help me."

"I'm shot to pieces, Holt.... I won't last long...."

"Aw, Lane, don't say that!"

"It's true. And if I'm to help you at all it must be now.... You haven't told me everything, boy—now have you?"

Holt dropped his head.

"I'll say—I haven't," he replied, haltingly. "Lane—the trouble is—I'm clean gone on Margie Maynard. But her mother hates the sight of me. She won't stand for me."

"Oho! So that's it?" ejaculated Lane, a light breaking in upon him. "Well, I'll be darned. It *is* serious, Holt.... Does Margie love you?"

"Sure she does. We've always cared. Don't you remember how Margie and I and Dal and you used to go to school together? And come home together? And play on Saturdays?... Ever since then!... But lately Margie and I are—we got—pretty badly mixed up."

"Yes, I remember those days," replied Lane, dreamily, and suddenly he recalled Dal's dark eyes, somehow haunting. He had to make an effort to get back to the issue at hand.

"If Margie loves you—why it's all right. Go back to work and marry her."

"Lane, it can't be all right. Mrs. Maynard has handed me the mitt," replied Holt, bitterly. "And Margie hasn't the courage to run off with me.... Her mother is throwing Margie at Swann—because he's rich."

"Oh Lord, no—Holt—you can't mean *it*!" exclaimed Lane, aghast.

"I'll say I do mean it. I *know* it," returned Holt, moodily. "So I let go—fell into the dumps—didn't care a d—— what became of me."

Lane was genuinely shocked. What a tangle he had fallen upon! Once again there seemed to confront him a colossal Juggernaut, a moving, crushing, intangible thing, beyond his power to cope with.

"Now, what can I do?" queried Holt, in sudden hope his friend might see a way out.

Despairingly, Lane racked his brain for some word of advice or assurance, if not of solution. But he found none. Then his spirit mounted, and with it passion.

"Holt, don't be a miserable coward," he began, in fierce scorn. "You're a soldier, man, and you've got your life to *live*!... The sun will rise—the days will be long and pleasant—you can work—*do* something. You can fish the streams in summer and climb the hills in autumn. You can enjoy. Bah! don't tell me one shallow girl means the world. If Margie hasn't courage enough to run off and marry you—*let her go!* But you can never tell. Maybe Margie will stick to you. I'll help you. Margie and I have always been friends and I'll try to influence her. Then think of your mother and sister. Work for *them*. Forget yourself—your little, miserable, selfish desires.... My God, boy, but it's a strange life the war's left us to face. I *hate* it. So do you hate it. Swann and Mackay giving nothing and getting all!... So it looks.... But it's false—false. God did not intend men to live solely for their bodies. A balance *must* be struck. They have *got* to pay. Their time will come.... As for you, the harder this job is the fiercer you should be. I've got to die, Holt. But if I could live I'd show these slackers, these fickle wild girls, what they're doing.... You can do it, Holt. It's the greatest part any man could be called upon to play. It will prove the difference between you and them...."

Holt Dalrymple crushed Lane's hand in both his own. On his face was a glow—his dark eyes flashed: "Lane—that'll be about all," he burst out with a kind of breathlessness. Then his head high, he stalked out.

The next day was bad. Lane suffered from both over-exertion and intensity of emotion. He remained at home all day, in bed most of the time. At supper time he went downstairs to find Lorna pirouetting in a new dress, more abbreviated at top and bottom than any costume he had seen her wear. The effect struck him at an inopportune time. He told her flatly that she looked like a French grisette of the music halls, and ought to be ashamed to be seen in such attire.

"Daren, I don't think you're a good judge of clothes these days," she observed, complacently. "The boys will say I look spiffy in this."

So many times Lorna's trenchant remarks silenced Lane. She hit the nail on the head. Practical, logical, inevitable were some of her speeches. She knew what men wanted. That was the pith of her meaning. What else mattered?

"But Lorna, suppose you don't look nice?" he questioned.

"I *do* look nice," she retorted.

"You don't look anything of the kind."

"What's nice? It's only a word. It doesn't mean much in my young life."

"Where are you going to-night?" he asked, sitting down to the table.

"To the armory—basketball game—and dance afterward."

"With whom?"

"With Harry. I suppose that pleases you, big brother?"

"Yes, it does. I like him. I wish he'd take you out oftener."

"*Take* me! Hot dog! He'd kill himself to take me all the time. But Harry's slow. He bores me. Then he hasn't got a car."

"Lorna, you may as well know now that I'm going to stop your car rides," said Lane, losing his patience.

"You are *not*," she retorted, and in the glint of the eyes meeting his, Lane saw his defeat. His patience was exhausted, his fear almost verified. He did not mince words. With his mother standing open-mouthed and shocked, Lane gave his sister to understand what he thought of automobile rides, and that as far as she was concerned they had to be stopped. If she would not stop them out of respect to her mother and to him, then he would resort to other measures. Lorna bounced up in a fury, and in the sharp quarrel that followed, Lane realized he was dealing with flint full of fire. Lorna left without finishing her supper.

"Daren, that's not the way," said his mother, shaking her head.

"What is the way, mother?" he asked, throwing up his hands.

"I don't know, unless it's to see her way," responded the mother. "Sometimes I feel so—so old-fashioned and ignorant before Lorna. Maybe she is right. How can we tell? What makes all the young girls like that?"

What indeed, wondered Lane! The question had been hammering at his mind for over a month. He went back to bed, weary and dejected, suffering spasms of pain, like blades, through his lungs, and grateful for the darkness. Almost he wished it was all over—this ordeal. How puny his efforts! Relentlessly life marched on. At midnight he was still fighting his pangs, still unconquered. In the night his dark room was not empty. There were faces, shadows, moving images and pictures, scenes of the war limned against the blackness. At last he rested, grew as free from pain as he ever grew, and slept. In the morning it was another day, and the past was as if it were not.

May the first dawned ideally springlike, warm, fresh, fragrant, with birds singing, sky a clear blue, and trees budding green and white.

Lane yielded to an impulse that had grown stronger of late. His steps drew him to the little drab house where Mel Iden lived with her aunt. On the way, which led past a hedge, Lane gathered a bunch of violets.

"'In the spring a young man's fancy lightly turns to thoughts of love,'" he mused. "It's good, even for *me*, to be alive this morning.... These violets, the birds, the fresh smells, the bursting green! Oh, well, regrets are idle. But just to think—I had to go through all I've known—right down to this moment—to realize how stingingly sweet life is...."

Mel answered his knock, and sight of her face seemed to lift his heart with an unwonted throb. Had he unconsciously needed that? The thought made his greeting, and the tender of the violets, awkward for him.

"Violets! Oh, and spring! Daren, it was good of you to gather them for me. I remember.... But I told you not to come again."

"Yes, I know you did," he replied. "But I've disobeyed you. I wanted to see you, Mel.... I didn't know how badly until I got here."

"You should not want to see me at all. People will talk."

"So you care what people say of you?" he questioned, feigning surprise.

"Of me? No. I was thinking of you."

"You fear the poison tongues for me? Well, they cannot harm me. I'm beyond tongues or minds like those."

She regarded him earnestly, with serious gravity and slowly dawning apprehension; then, turning to arrange the violets in a tiny vase, she shook her head.

"Daren, you're beyond me, too. I feel a—a change in you. Have you had another sick spell?"

"Only for a day off and on. I'm really pretty well to-day. But I have changed. I feel that, yet I don't know how."

Lane could talk to her. She stirred him, drew him out of himself. He felt a strange desire for her sympathy, and a keen curiosity concerning her opinions.

"I thought maybe you'd been ill again or perhaps upset by the consequences of your—your action at Fanchon Smith's party."

"Who told you of that?" he asked in surprise.

"Dal. She was here yesterday. She will come in spite of me."

"So will I," interposed Lane.

She shook her head. "No, it's different for a man.... I've missed the girls. No one but Dal ever comes. I thought Margie would be true to me—no matter what had befallen.... Dal comes, and oh, Daren, she is good. She helps me so.... She told me what you did at Fanchon's party."

"She did! Well, what's your verdict?" he queried, grimly. "That break queered me in Middleville."

"I agree with what Doctor Wallace said to his congregation," returned Mel.

As Lane met the blue fire of her eyes he experienced another singularly deep and profound thrill, as if the very depths of him had been stirred. He seemed to have suddenly discovered Mel Iden.

"Doctor Wallace did back me up," said Lane, with a smile. "But no one else did."

"Don't be so sure of that. Harsh conditions require harsh measures. Dal said you killed the camel-walk dance in Middleville."

"It surely was a disgusting sight," returned Lane, with a grimace. "Mel, I just saw red that night."

"Daren," she asked wistfully, following her own train of thought, "do you know that most of the girls consider me an outcast? Fanchon rides past me with her head up in the air. Helen Wrapp cuts me. Margie looks to see if her mother is watching when she bows to me. Isn't it strange, Daren, how things turn out? Maybe my old friends are right. But I don't *feel* that I am what they think I am.... I would do what I did—over and over."

Her eyes darkened under his gaze, and a slow crimson tide stained her white face.

"I understand you, Mel," he said, swiftly. "You must forgive me that I didn't understand at once.... And I think you are infinitely better, finer, purer than these selfsame girls who scorn you."

"Daren! You—understand?" she faltered.

And just as swiftly he told her the revelation that thinking had brought to him. When he had finished she looked at him for a long while. "Yes, Daren," she finally said, "you understand, and you have made me understand. I always felt"—and her hand went to her heart—"but my mind did not grasp.... Oh, Daren, how I thank you!" and she held her hands out to him.

Lane grasped the outstretched hands, and loosed the leaping thought her words and action created.

"Mel, let me give your boy a father—a name."

No blow could have made her shrink so palpably. It passed—that shame. Her lips parted, and other emotions claimed her.

"Daren—you would—marry me?" she gasped.

"I am asking you to be my wife for your child's sake," he replied.

Her head bowed. She sank against him, trembling. Her hands clung tightly to his. Lane divined something of her agitation from the feel of her slender form. And then again that deep and profound thrill ran over him. It was followed by an instinct to wrap her in his arms, to hold her, to share her trouble and to protect her.

Strong reserve force suddenly came to Mel. She drew away from Lane, still quivering, but composed.

"Daren, all my life I'll thank you and bless you for that offer," she said, very low. "But, of course it is impossible."

She disengaged her hands, and, turning away, looked out of the window. Lane rather weakly sat down. What had come over him? His blood seemed bursting in his veins. Then he gazed round the dingy little parlor and at this girl of twenty, whose beauty did not harmonize with her surroundings. Fair-haired, white-faced, violet-eyed, she emanated tragedy. He watched her profile, clear cut as a cameo, fine brow, straight nose, sensitive lips, strong chin. She was biting those tremulous lips. And when she turned again to him they were red. The short-bowed upper lip, full and sweet, the lower, with its sensitive droop at the corner, eloquent of sorrow—all at once Lane realized he wanted to kiss that mouth more than he had ever wanted anything. The moment was sudden and terrible, for it meant love—love such as he had never known.

"Daren," she said, turning, "tell me how you got the *Croix de Guerre*."

By the look of her and the hand that moved toward his breast, Lane felt his power over her. He began his story and it was as if he heard some one else talking. When he had finished, she asked, "The French Army honored you, why not the American?"

"It was never reported."

"How strange! Who was your officer?"

"You'll laugh when you hear," he replied, without hint of laugh himself. "Heavens, how things come about! My officer was from Middleville."

"Daren! Who?" she asked, quickly, her eyes darkening with thought.

"Captain Vane Thesel."

How singular to Lane the fact she did not laugh! She only stared. Then it seemed part of her warmth and glow, her subtle response to his emotion, slowly receded. He felt what he could not see.

"Oh! He. Vane Thesel," she said, without wonder or surprise or displeasure, or any expression Lane anticipated.

Her strange detachment stirred a hideous thought—could Thesel have been.... But Lane killed the culmination of that thought. Not, however, before dark, fiery jealousy touched him with fangs new to his endurance.

To drive it away, Lane launched into more narrative of the war. And as he talked he gradually forgot himself. It might be hateful to rake up the burning threads of memory for the curious and the soulless, but to tell Mel Iden it was a keen, strange delight. He watched the changes of her expression. He learned to bring out the horror, sadness, glory that abided in her heart. And at last he cut himself off abruptly: "But I must save something for another day."

That broke the spell.

"No, you must never come back."

He picked up his hat and his stick.

"Mel, would you shut the door in my face?"

"No, Daren—but I'll not open it," she replied resolutely.

"Why?"

"You must not come."

"For my sake—or yours?"

"Both our sakes."

He backed out on the little porch, and looked at her as she stood there. Beyond him, indeed, were his emotions then. Sad as she seemed, he wanted to make her suffer more—an inexplicable and shameful desire.

"Mel, you and I are alike," he said.

"Oh, no, Daren; you are noble and I am...."

"Mel, in my dreams I see myself standing—plodding along the dark shores of a river—that river of tears which runs down the vast naked stretch of our inner lives.... I see you now, on the opposite shore. Let us reach our hands across—for the baby's sake."

"Daren, it is a beautiful thought, but it—it can't be," she whispered.

"Then let me come to see you when I need—when I'm down," he begged.

"No."

"Mel, what harm can it do—just to let me come?"

"No—don't ask me. Daren, I am no stone."

"You'll be sorry when I'm out there in—Woodlawn.... That won't be long."

That broke her courage and her restraint.

"Come, then," she whispered, in tears.

CHAPTER VIII

Lane's intentions and his spirit were too great for his endurance. It was some time before he got downtown again. And upon entering the inn he was told some one had just called him on the telephone.

"Hello, this is Lane," he answered. "Who called me?"

"It's Blair," came the reply. "How are you, old top?"

"Not so well. I've been down and out."

"Sorry. Suppose that's why you haven't called me up for so long?"

"Well, Buddy, I can't lay it all to that.... And how're you?"

The answer did not come. So Lane repeated his query.

"Well, I'm still hobbling round on one leg," replied Blair.

"That's good. Tell me about Reddie."

Again the reply was long in coming....

"Haven't you heard—about Red?"

"No."

"Haven't seen the newspapers lately?"

"I never read the papers, Blair."

"Right-o. But I had to.... Buck up, now, Dare!"

"All right. Shoot it quick," returned Lane, feeling his breast contract and his skin tighten with a chill.

"Red Payson has gone west."

"Blair! You don't mean—dead?" exclaimed Lane.

"Yes, Reddie's gone—and I guess it's just as well, poor devil!"

"How? When?"

"Two days ago, according to papers.... He died in Washington, D.C. Fell down in the vestibule of one of the government offices—where he was waiting.... fell with another hemorrhage—and died right there—on the floor—quick."

"My—God!" gasped Lane.

"Yes, it's tough. You see, Dare, I couldn't keep Reddie here. Heaven knows I tried, but he wouldn't stay.... I'm afraid he heard my mother complaining. Say, Dare, suppose I have somebody drive me in town to see you."

"I'd like that, Blair."

"You're on. And say, I've another idea. Tonight's the Junior Prom—did you know that?"

"No, I didn't."

"Well, it is. Suppose we go up? My sister can get me cards.... I tell you, Dare, I'd like to see what's going on in that bunch. I've heard a lot and seen some things."

"Did you hear how I mussed up Fanchon Smith's party?"

"You bet I did. That's one reason I want to see some of this dancing. Will you go?"

"Yes, I can stand it if you can."

"All right, Buddy, I'll meet you at the inn—eight o'clock."

Lane slowly made his way to a secluded corner of the lobby, where he sat down. Red Payson dead! Lane felt that he should not have been surprised or shocked. But he was both. The strange, cold sensation gradually wore away and with it the slight trembling of his limbs. A mournful procession of thoughts and images returned to his mind and he sat and brooded.

At the hour of his appointment with his friend, Lane went to the front of the lobby. Blair was on time. He hobbled in, erect and martial of bearing despite the crutch, and his dark citizen's suit emphasized the whiteness of his face. Being home had softened Blair a little. Yet the pride and tragic bitterness were there. But when Blair espied Lane a warmth burned out of the havoc in his face. Lane's conscience gave him a twinge. It dawned upon him that neither his spells of illness, nor his distress over his sister Lorna, nor his obsession to see and understand what the young people were doing could hold him wholly excusable for having neglected his comrade.

Their hand-clasp was close, almost fierce, and neither spoke at once. But they looked intently into each other's faces. Emotion stormed Lane's heart. He realized that Blair loved him and that he loved Blair—and that between them was a measureless bond, a something only separation could make tangible. But little of what they felt came out in their greetings.

"Dare, why the devil don't you can that uniform," demanded Blair, cheerfully. "People might recognize you've been 'over there.'"

"Well, Blair, I expected you'd have a cork leg by this time," said Lane.

"Nothing doing," returned the other. "I want to be perpetually reminded that I was in the war. This 'forget the war' propaganda we see and hear all over acts kind of queer on a soldier.... Let's find a bench away from these people."

After they were comfortably seated Blair went on: "Do you know, Dare, I don't miss my leg so much when I'm crutching around. But when I try to sit down or get up! By heck, sometimes I forget it's gone. And sometimes I want to scratch my lost foot. Isn't that hell?"

"I'll say so, Buddy," returned Lane, with a laugh.

"Read this," said Blair, taking a paper from his pocket, and indicating a column.

Whereupon Lane read a brief Associated Press dispatch from Washington, D.C., stating that one Payson, disabled soldier of twenty-five, suffering with tuberculosis caused by gassed lungs, had come to Washington to make in person a protest and appeal that had been unanswered in letters. He wanted money from the government to enable him to travel west to a dry climate, where doctors assured him he might get well. He made his statement to several clerks and officials, and waited all day in the vestibule of the department. Suddenly he was seized with a hemorrhage, and, falling on the floor, died before aid could be summoned.

Without a word Lane handed the paper back to his friend.

"Red was a queer duck," said Blair, rather hoarsely. "You remember when I 'phoned you last over two weeks ago?... Well, just after that Red got bad on my hands. He wouldn't accept charity, he said. And he wanted to beat it. He got wise to my mother. He wouldn't give up trying to get money from the government—back money owed him, he swore—and the idea of being turned down at home seemed to obsess him. I talked and cussed myself weak. No good! Red beat it soon after that—beat it from Middleville on a freight train. And I never heard a word from him.... Not a word...."

"Blair, can't you see it Red's way?" queried Lane, sadly.

"Yes, I can," responded Blair, "but hell! he might have gotten well. Doc Bronson said Red had a chance. I could have borrowed enough money to get him out west. Red wouldn't take it."

"And he ran off—exposed himself to cold and starvation—over-exertion and anger," added Lane.

"Exactly. Brought on that hemorrhage and croaked. All for nothing!"

"No, Blair. All for a principle," observed Lane. "Red was fired out of the hospital without a dollar. There was something terribly wrong."

"Wrong?... God Almighty!" burst out Blair, with hard passion. "Let me read you something in this same paper." With shaking hands he unfolded it, searched until he found what he wanted, and began to read:

"'If the *actual* needs of disabled veterans require the expenditure of much money, then unquestionably a majority of the taxpayers of the country will favor spending it. Despite the insistent demand for economy in Washington that is arising from every part of the country, no member of House or Senate will have occasion to fear that he is running counter to popular opinion when eventually he votes to take generous care of disabled soldiers.'"

Blair's trembling voice ceased, and then twisting the newspaper into a rope, he turned to Lane. "Dare, can you understand that?... Red Payson was a bull-headed boy, not over bright. But you and I have some intelligence, I hope. We can allow for the immense confusion at Washington—the senselessness of red tape—the callosity of politicians. But when we remember the eloquent calls to us boys—the wonderfully worded appeals to our patriotism, love of country and home—the painted posters bearing the picture of a beautiful American girl—or a young mother with a baby— remembering these deep, passionate calls to the best in us, can you understand *that* sort of talk now?"

"Blair, I think I can," replied Lane. "Then—before and after the draft—the whole country was at a white heat of all that the approach of war rouses. Fear, self- preservation, love of country, hate of the Huns, inspired patriotism, and in most everybody the will to fight and to sacrifice.... The war was a long, hideous, soul-racking, nerve-destroying time. When it ended, and the wild period of joy and relief had its run, then all that pertained to the war sickened and wearied and disgusted the majority of people. It's 'forget the war.' You and Payson and I got home a year too late."

"Then—it's just—monstrous," said Blair, heavily.

"That's all, Blair. Just monstrous. But we can't beat our spirits out against this wall. No one can understand us—how alone we are. Let's forget *that*—this wall—this thing called government. Shall we spend what time we have to live always in a thunderous atmosphere of mind—hating, pondering, bitter?"

"No. I'll make a compact with you," returned Blair, with flashing eyes. "Never to speak again of *that*—so long as we live!"

"Never to a living soul," rejoined Lane, with a ring in his voice.

They shook hands much the same as when they had met half an hour earlier.

"So!" exclaimed Blair, with a deep breath. "And now, Dare, tell me how you made out with Helen. You cut me short over the 'phone."

"Blair, that day coming into New York on the ship, you didn't put it half strong enough," replied Lane. Then he told Blair about the call he had made upon Helen, and what had transpired at her studio.

Blair did not voice the scorn that his eyes expressed. And, in fact, most of his talking was confined to asking questions. Lane found it easy enough to unburden himself, though he did not mention his calls on Mel Iden, or Colonel Pepper's disclosures.

"Well, I guess it's high time we were meandering up to the hall," said Blair, consulting his watch. "I'm curious about this Prom. Think we're in for a jolt. It's four years since I went to a Prom. Now, both of us, Dare, have a sister who'll be there, besides all our old friends.... And we're not dancing! But I want to look on. They've got an out-of-town orchestra coming—a jazz orchestra. There'll probably be a hot time in the old town to-night."

"Lorna did not tell me," replied Lane, as they got up to go. "But I suppose she'd rather I didn't know. We've clashed a good deal lately."

"Dare, I hear lots of talk," said Blair. "Margaret is chummy with me, and some of her friends are always out at the house. I hear Dick Swann is rushing Lorna. Think he's doing it on the q-t."

"I know he is, Blair, but I can't catch them together," returned Lane. "Lorna is working now. Swann got her the job."

"Looks bad to me," replied Blair, soberly. "Swann is cutting a swath. I hear his old man is sore on him.... I'd take Lorna out of that office quick."

"Maybe you would," declared Lane, grimly. "For all the influence or power I have over Lorna I might as well not exist."

They walked silently along the street for a little while. Lane had to accommodate his step to the slower movement of his crippled friend. Blair's crutch tapped over the stone pavement and clicked over the curbs. They crossed the railroad tracks and turned off the main street to go down a couple of blocks.

"Shades of the past!" exclaimed Blair, as they reached a big brick building, well-lighted in front by a sizzling electric lamp. The night was rather warm and clouds of insects were wheeling round the light. "The moths and the flame!" added Blair, satirically. "Well, Dare, old bunkie, brace up and we'll go over the top. This ought to be fun for us."

"I don't see it," replied Lane. "I'll be about as welcome as a bull in a china shop."

"Oh, I didn't mean any one would throw fits over us," responded Blair. "But we ought to get some fun out of the fact."

"What fact?" queried Lane, puzzled.

"Rather far-fetched, maybe. But I'll get a kick out of looking on—watching these swell slackers with the girls *we* fought for."

"Wonder why they didn't give the dance at the armory, where they'd not have to climb stairs, and have more room?" queried Lane, as they went in under the big light.

"Dare, you're far back in the past," said Blair, sardonically. "The armory is on the ground floor—one big hall—open, you know. The Assembly Hall is a regular maze for rooms and stairways."

Blair labored up the stairway with Lane's help. At last they reached the floor from which had blared the strains of jazz. Wide doors were open, through which Lane caught the flash of many colors. Blair produced his tickets at the door. There did not appear to be any one to take them.

Lane experienced an indefinable thrill at the scene. The air seemed to reek with a mixed perfume and cigarette smoke—to resound with high-keyed youthful laughter, wild and sweet and vacant above the strange, discordant music. Then the flashing, changing, whirling colors of the dancers struck Lane as oriental, erotic, bizarre—gorgeous golds and greens and reds striped by the conventional black. Suddenly the blare ceased, and the shrill, trilling laughter had dominance. The rapid circling of forms came to a sudden stop, and the dancers streamed in all directions over the floor.

"Dare, they've called time," said Blair. "Let's get inside the ropes so we can see better."

The hall was not large, but it was long, and shaped like a letter L with pillars running down the center. Countless threads of many-colored strings of paper had been stretched from pillars to walls, hanging down almost within reach of the dancers. Flags and gay bunting helped in the riotous effect of decoration. The black-faced orchestra held forth on a raised platform at the point where the hall looked two ways. Recesses, alcoves and open doors to other rooms, which the young couples were piling over each other to reach, gave Lane some inkling of what Blair had hinted.

"Now we're out in the limelight," announced Blair, as he halted. "Let's stand here and run the gauntlet until the next dance—then we can find seats."

Almost at once a stream of gay couples enveloped them in passing. Bright, flashing, vivid faces and bare shoulders, arms and breasts appeared above the short bodices of the girls. Few of them were gowned in white. The colors seemed too garish for anything but musical comedy. But the freshness, the vividness of these girls seemed exhilarating. The murmur, the merriment touched a forgotten chord in Lane's heart. For a moment it seemed sweet to be there, once more in a gathering where pleasure was the pursuit. It breathed of what seemed long ago, in a past that was infinitely more precious to remember because he had no future of hope or of ambition or dream. Something had happened to him that now made the sensations of the moment stingingly bitter-sweet. The freshness and fragrance, the color and excitement, the beauty and gayety were not for him. Youth was dead. He could never enter the lists with these young men, many no younger than he, for the favor and smile of a girl. Resignation had not been so difficult in the spiritual moment of realization and resolve, but to be presented with one concrete and stunning actuality after another, each with its mocking might-have-been, had grown to be a terrible ordeal.

Lane looked for faces he knew. On each side of the pillar where he and Blair stood the stream of color and gayety flowed. Helen and Margaret Maynard went by on the far edge of that stream. Across the hall he caught a glimpse of the flashing golden beauty of Bessy Bell. Then near at hand he recognized Fanchon Smith, a petite, smug-faced little brunette, with naked shoulders bulging out of a piebald gown. She espied Lane and her face froze. Then there were familiar faces near and far, to which Lane could not attach names.

All at once he became aware that other of his senses besides sight were being stimulated. He had been hearing without distinguishing what he heard. And curiously he listened, still with that strange knock of memory at his heart. Everybody was talking, some low, some high, all in the spirit of the hour. And in one moment he had heard that which killed the false enchantment.

"Not a chance!...."

"Hot dog—she's some Jane!"

"Now to the clinch—"

"What'll we do till the next spiel—"

"Have a shot?——"

"Boys, it's only the shank of the evening. Leave something peppy for the finish."

"Mame, you look like a million dollars in that rag."

"She shakes a mean shimmy, believe me...."

"That egg! Not on your life!"

"Cut the next with Ned. We'll sneak down and take a ride in my car...."

"Oh, spiffy!"

Lane's acutely strained attention was diverted by Blair's voice.

"Look who's with my sister Margie."

Lane turned to look through an open space in the dispersing stream. Blair's sister was passing with Dick Swann. Elegantly and fastidiously attired, the young millionaire appeared to be attentive to his partner. Margaret stood out rather strikingly from the other girls near her by reason of the simplicity and modesty of her dress. She did not look so much bored as discontented. Lane saw her eyes rove to and fro from the entrance of the hall. When she espied Lane she nodded and spoke with a smile and made an evident move toward him, but was restrained by Swann. He led her past Lane and Blair without so much as glancing in their direction. Lane heard Blair swear.

"Dare, if my mother throws Marg at that—slacker, I'll block the deal if it's the last thing I ever do," he declared, violently.

"And I'll help you," replied Lane, instantly.

"I know Margie hates him."

"Blair, your sister is in love with Holt Dalrymple."

"No! Not really? Thought that was only a boy-and-girl affair.... Aha! the nigger music again! Let's find a seat, Dare."

Saxophone, trombone, piccolo, snare-drum and other barbaric instruments opened with a brazen defiance of music, and a vibrant assurance of quick, raw, strong sounds. Lane himself felt the stirring effect upon his nerves. He had difficulty in keeping still. From the lines of chairs along the walls and from doors and alcoves rushed the gay-colored throng to leap, to close, to step, to rock and sway, until the floor was full of a moving mass of life.

The first half-dozen couples Lane studied all danced more or less as Helen and Swann had, that day in Helen's studio. Then, by way of a remarkable contrast, there passed two young people who danced decently. Lane descried his sister Lorna in the throng, and when she and her partner came round in the giddy circle, Lane saw that she wiggled and toddled like the others. Lane, as she passed him, caught a glance of her eyes, flashing, reproachful, furious, directed at some one across her partner's shoulder. Lane followed that glance and saw Swann. Apparently he did not notice Lorna, and was absorbed in the dance with his own partner, Helen Wrapp. This byplay further excited Lane's curiosity. On the whole, it was an ungraceful, violent mob, almost totally lacking in restraint, whirling, kicking, swaying, clasping, instinctively physical, crude, vulgar and wild. Down the line of chairs from his position, Lane saw the chaperones of the Prom, no doubt mothers of some of these girls. Lane wondered at them with sincere and persistent amaze. If they were respectable, and had even a slight degree of intelligence, how could they look on at this dance with complacence? Perhaps after all the young people were not wholly to blame for an abnormal expression of instinctive action.

That dance had its several encores and finally ended.

Margaret and Holt made their way up to Lane and Blair. The girl was now radiant. It took no second glance for Lane to see how matters stood with her at that moment.

"Say, beat it, you two," suddenly spoke up Blair. "There comes Swann. He's looking for you. Chase yourselves, now, Marg—Holt. Leave that slacker to *us*!"

Margaret gave a start, a gasp. She looked hard at her brother. Blair wore a cool smile, underneath which there was sterner hidden meaning. Then Margaret looked at Lane with slow, deep blush, making her really beautiful.

"Margie, we're for you two, strong," said Lane, with a smile. "Go hide from Swann."

"But I—I came with him," she faltered.

"Then let him find you—in other words, let him *get* you.... 'All's fair in love and war.'"

Lane had his reward in the sweet amaze and confusion of her face, as she turned away. Holt rushed her off amid the straggling couples.

"Dare, you're a wiz," declared Blair. "Margie's strong for Holt—I'm glad. If we could only put Swann out of the running."

"It's a cinch," returned Lane, with sudden heat.

"Pard, you don't know my mother. If she has picked out Swann for Margie—all I've got to say is—good night!"

"Even if we prove Swann——"

"No matter what we prove," interrupted Blair. "No matter what, so long as he's out of jail. My mother is money mad. She'd sell Margie to the devil himself for gold, position—the means to queen it over these other mothers of girls."

"Blair, you're—you're a little off your nut, aren't you?"

"Not on your life. That talk four years ago might have been irrational. But now—not on your life.... The world has come to an end.... Oh, Lord, look who's coming! Lane, did you ever in your life see such a peach as that?"

Bessy Bell had appeared, coming toward them with a callow youth near her own age. Her dress was some soft, pale blue material that was neither gaudy nor fantastical. But it was far from modest. Lane had to echo Blair's eulogy of this young specimen of the new America. She simply verified and stabilized the assertion that physically the newer generations of girls were markedly more beautiful than those of any generation before.

Bessy either forgot to introduce her escort or did not care to. She nodded a dismissal to him, spoke sweetly to Blair, and then took the empty chair next to Lane.

"You're having a rotten time," she said, leaning close to him. She seemed all fragrance and airy grace and impelling life.

Lane had to smile. "How do you know?"

"I can tell by your face. Now aren't you?"

"Well, to be honest, Miss Bessy"

"For tripe's sake, don't be so formal," she interrupted. "Call me Bessy."

"Oh, very well, Bessy. There's no use to lie to you. I'm not very happy at what I see here."

"What's the matter with it—with us?" she queried, quickly. "Everybody's doing it."

"That is no excuse. Besides, that's not so. Everybody is not—not——"

"Well, not what?"

"Not doing it, whatever you meant by that," returned Lane, with a laugh.

"Tell me straight out what *you* think of us," she shot at Lane, with a purple flash of her eyes.

She irritated Lane. Stirred him somehow, yet she seemed wholesome, full of quick response. She was daring, sophisticated, provocative. Therefore Lane retorted in brief, blunt speech what he thought of the majority of the girls present.

Bessy Bell did not look insulted. She did not blush. She did not show shame. Her eyes darkened. Her rosy mouth lost something of its soft curves.

"Daren Lane, we're not all rotten," she said.

"I did not say or imply you *all* were," he replied.

She gazed up at him thoughtfully, earnestly, with an unconscious frank interest, curiosity, and reverence.

"You strike me funny," she mused. "I never met a soldier like you."

"Bessy, how many soldiers have you met who have come back from France?"

"Not many, only Blair and you, and Captain Thesel, though I really didn't meet him. He came up to me at the armory and spoke to me. And to-night he cut in on Roy's dance. Roy was sore."

"Three. Well, that's not many," replied Lane. "Not enough to get a line on two million, is it?"

"Captain Thesel is just like all the other fellows.... But you're not a bit like them."

"Is that a compliment or otherwise?"

"I'll say it's a compliment," she replied, with arch eyes on his.

"Thank you."

"Well, you don't deserve it.... You promised to make a date with me. Why haven't you?"

"Why child, I—I don't know what to say," returned Lane, utterly disconcerted. Yet he liked this amazing girl. "I suppose I forgot. But I've been ill, for one reason."

"I'm sorry," she said, giving his arm a squeeze. "I heard you were badly hurt. Won't you tell me about your—your hurts?"

"Some day, if opportunity affords. I can't here, that's certain."

"Opportunity! What do you want? Haven't I handed myself out on a silver platter?"

Lane could find no ready retort for this query. He gazed at her, marveling at the apparently measureless distance between her exquisite physical beauty and the spiritual beauty that should have been harmonious with it. Still he felt baffled by this young girl. She seemed to resemble Lorna, yet was different in a way he could not grasp. Lorna had coarsened in fibre. This girl was fine, despite her coarse speech. She did not repel.

"Mr. Lane, will you dance with me?" she asked, almost wistfully. She liked him, and was not ashamed of it. But she seemed pondering over what to make of him—how far to go.

"Bessy, I dare not exert myself to that extent," he replied, gently. "You forget I am a disabled soldier."

"Forget that? Not a chance," she flashed. "But I hoped you might dance with me once—just a little."

"No. I might keel over."

She shivered and her eyes dilated. "You mean it as a joke. But it's no joke.... I read about your comrade—that poor Red Payson!" ... Then both devil of humor and woman of fire shone in her glance. "Daren, if you *did* keel over—you'd die in my arms—not on the floor!"

Then another partner came up to claim her. As the orchestra blurted forth and Bessy leaned to the dancer's clasp she shouted audaciously at Lane: "Don't forget that silver platter!"

Lane turned to Blair to find that worthy shaking his handsome head.

"Did you hear what she said?" asked Lane, close to Blair's ear.

"Every word," replied Blair. "Some kid!... She's like the girl in the motion-pictures. She comes along. She meets the fellow. She looks at him—she says 'good day'—then *Wham*, into his arms.... My God!... Lane, is that kid good or bad?"

"Good!" exclaimed Lane, instantly.

"Bah!"

"Good—still," returned Lane. "But alas! She is brazen, unconscious of it. But she's no fool, that kid. Lorna is an absolute silly bull-headed fool. I wish Bessy Bell was my sister—or I mean that Lorna was like her."

"Here comes Swann without Margie. Looks sore as a pup. The——"

"Shut up, Blair. I want to listen to this jazz."

Lane shut his eyes during the next number and listened without the disconcerting spectacle in his sight. He put all the intensity of which he was capable into his attention. His knowledge of music was not extensive, but on the other hand it was enough to enable him to analyze this jazz. Neither music nor ragtime, it seemed utterly barbarian in character. It appealed only to primitive, physical, sensual instincts. It could not be danced to sanely and gracefully. When he opened his eyes again, to see once more the disorder of dancers in spirit and action, he seemed to have his analysis absolutely verified.

These dances were short, the encores very brief, and the intermissions long. Perhaps the dancers needed to get their breath and rearrange their apparel.

After this number, Lane left Blair talking to friends, and made his way across the hall to where he espied Lorna. She did not see him. She looked ashamed, hurt, almost sullen. Her young friend, Harry, was bending over talking earnestly. Lane caught the words: "Lorna dear, that Swann's only stringing you—rushing you on the sly. He won't dance with you *here*—not while he's with that swell crowd."

"It's a lie," burst out Lorna. She was almost in tears.

Lane took her arm, making her start.

"Well, kids, you're having some time, aren't you," he said, cheerfully.

"Sure—are," gulped Harry.

Lorna repressed her grief, but not her sullen resentment.

Lane pretended not to notice anything unusual, and after a few casual remarks and queries he left them. Strolling from place to place, mingling with the gay groups, in the more secluded alcoves and recesses where couples appeared, oblivious to eyes, in the check room where a sign read: "check your corsets," out in the wide landing where the stairway came up, Lane passed, missing little that might have been seen or heard. He did not mind that two of the chaperones stared at him in supercilious curiosity, as if speculating on a possible *faux pas* of his at this dance. Both boys and girls he had met since his return to Middleville, and some he had known before, encountered him face to face, and cut him dead. He heard sarcastic remarks. He was an outsider, a "dead one," a "has been" and a "lemon." But Margaret was gracious to him, and Flossie Dickerson made no bones of her regard. Dorothy, he was relieved and glad to see, was not present.

Lane had no particular object in mind. He just wanted to rub elbows with this throng of young people. This was the joy of life he had imagined he had missed while in France. How much vain longing! He had missed nothing. He had boundlessly gained.

Out on this floor a railing ran round the curve of the stairway. Girls were sitting on it, smoking cigarettes, and kicking their slipper-shod feet. Their partners were lounging close. Lane passed by, and walking to a window in the shadow he stood there. Presently one of the boys threw away his cigarette and said: "Come on, Ironsides. I gotta dance. You're a rotten dancer, but I love you."

They ran back into the hall. The young fellow who was left indolently attempted to kiss his partner, who blew smoke in his face. Then at a louder blast of jazz they bounced away. The next moment a third couple appeared, probably from another door down the hall. They did not observe Lane. The girl was slim, dainty, gorgeously arrayed, and her keen, fair face bore traces of paint wet by perspiration. Her companion was Captain Vane Thesel, in citizen's garb, well-built, ruddy-faced, with tiny curled moustache.

"Hurry, kid," he said, breathlessly, as he pulled at her. "We'll run down and take a spin."

"Spiffy! But let's wait till after the next," she replied. "It's Harold's and I came with him."

"Tell him it was up to him to find you."

"But he might get wise to a car ride."

"He'd do the same. Come on," returned Thesel, who all the time was leading her down the stairway step by step.

They disappeared. From the open window Lane saw them go down the street and get into a car and ride away. He glanced at his watch, muttering. "This is a new stunt for dances. I just wonder." He watched, broodingly and sombrely. It was not his sister, but it might just as well have been. Two dances and a long intermission ended before Lane saw the big auto return. He watched the couple get out, and hurry up, to disappear at the entrance. Then Lane changed his position, and stood directly at the head of the stairway under the light. He had no interest in Captain Vane Thesel. He just wanted to get a close look at the girl.

Presently he heard steps, heavy and light, and a man's deep voice, a girl's low thrill of laughter. They turned the curve in the stairway and did not see Lane until they had mounted to the top.

With cool steady gaze Lane studied the girl. Her clear eyes met his. If there was anything unmistakable in Lane's look at her, it was not from any deception on his part. He tried to look into her soul. Her smile—a strange indolent little smile, remnant of excitement—faded from her face. She stared, and she put an instinctive hand up to her somewhat dishevelled hair. Then she passed on with her companion.

"Of all the nerve!" she exclaimed. "Who's that soldier boob?"

Lane could not catch the low reply. He lingered there a while longer, and then returned to the hall, much surprised to find it so dark he could scarcely distinguish the dancers. The lights had been lowered. If the dance had been violent and strange before this procedure, it was now a riot. In the semi-darkness the dancers cut loose. The paper strings had been loosened and had fallen down to become tangled with the flying feet and legs. Confetti swarmed like dark snowdrops in the hot air. Lane actually smelled the heat of bodies—a strangely stirring and yet noxious sensation. A rushing, murmuring, shrill sound—voices, laughter, cries, and the sliding of feet and brushing of gowns— filled the hall—ominous to Lane's over-sensitive faculties, swelling unnaturally, the expression of unrestrained physical abandon. Lane walked along the edge of this circling, wrestling melee, down to the corner where the orchestra held forth. They seemed actuated by the same frenzy which possessed the dancers. The piccolo player lay on his back on top of the piano, piping his shrill notes at the ceiling. And Lane made sure this player was drunk. On the moment then the jazz came to an end with a crash. The lights flashed up. The dancers clapped and stamped their pleasure.

Lane wound his way back to Blair.

"I've had enough, Blair," he said. "I'm all in. Let's go."

"Right-o," replied Blair, with evident relief. He reached a hand to Lane to raise himself, an action he rarely resorted to, and awkwardly got his crutch in place. They started out, with Lane accommodating his pace to his crippled comrade. Thus it happened that the two ran a gauntlet with watching young people on each side, out to the open part of the hall. There directly in front they encountered Captain Vane Thesel, with Helen Wrapp on his arm. Her red hair, her green eyes, and carmined lips, the white of her voluptuous neck and arms, united in a singular effect of allurement that Lane felt with scorn and melancholy.

Helen nodded to Blair and Lane, and evidently dragged at her escort's arm to hold him from passing on.

"Look who's here! Daren, old boy—and Blair," she called, and she held the officer back. The malice in her green glance did not escape Lane, as he bowed to her. She gloried in that situation. Captain Thesel had to face them.

It was Blair's hand that stiffened Lane. They halted, erect, like statues, with eyes that failed to see Thesel. He did not exist for them. With a flush of annoyance he spoke, and breaking from Helen, passed on. A sudden silence in the groups nearby gave evidence that the incident had been observed. Then whispers rose.

"Boys, aren't you dancing?" asked Helen, with a mocking sweetness. "Let me teach you the new steps."

"Thanks, Helen," replied Lane, in sudden weariness. "But I couldn't go it."

"Why did you come? To blow us up again? Lose your nerve?"

"Yes, I lost it to-night—and something more."

"Blair, you shouldn't have left one of your legs in France," she said, turning to Blair. She had always hated Blair, a fact omnipresent now in her green eyes.

Blair had left courtesy and endurance in France, as was evinced by the way he bent closer to Helen, to speak low, with terrible passion.

"If I had it to do over again—I'd see *you* and *your* kind—your dirt-cheap crowd of painted hussies where you belong—in the clutch of the Huns!"

CHAPTER IX

Miss Amanda Hill, teacher in the Middleville High School, sat wearily at her desk. She was tired, as tired as she had ever been on any day of the fifteen long years in which she had wrestled with the problems of school life. Her hair was iron gray and she bent a worn, sad, severe face over a mass of notes before her.

At that moment she was laboring under a perplexing question that was not by any means a new one. Only this time it had presented itself in a less insidious manner than usual, leaving no loophole for charitable imagination. Presently she looked up and rapped on her desk.

"These young ladies will remain after school is dismissed," she said, in her authoritative voice: "Bessy Bell—Rose Clymer—Gail Matthews—Helen Tremaine—Ruth Winthrop.... Also any other girls who are honest enough to admit knowledge of the notes found in Rose Clymer's desk."

The hush that fell over the schoolroom was broken by the gong in the main hall, sounding throughout the building. Then followed the noise of shutting books and closing desks, and the bustle and shuffling of anticipated dismissal.

In a front seat sat a girl who did not arise with the others, and as one by one several girls passed her desk with hurried step and embarrassed snicker she looked at them with purple, blazing eyes.

Miss Hill attended to her usual task with the papers of the day's lessons and the marking of the morrow's work before she glanced up at the five girls she had detained. They sat in widely separated sections of the room. Rose Clymer, pretty, fragile, curly-haired, occupied the front seat of the end row. Her face had no color and her small mouth was set in painful lines. Four seats across from her Bessy Bell leaned on her desk, with defiant calmness, and traces of scorn still in her expressive eyes. Gail Matthews looked frightened and Helen Tremaine was crying. Ruth Winthrop bent forward with her face buried in her arms.

"Girls," began Miss Hill, presently. "I know you regard me as a cross old schoolteacher."

She had spoken impulsively, a rare thing with her, and occasioned in this instance by the painful consciousness of how she was judged, when she was really so kindly disposed toward the wayward girls.

"Girls, I've tried to get into close touch with you, to sympathize, to be lenient; but somehow, I've failed," she went on. "Certainly I have failed to stop this note-writing. And lately it has become—beyond me to understand. Now won't you help me to get at the bottom of the matter? Helen, it was you who told me these notes were in Rose's desk. Have you any knowledge of more?"

"Ye—s—m," said Helen, raising her red face. "I've—I've one—I—was afraid to g—give up."

"Bring it to me."

Helen rose and came forward with an expressive little fist and opening it laid a crumpled paper upon Miss Hill's desk. As Helen returned to her seat she met Bessy Bell's fiery glance and it seemed to wither her.

The teacher smoothed out the paper and began to read. "Good Heavens!" she breathed, in amaze and pain. Then she turned to Helen. "This verse is in your handwriting."

"Yes'm—but I—I only copied it," responded the culprit.

"Who gave you the original?"

"Rose."

"Where did she get it?"

"I—I don't know—Miss Hill. Really and tru—truly I don't," faltered Helen, beginning to cry again.

Gail and Ruth also disclaimed any knowledge of the verse, except that it had been put into their hands by Rose. They had read it, copied it, written notes about it and discussed it.

"You three girls may go home now," said Miss Hill, sadly.

The girls hastily filed out and passed the scornful Bessy Bell with averted heads.

"Rose, can you explain the notes found in your possession?" asked the teacher.

"Yes, Miss Hill. They were written to me by different boys and girls," replied Rose.

"Why do you seem to have all these writings addressed to you?"

"I didn't get any more than any other girl. But I wasn't afraid to keep mine."

"Do you know where these verses came from, before Helen had them?"

"Yes, Miss Hill."

"Then you know who wrote them?"

"Yes."

"Who?"

"I won't tell," replied Rose, deliberately. She looked straight into her teacher's eyes.

"You refuse when I've assured you I'll be lenient?" demanded Miss Hill.

"I'm no tattletale." Rose's answer was sullen.

"Rose, I ask you again. A great deal depends on your answer. Will you tell me?"

The girl's lip curled. Then she laughed in a way that made Miss Hill think of her as older. But she kept silent.

"Rose, you're expelled until further notice." Miss Hill's voice trembled with disappointment and anger. "You may go now."

Rose gathered up her books and went into the cloakroom. The door in the outer hall opened and closed.

"Miss Hill, it wasn't fair!" exclaimed Bessy Bell, hotly. "It wasn't fair. Rose is no worse than the other girls. She's not as bad, for she isn't sly and deceitful. There were a dozen girls who lied when they went out. Helen lied. Ruth lied. Gail lied. But Rose told the truth so far as she went. And she wouldn't tell all because she wanted to shield me."

"Why did she want to shield you?"

"Because I wrote the verses."

"You mean you copied them?"

"I composed them," Bessy replied coolly. Her blue eyes fearlessly met Miss Hill's gaze.

"Bessy Bell!" ejaculated the teacher.

The girl stood before her desk and from the tip of her dainty boot to the crown of her golden hair breathed forth a strange, wilful and rebellious fire.

Miss Hill's lips framed to ask a certain question of Bessy, but she refrained and substituted another.

"Bessy, how old are you?"

"Fifteen last April."

"Have you any intelligent idea of—do you know—Bessy, *how* did you write those verses?" asked Miss Hill, in bewilderment.

"I know a good deal and I've imagination," replied Bessy, candidly.

"That's evident," returned the teacher. "How long has this note-and verse-writing been going on?"

"For a year, at least, among us."

"Then you caught the habit from girls gone higher up?"

"Certainly."

Bessy's trenchant brevity was not lost upon Miss Hill.

"We've always gotten along—you and I," said Miss Hill, feeling her way with this strange girl.

"It's because you're kind and square, and I like you."

Something told the teacher she had never been paid a higher compliment.

"Bessy, how much will you tell me?"

"Miss Hill, I'm in for it and I'll tell you everything, if only you won't punish Rose," replied the girl, impulsively. "Rose's my best friend. Her father's a mean, drunken brute. I'm afraid of what he'll do if he finds out. Rose has a hard time."

"You say Rose is no more guilty than the other girls?"

"Rose Clymer never had an idea of her own. She's just sweet and willing. I hate deceitful girls. Every one of them wrote notes to the boys—the same kind of notes—and some of them tried to write poetry. Most of them had a copy of the piece I wrote. They had great fun over it—getting the boys to guess what girl wrote it. I've written a dozen pieces before this and they've all had them."

"Well, that explains the verses.... Now I read in these notes about meetings with the boys?"

"That refers to mornings before school, and after school, and evenings when it's nice weather. And the literary society."

"You mean the Girl's Literary Guild, with rooms at the Atheneum?"

"Yes. But, Miss Hill, the literary part of it is bunk. We meet there to dance. The boys bring the girls cigarettes. They smoke, and sometimes the boys have something with them to drink."

"These—these girls—hardly in their teens—smoke and drink?" gasped Miss Hill.

"I'll say they do," replied Bessy Bell.

"What—does the 'Bell-garter' mean?" went on the teacher, presently.

"One of the boys stole my garter and fastened a little bell to it. Now it's going the rounds. Every girl who could has worn it."

"What's the 'Old Bench'?"

"Down in the basement here at school there's a bench under the stairway in the dark. The boys and girls have signals. One boy will get permission to go out at a certain time, and a girl from his room, or another room, will go out too. It's all arranged beforehand. They meet down on the Old Bench."

"What for?"

"They meet to spoon."

"I find the names Hardy Mackay, Captain Thesel, Dick Swann among these notes. What can these young society men be to my pupils?"

"Some of the jealous girls have been tattling to each other and mentioning names."

"Bessy! Do you imply these girls who talk have had the—the interest or attention of these young gentlemen named?"

"Yes."

"In what way?"

"I mean they've had dates to meet in the park—and other places. Then they go joy riding."

"Bessy, have you?"

"Yes—but only just lately."

"Thank you Bessy, for your—your frankness," replied Miss Hill, drawing a long breath. "I'll have another talk with you, after I see your mother. You may go now."

It was an indication of Miss Hill's mental perturbation that for once she broke her methodical routine. For many years she had carried a lunch-basket to and from school; for so many in fact that now on Saturdays when she went to town without it she carried her left hand forward in the same position that had grown habitual to her while holding it. But this afternoon, as she went out, she forgot the basket entirely.

"I'll go to Mrs. Bell," soliloquized the worried schoolteacher. "But how to explain what I can't understand! Some people would call this thing just natural depravity. But I love these girls. As I think back, every year, in the early summer, I've always had something of this sort of thing to puzzle over. But the last few years it's grown worse. The war made a difference. And since the war—how strange the girls are! They seem to feel more. They're bolder. They break out oftener. They dress so immodestly. Yet they're less deceitful. They have no shame. I can blind myself no longer to that. And this last is damning proof of—of wildness. Some of them have taken the fatal step!... Yet—yet I seem to feel somehow Bessy Bell isn't *bad*. I wonder if my hope isn't responsible for that feeling. I'm old-fashioned. This modern girl is beyond me. How clearly she spoke! She's a wonderful, fearless, terrible girl. I never saw a girl so alive. I can't—can't understand her."

In the swift swinging from one consideration of the perplexing question to another Miss Hill's mind naturally reverted to her errand, and to her possible reception. Mrs. Bell was a proud woman. She had married against the wishes of her blue-blooded family, so rumor had it, and her husband was now Chief of Police in Middleville. Mrs. Bell had some money of her own and was slowly recovering her old position in society.

It was not without misgivings that Miss Hill presented herself at Mrs. Bell's door and gave her card to a servant. The teacher had often made thankless and misunderstood calls upon the mothers of her pupils. She was admitted and shown to a living room where a woman of fair features and noble proportions greeted her.

"Bessy's teacher, I presume?" she queried, graciously, yet with just that slight touch of hauteur which made Miss Hill feel her position.

"I am Bessy's teacher," she replied, with dignity. "Can you spare me a few minutes?"

"Assuredly. Please be seated. I've heard Bessy speak of you. By the way, the child hasn't come home yet. How late she always is!"

Miss Hill realized, with a protest at the unfairness of the situation, that to face this elegant lady, so smiling, so suave, so worldly, so graciously superior, and to tell her some unpleasant truths about her daughter, was a task by no means easy, and one almost sure to prove futile. But Miss Hill never shirked her duty, and after all, her motive was a hope to help Bessy.

"Mrs. Bell, I've come on a matter of importance," began Miss Hill. "But it is so delicate a one I don't know how to broach it. I believe plain speaking best."

Here Miss Hill went into detail, sparing not to call a spade a spade. But she held back the names of the young society gentlemen mentioned in the notes. Miss Hill was not sure of her ground there and her revelation was grave enough for any intelligent mother.

"Really, Miss Hill, you amaze me!" exclaimed Mrs. Bell. "Bessie has fallen into bad company. Oh, these public schools! I never attended one, but I've heard what they are."

"The public schools are not to blame," replied Miss Hill, bluntly.

Mrs. Bell gave her visitor a rather supercilious stare.

"May I ask you to explain?"

"I'm afraid I can't explain," replied Miss Hill, conscious of a little heat. "I've proofs of the condition. But as I can't understand it, how can I explain? I have my own peculiar ideas, only, lately, I've begun to doubt them. A year or so ago I would have said girls had their own way too much—too much time to themselves—too much freedom. But now I seem to feel life isn't like what it was a few years ago. Girls are bound to learn. And they never learn at home, that's sure. The last thing a mother will do is to tell her daughter what she *ought* to know. There's always been a shadow between most mothers and daughters. And in these days of jazz it has become a wall. Perhaps that's why girls don't confide in their mothers.... Mrs. Bell, I considered it my duty to acquaint you with the truth about these verses and notes, and what they imply. Would you care to read some of them?"

"Thank you, but they wouldn't interest me in the least," replied Mrs. Bell, coldly. "I wouldn't insult Bessy or her girl friends. I imagine it's all some risque suggestion overheard and made much of or a few verses mischievously plagiarized. I'm no prude, Miss Hill. I know enough not to be strict, which is apparently the fault of the school system. As for my own daughter I understand her perfectly and trust her implicitly. I know the blood in her. And I shall remove her from public school and place her in a private institution under a tutor, where she'll no longer be exposed to contaminating influences.... I thank you for your intention, which I'm sure is kind—and, will you please excuse me? I must dress for my bridge party. Good afternoon, Miss Hill."

The schoolteacher plodded homeward, her eyes downcast and sad. The snub given her by the mother had not hurt her as had the failure to help the daughter.

"I knew it—I knew it. I'll never try again. That woman's mind is a wilderness where her girl is concerned. How brainless these mothers are!... Yet if I'd ever had a girl—I wonder—would I have been blind? One's own blood—that must be the reason. Pride. Could I have believed of *my* girl what I admitted of hers? Perhaps not till too late. That would be so human. But, oh! the mystery—the sadness of it—the fatality!"

Rose Clymer left the High School with the settled, indifferent bitterness of one used to trouble. Every desire she followed, turn what way she would, every impulse reaching to grasp some girlish gleam of happiness, resulted in the inevitable rebuke. And this time it had been disgrace. But Rose felt she did not care if she could only deceive her father. No cheerful task was it to face him. Shivering at the thought she resolved to elude the punishment he was sure to inflict if he learned why she had been expelled.

She had no twinge of conscience. She was used to slights and unkindness, and did not now reflect upon the justice of her dismissal. What little pleasure she got came from friendships with boys, and these her father had forbidden her to have. In the bitter web of her thought ran the threads that if she had pretty clothes like Helen, and a rich mother like Bessy, and a father who was not a drunkard, her lot in life would have been happy.

Rose lived with her stepfather in three dingy rooms in the mill section of Middleville. She never left the wide avenues and lawns and stately residences, which she had to pass on her way to and from school, without contrasting them with the dirty alleys and grimy walls and squalid quarters of the working-class. She had grown up in that class, but in her mind there was always a faint vague recollection of a time when her surroundings had been bright and cheerful, where there had been a mother who had taught her to love beautiful things. To-day she climbed the rickety stairs to her home and pushed open the latchless door with a revolt brooding in her mind.

A man in his shirt sleeves sat by the little window.

"Why father—home so early?" she asked.

"Yes lass, home early," he replied wearily. "I'm losing my place again."

He had straggling gray hair, bleared eyes with an opaque, glazy look and a bluish cast of countenance. His chin was buried in the collar of his open shirt; his shoulders sagged, and he breathed heavily.

One glance assured Rose her father was not very much under the influence of drink. And fear left her. When even half-sober he was kind.

"So you've lost your place?" she asked.

"Yes. Old Swann is layin' off."

This was an untruth, Rose knew, because the mills had never been so full, and men never so in demand. Besides her father was an expert at his trade and could always have work.

"I'm sorry," she said, slowly. "I've been thinking lately that I'll give up school and go to work. In an office uptown or a department store."

"Rose, that'd be good of you," he replied. "You could help along a lot. I don't do my work so well no more. But your poor mother won't rest in her grave. She was so proud of you, always dreamin'."

The lamp Rose lighted showed comfortless rooms, with but few articles of furniture. It was with the deft fingers of long practice that the girl spread the faded table-cloth, laid the dishes, ground the coffee, peeled the potatoes, and cut the bread. Then presently she called her father to the meal. He ate in silence, having relapsed once more into the dull gloom natural to him. When he had finished he took up his hat and with slow steps left the room.

"No more study for me," mused Rose, and she felt both glad and sorry. "What will Bessy say? She won't like it. I wonder what old Hill did to her. Let her off easy. I won't get to see Bessy so much now. No more afternoons in the park. But I'll have the evenings. Best of all, some nice clothes to wear. I might some day have a lovely gown like that Miss Maynard wore the night of the Prom."

Rose washed and dried the dishes, put them away, and cleaned up the little kitchen in a way that spoke well for her. And she did it cheerfully, for in the interest of this new idea of work she forgot her trouble and discontent. Taking up the lamp she went to her room. It contained a narrow bed, a bureau, a small wardrobe and a rug. The walls held several pictures, and some touches of color in the way of ribbons, bright posters, and an orange-and-blue banner. A photograph of Bessy Bell stood on the bureau and the girl's beauty seemed like a light in the dingy room.

Rose looked in the mirror and smiled and tossed her curly head. She studied the oval face framed in its mass of curls, the steady gray-blue eyes, the soft, wistful, tenderly curved lips. "Yes, I'm pretty," she said. "And I'm going to buy nice things to wear."

Suddenly she heard a pattering on the roof.

"Rain! What do you know about that? I've got to stay in. If I spoil that relic of a hat I'll never have the nerve to go ask for a job."

She prepared for bed, and placing the lamp on the edge of the bureau, she lay down to become absorbed in a paper-backed novel. The mill-clock was striking ten when she finished. There was a dreamy light in her eyes and a glow upon her face.

"How grand to be as beautiful as she was and turn out to be an heiress with blue blood, and a lovely mother, and handsome lovers dying for her!"

Then she flung the novel against the wall.

"It's only a book. It's not true."

Rose blew out the lamp and went to sleep.

During the night she dreamed that the principal of the High School had called to see her father, and she awoke trembling.

The room was dark as pitch; the rain pattered on the roof; the wind moaned softly under the eaves. A rat somewhere in the wall made a creaking noise. Rose hated to awaken in the middle of the night. She listened for her father's breathing, and failing to hear it, knew he had not yet come home. Often she was left alone until dawn. She tried bravely to go to sleep again but found it impossible; she lay there listening, sensitive to every little sound. The silence was almost more dreadful than the stealthy unknown noises of the night. Vague shapes seemed to hover over her bed. Somehow to-night she dreaded them more. She was sixteen years old, yet there abided with her the terror of the child in the dark.

She cried out in her heart—why was she alone? It was so dark, so silent. Mother! Mother!... She would never—never say her prayers again!

The brazen-tongued mill clock clanged the hour of two, when shuffling uncertain footsteps sounded on the hollow stairs. Rose raised her head to listen. With slow, weary, dragging steps her father came in. Then she lay back on the pillow with a sigh of relief.

CHAPTER X

In the following week Rose learned that work was not to be had for the asking. Her love of pretty things and a desire to be independent of her father had occupied her mind to the exclusion of a consideration of what might be demanded of a girl seeking a position. She had no knowledge of stenography or bookkeeping; her handwriting was poor. Moreover, references from former employers were required and as she had never been employed, she was asked for recommendations from the principal of her school. These, of course, she could not supply. The stores of the better class had nothing to offer her except to put her name on the waiting-list.

Finally Rose secured a place in a second-rate establishment on Main Street. The work was hard; it necessitated long hours and continual standing on her feet. Rose was not rugged enough to accustom herself to the work all at once, and she was discharged. This disheartened her, but she kept on trying to find other employment.

One day in the shopping district, some one accosted her. She looked up to see a young man, slim, elegant, with a curl of his lips she remembered. He raised his hat.

"How do you do, Mr. Swann," she answered.

"Rose, are you on the way home?"

"Yes."

"Let's go down this side street," he said, throwing away his cigarette. "I've been looking for you."

They turned the corner. Rose felt strange to be walking alone with him, but she was not embarrassed. He had danced with her once. And she knew his friend Hardy Mackay.

"What're you crying about?" he said.

"I'm not."

"You have been then. What for?"

"Oh, nothing."

"Come, tell me."

"I—I've been disappointed."

"What about?" He was persistent, and Rose felt that he must be used to having his own way.

"It was about a job I didn't get," replied Rose, trying to laugh.

"So you're looking for a job. Heard you'd been fired by old Hill. Gail told me. I had her out last night in my new car."

"I could go back to school. Miss Hill sent for me.... Was Bessy with you and Gail?"

"No. Gail and I were alone. We had a dandy time.... Rose, will you meet me some night and take a ride? It'll be fine and cool."

"Thank you, Mr. Swann. It's very kind of you to ask me."

"Well, will you go?" he queried, impatiently.

"No," she replied, simply.

"Why not?"

"I don't want to."

"Well, that's plain enough," he said, changing his tone. "Say, Rose, you're in Clark's store, aren't you?"

"I was. But I lost the place."

"How's that?"

"I couldn't stand on my feet all day. I fainted. Then he fired me."

"So you're hunting for another job?" inquired Swann, thoughtfully.

"Yes."

"Sorry. It's too bad a sweet kid like you has to work. You're not strong, Rose.... Well, I'll turn off at this corner. You won't meet me to-night?"

"No, thanks."

Swann pulled a gold case from his pocket, and extracting a cigarette, tilted it in his lips as he struck a match. His face wore a careless smile Rose did not like. He was amiable, but he seemed so sure, so satisfied, almost as if he believed she would change her mind.

"Rose, you're turning me down cold, then?"

"Take it any way you like, Mr. Swann," she replied. "Good day."

Rose forgot him almost the instant her back was turned. He had only annoyed her. And she had her stepfather to face, with news of her discharge from the store. Her fears were verified; he treated her brutally. Next day Rose went to work in a laundry.

And then, very soon it seemed, her school days, the merry times with the boys, and Bessy—all were far back in the past. She did not meet any one who knew her, nor hear from any one. They had forgotten her. At night, after coming home from the laundry and doing the housework, she was so tired that she was glad to crawl into bed.

But one night a boy brought her a note. It was from Dick Swann. He asked her to go to Mendleson's Hall to see the moving-pictures. She could meet him uptown at the entrance. Rose told the boy to tell Swann she would not come.

This invitation made her thoughtful. If Swann had been ashamed to be seen with her he would not have invited her to go there. Mendleson's was a nice place; all the nice people of Middleville went there. Rose found herself thinking of the lights, the music, the well-dressed crowd, and then the pictures. She loved moving-pictures, especially those with swift horses and cowboys and a girl who could ride. All at once a wave of the old thrilling excitement rushed over her. Almost she regretted having sent back a refusal. But she would not go with Swann. And it was not because she knew what kind of a young man he was—what he wanted. Rose refused from dislike, not scruples.

Then came a Saturday night which seemed a climax of her troubles. She was told not to come back to work until further notice, and that was as bad as being discharged. How could she tell her stepfather? Of late he had been hard with her. She dared not tell him. The money she earned was little enough, but during his idleness it had served to keep them.

Rose had scarcely gone a block when she encountered Dick Swann. He stopped her—turned to walk with her. It was a melancholy gift of Rose's that she could tell when men were even in the slightest under the influence of drink. Swann was not careless now or indifferent. He seemed excited and gay.

"Rose, you're just the girl I'm looking for," he said. "I really was going to your home. Got that job yet?"

"No," she replied.

"I've got one for you. It's at the Telephone Exchange. They need an operator. My dad owns the telephone company. I've got a pull. I'll get you the place. You can learn it easy. Nice job—short hours—you sit down all the time—good pay. What do you say, Rose?"

"I—I don't know—what to say," she faltered. "Thanks for thinking of me."

"I've had you in mind for a month. Rose, you take this job. Take it whether you've any use for me or not. I'm not rotten enough to put this in your way just to make you under obligations to me."

"I'll think about it. I—I do need a place. My father's out of work. And he's—he's not easy to get along with."

"I tell you what, Rose. You meet me to-night. We'll take a spin in my car. It'll be fine down the river road. Then we can talk it over. Will you?"

Rose looked at him, and thought how strange it was that she did not like him any better, now when she ought to.

"Why have you tried to—to rush me?" she asked.

"I like you, Rose."

"But you don't want me to meet you—go with you, when I—I can't feel as you do?"

"Sure, I want you to, Rose. Nobody ever likes me right off. Maybe you will, after you know me. The job is yours. Don't make any date with me for that. I say here's your chance to have a ride, to win a friend. Take it or not. It's up to you. I won't say another word."

Rose's hungry, lonely heart warmed toward Swann. He seemed like a ray of light in the gloom.

"I'll meet you," she said.

They arranged the hour and then she went on her way home.

The big car sped through River Park. Rose shivered a little as she peered into the darkness of the grove. Then the car shot under the last electric light, out into the country, with the level road white in the moonlight, and the river gleaming below. There was a steady, even rush of wind. The car hummed and droned and sang. And mingled with the dry scent of dust was the sweet fragrance of new-mown hay. Far off a light twinkled or it might have been a star.

Swann put his arm around Rose. She did not shrink—she did not repulse him—she did not move. Something strange happened in her mind or heart. It was that moment she fell.

And she fell wide-eyed, knowing what she was doing, not in a fervor of excitement, without pleasure or passion, bitterly sure that it was better to be with some one she could not like than to be alone forever. The wrong to herself lay only in the fact that she could not care.

CHAPTER XI

Toward the end of June, Lane's long vigil of watchfulness from the vantage-point at Colonel Pepper's apartment resulted in a confirmation of his worst fears.

One afternoon and evening of a warm, close day in early summer he lay and crouched on the attic floor above the club-rooms from three o'clock until one the next morning. From time to time he had changed his position to rest. But at the expiration of that protracted period of spying he was so exhausted from the physical strain and mental shock that he was unable to go home. All the rest of the night he lay upon Colonel Pepper's couch, wide awake, consumed by pain and distress. About daylight he fell into a sleep, fitful and full of nightmares, to be awakened around nine o'clock by Pepper. The old gambler evinced considerable alarm until Lane explained how he happened to be there; and then his feeling changed to solicitude.

"Lane, you look awful," he said.

"If I look the way I feel it's no wonder you're shocked," returned Lane.

"Ahuh! What'd you see?" queried the other, curiously.

"When?"

"Why, you numskull, while you were peepin' all that time."

Lane sombrely shook his head. "I couldn't tell—what I saw. I want to forget.... Maybe in twenty-four hours I'll believe it was a nightmare."

"Humph! Well, I'm here to tell you what *I've* seen wasn't any nightmare," returned Pepper, with his shrewd gaze on Lane. "But we needn't discuss that. If it made an old bum like me sick what might not it do to a sensitive high-minded chap like you.... The question is are you going to bust up that club."

"I am," declared Lane, grimly.

"Good! But how—when? What's the sense in lettin' them carry on any longer?"

"I had to fight myself last night to keep from breaking in on them.... But I want to catch this fellow Swann with my sister. She wasn't there."

"Lane, don't wait for that," returned Pepper, nervously. "You might never catch him.... And if you did...."

His little plump well-cared-for hand shook as he extended it.

"I don't know what I'll do.... I don't know," said Lane, darkly, more to himself.

"Lane, this—this worry will knock you out."

"No matter. All I ask is to stand up—long enough—to do what I want to do."

"Go home and get some breakfast—and take care of yourself," replied Pepper, gruffly. "Damn me if I'm not sorry I gave Swann's secret away."

"Oh no, you're not," said Lane, quickly. "But I'd have found it out by this time."

Pepper paced up and down the faded carpet, his hands behind his back, a plodding, burdened figure.

"Have you any—doubts left?" he asked, suddenly.

"Doubts!" echoed Lane, vaguely.

"Yes—doubts. You're like most of these mothers and fathers.... You couldn't believe. You made excuses for the smoke—saying there was no fire."

"No more doubts, alas!... My God! I *saw*," burst out Lane.

"All right. Buck up now. It's something to be sure.... You've overdone your strength. You look...."

"Pepper, do me a favor," interposed Lane, as he made for the door. "Get me an axe and leave it here in your rooms. In case I want to break in on those fellows some time—quick—I'll have it ready."

"Sure, I'll get you anything. And I want to be around when you butt in on them."

"That's up to you. Good-bye now. I'll run in to-morrow if I'm up to it."

Lane went home, his mind in a tumult. His mother had just discovered that he had not slept in his bed, and was greatly relieved to see him. Breakfast was waiting, and after partaking of it Lane felt somewhat better. His mother appeared more than usually sombre. Worry was killing her.

"Lorna did not sleep at home last night," she said, presently, as if reluctantly forced to impart this information.

"Where was she?" he queried, blankly.

"She said she would stay with a friend."

"What friend?"

"Some girl. Oh, it's all right I suppose. She's stayed away before with girl friends.... But what worried me...."

"Well," queried Lane, as she paused.

"Lorna was angry again last night. And she told me if you didn't stop your nagging she'd go away from home and stay. Said she could afford to pay her board."

"She told me that, too," replied Lane, slowly. "And—I'm afraid she meant it."

"Leave her alone, Daren."

"Poor mother! I'm afraid I'm a—a worry to you as well as Lorna," he said, gently, with a hand going to her worn cheek. She said nothing, although her glance rested upon him with sad affection.

Lane clambered wearily up to his little room. It had always been a refuge. He leaned a moment against the wall, and felt in his extremity like an animal in a trap. A thousand pricking, rushing sensations seemed to be on the way to his head. That confusion, that sensation as if his blood vessels would burst, yielded to his will. He sat down on his bed. Only the physical pains and weariness, and the heartsickness abided with him. These had been nothing to daunt his spirit. But to-day was different. The dark, vivid, terrible picture in his mind unrolled like a page. Yesterday was different. To-day he seemed a changed man, confronted by imperious demands. Time was driving onward fast.

As if impelled by a dark and sinister force, he slowly leaned down to pull his bag from under the bed. He opened it, and drew out his Colt's automatic gun. Though the June day was warm this big worn metal weapon had a cold touch. He did not feel that he wanted to handle it, but he did. It seemed heavy, a thing of subtle, latent energy, with singular fascination for him. It brought up a dark flowing tide of memory. Lane shut his eyes, and saw the tide flow by with its conflict and horror. The feel of his gun, and the recall of what it had meant to him in terrible hours, drove away a wavering of will, and a still voice that tried to pierce his consciousness. It fixed his sinister intention. He threw the gun on the bed, and rising began to pace the floor.

"If I told what I saw—no jury on earth would convict me," he soliloquized. "But I'll kill him—and keep my mouth shut."

Plan after plan he had pondered in mind—and talked over with Blair—something to thwart Richard Swann—to give Margaret the chance for happiness and love her heart craved—to put out of Lorna's way the evil influence that had threatened her. Now the solution came to him. Sooner or later he would catch Swann with his sister in an automobile, or at the club rooms, or at some other questionable place. He knew Lorna was meeting Swann. He had tried to find them, all to no avail. What he might have done heretofore was no longer significant; he knew what he meant to do now.

But all at once Lane was confronted with remembrance of another thing he had resolved upon—equally as strong as his determination to save Lorna—and it was his intention to persuade Mel Iden to marry him.

He loved his sister, but not as he loved Mel Iden. Whatever had happened to Lorna or might happen, she would be equal to it. She had the boldness, the cool, calculating selfishness of the general run of modern girls. Her reactions were vastly different front Mel Iden's. Lane had lost hope of saving Lorna's soul. He meant only to remove a baneful power from her path, so that she might lean to the boy who wanted to marry her. When in his sinister intent he divined the passionate hate of the soldier for the slacker he refused to listen to his conscience. The way out in Lorna's case he had discovered. But what relation had this new factor of his dilemma to Mel Iden? He could never marry her after he had killed Swann.

Lane went to bed, and when he rested his spent body, he pondered over every phase of the case. Reason and intelligence had their say. He knew he had become morbid, sick, rancorous, base, obsessed with this iniquity and his passion to stamp on it, as if it were a venomous serpent. He would have liked to do some magnificent and awful deed, that would show this little, narrow, sordid world at home the truth, and burn forever on their memories the spirit of a soldier. He had made a sacrifice that few understood. He had no reward except a consciousness that grew more luminous and glorious in its lonely light as time went on. He had endured the uttermost agonies of hell, a thousand times worse than death, and he had come home with love, with his faith still true. To what had he returned?

No need for reason or intelligence to knock at the gates of his passion! The war had left havoc. The physical, the sensual, the violent, the simian—these instincts, engendering the Day of the Beast, had come to dominate the people he had fought for. Why not go out and deliberately kill a man, a libertine, a slacker? He would still be acting on the same principle that imbued him during the war.

His thoughts drifted to Mel Iden. Strange how he loved her! Why? Because she was a lonely soul like himself—because she was true to her womanhood—because she had fallen for the same principle for which he had sacrificed all—because she had been abandoned by family and friends—because she had become beautiful, strange, mystic, tragic. Because despite the unnamed child, the scarlet letter upon her breast, she seemed to him infinitely purer than the girl who had jilted him.

Lane now surrendered to the enchantment of emotion embodied in the very name of Mel Iden. He had long resisted a sweet, melancholy current. He had driven Mel from his mind by bitter reflection on the conduct of the people who had ostracized her. Thought of her now, of what he meant to do, of the mounting love he had so strangely come to feel for her, was his only source of happiness. She would never know his secret love; he could never tell her that. But it was something to hold to his heart, besides that unquenchable faith in himself, in some unseen genius for far-off good.

The next day Lane, having ascertained where Joshua Iden was employed, betook himself that way just at the noon hour. Iden, like so many other Middleville citizens, gained a livelihood by working for the rich Swann. In his best days he had been a master mechanic of the railroad shops; at sixty he was foreman of one of the steel mills.

As it chanced, Iden had finished his noonday meal and was resting in the shade, apart from other laborers there. Lane remembered him, in spite of the fact that the three years had aged and bowed him, and lined his face.

"Mr. Iden, do you remember me?" asked Lane. He caught the slight averting of Iden's eyes from his uniform, and divined how the father of Mel Iden hated soldiers. But nothing could daunt Lane.

"Yes, Lane, I remember you," returned Iden. He returned Lane's hand-clasp, but not cordially.

Lane had mapped out in his mind this little interview. Taking off his hat, he carefully lowered himself until his back was propped against the tree, and looked frankly at Iden.

"It's warm. And I tire so easily. The damned Huns cut me to pieces.... Not much like I was when I used to call on Mel!"

Iden lowered his shadowed face. After a moment he said: "No, you're changed, Lane.... I heard you were gassed, too."

"Oh, everything came my way, Mr. Iden.... And the finish isn't far off."

Iden shifted his legs uneasily, then sat more erect, and for the first time really looked at Lane. It was the glance of a man who had strong aversion to the class Lane represented, but who was fair-minded and just, and not without sympathy.

"That's too bad, Lane. You're a young man.... The war hit us all, I guess," he said, and at the last, sighed heavily.

"It's been a long pull—Blair Maynard and I were the first to enlist, and we left Middleville almost immediately," went on Lane.

He desired to plant in Iden's mind the fact that he had left Middleville long before the wild era of soldier-and-girl attraction which had created such havoc. Acutely sensitive as Lane was, he could not be sure of an alteration in Iden's aloofness, yet there was some slight change. Then he talked frankly about specific phases of the war. Finally, when he saw that he had won interest and sympathy from Iden he abruptly launched his purpose.

"Mr. Iden, I came to ask if you will give your consent to my marrying Mel."

The older man shrank back as if he had been struck. He stared. His lower jaw dropped. A dark flush reddened his cheek.

"What!... Lane, you must be drunk," he ejaculated, thickly.

"No. I never was more earnest in my life. I want to marry Mel Iden."

"Why?" rasped out the father, hoarsely.

"I understand Mel," replied Lane, and swiftly he told his convictions as to the meaning and cause of her sacrifice. "Mel is good. She never was bad. These rotten people who see dishonor and disgrace in her have no minds, no hearts. Mel is far above these painted, bare-kneed girls who scorn her.... And I want to show them what *I* think of her. I want to give her boy a name—so he'll have a chance in the world. I'll not live long. This is just a little thing I can do to make it easier for Mel."

"Lane, you can't be the father of her child," burst out Iden.

"No. I wish I were. I was never anything to Mel but a friend. She was only a girl—seventeen when I left home."

"So help me God!" muttered Iden, and he covered his face with his hands.

"Say yes, Mr. Iden, and I'll go to Mel this afternoon."

"No, let me think.... Lane, if you're not drunk, you're crazy."

"Not at all. Why, Mr. Iden, I'm perfectly rational. Why, I'd glory in making that splendid girl a little happier, if it's possible."

"I drove my—my girl from her mother—her home," said Iden, slowly.

"Yes, and it was a hard, cruel act," replied Lane, sharply. "You were wrong. You—"

The mill whistle cut short Lane's further speech. When its shrill clarion ended, Iden got up, and shook himself as if to reestablish himself in the present.

"Lane, you come to my house to-night," he said. "I've got to go back to work.... But I'll think—and we can talk it over. I still live where you used to come as a boy.... How strange life is!... Good day, Lane."

Lane felt more than satisfied with the result of that interview. Joshua Iden would go home and tell Mel's mother, and that would surely make the victory easier. She would be touched in her mother's heart; she would understand Mel now, and divine Lane's mission; and she would plead with her husband to consent, and to bring Mel back home. Lane was counting on that. He must never even hint such a hope, but nevertheless he had it, he believed in it. Joshua Iden would have the scales torn from his eyes. He would never have it said that a dying soldier, who owed neither him nor his daughter anything, had shown more charity than he.

Therefore, Lane went early to the Iden homestead, a picturesque cottage across the river from Riverside Park. The only change Lane noted was a larger growth of trees and a fuller foliage. It was warm twilight. The frogs had begun to trill, sweet and melodious sound to Lane, striking melancholy chords of memory. Joshua Iden was walking on his lawn, his coat off, his gray head uncovered. Mrs. Iden sat on the low-roofed porch. Lane expected to see a sad change in her, something the same as he had found in his own mother. But he was hardly prepared for the frail, white-haired woman unlike the image he carried in his mind.

"Daren Lane! You should have come to see me long ago," was her greeting, and in her voice, so like Mel's, Lane recognized her. Some fitting reply came to him, and presently the moment seemed easier for all. She asked about his mother and Lorna, and then about Blair Maynard. But she did not speak of his own health or condition. And presently Lane thought it best to come to the issue at hand.

"Mr. Iden, have you made up your mind to—to give me what I want?"

"Yes, I have, Lane," replied Iden, simply. "You've made me see what Mel's mother always believed, though she couldn't make it clear to me.... I have much to forgive that girl. Yet, if you, who owe her nothing—who have wasted your life in vain sacrifice—if you can ask her to be your wife, I can ask her to come back home."

That was a splendid, all-satisfying moment for Lane. By his own grief he measured his reward. What had counted with Joshua Iden had been his faith in Mel's innate goodness. Then Lane turned to the mother. In the dusk he could see the working of her sad face.

"God bless you, my boy!" she said. "You feel with a woman's heart. I thank you.... Joshua has already sent word for Mel to come home. She will be back to-morrow.... You must come here to see her. But, Daren, she will never marry you."

"She will," replied Lane.

"You do not know Mel. Even if you had only a day to live she would not let you wrong yourself."

"But when she learns how much it means to me? The army ruined Mel, as it ruined hundreds of thousands of other girls. She will let one soldier make it up to her. She will let me go to my death with less bitterness."

"Oh, my poor boy, I don't know—I can't tell," she replied, brokenly. "By God's goodness you have brought about one miracle. Who knows? You might change Mel. For you have brought something great back from the war."

"Mrs. Iden, I will persuade her to marry me," said Lane. "And then, Mr. Iden, we must see what is best for her and the boy—in the future."

"Aye, son. One lesson learned makes other lessons easy. I will take Mel and her mother far away from Middleville—where no one ever heard of us."

"Good! You can all touch happiness again.... And now, if you and Mrs. Iden will excuse me—I will go."

Lane bade the couple good night, and slowly, as might have a lame man, he made his way through the gloaming, out to the road, and down to the bridge, where as always he lingered to catch the mystic whispers of the river waters, meant only for his ear. Stronger to-night! He was closer to that nameless thing. The shadows of dusk, the dark murmuring river, held an account with him, sometime to be paid. How blessed to fall, to float down to that merciful oblivion.

CHAPTER XII

Several days passed before Lane felt himself equal to the momentous interview with Mel Iden. After his call upon Mel's father and mother he was overcome by one of his sick, weak spells, that happily had been infrequent of late. This one confined him to his room. He had about fought and won it out, when the old injury at the base of his spine reminded him that misfortunes did not come singly. Quite unexpectedly, as he bent over with less than his usual caution, the vertebra slipped out; and Lane found his body twisted like a letter S. And the old pain was no less terrible for its familiarity.

He got back to his bed and called his mother. She sent for Doctor Bronson. He came at once, and though solicitous and kind he lectured Lane for neglecting the osteopathic treatment he had advised. And he sent his chauffeur for an osteopath.

"Lane," said the little physician, peering severely down upon him, "I didn't think you'd last as long as this."

"I'm tough, Doctor—hard to kill," returned Lane, making a wry face. "But I couldn't stand this pain long."

"It'll be easier presently. We can fix that spine. Some good treatments to strengthen ligaments, and a brace to wear—we can fix that.... Lane, you've wonderful vitality."

"A doctor in France told me that."

"Except for your mental condition, you're in better shape now than when you came home." Doctor Bronson peered at Lane from under his shaggy brows, walked to the window, looked out, and returned, evidently deep in thought.

"Boy, what's on your mind?" he queried, suddenly.

"Oh, Lord! listen to him," sighed Lane. Then he laughed. "My dear Doctor, I have nothing on my mind—absolutely nothing.... This world is a beautiful place. Middleville is fine, clean, progressive. People are kind—thoughtful—good. What could I have on my mind?"

"You can't fool me. You think the opposite of what you say.... Lane, your heart is breaking."

"No, Doctor. It broke long ago."

"You believe so, but it didn't. You can't give up.... Lane, I want to tell you something. I'm a prohibitionist myself, and I respect the law. But there are rare cases where whiskey will effect a cure. I say that as a physician. And I am convinced now that your case is one where whiskey might give you a fighting chance."

"Doctor! What're you saying?" ejaculated Lane, wide-eyed with incredulity.

Doctor Bronson enlarged upon and emphasized his statement.

"I might *live*!" whispered Lane. "My God!... But that is ridiculous. I'm shot to pieces. I'm really tired of living. And I certainly wouldn't become a drunkard to save my life."

At this juncture the osteopath entered, putting an end to that intimate conversation. Doctor Bronson explained the case to his colleague. And fifteen minutes later Lane's body was again straight. Also he was wringing wet with cold sweat and quivering in every muscle.

"Gentlemen—your cure is—worse than—the disease," he panted.

Manifestly Doctor Branson's interest in Lane had advanced beyond the professional. His tone was one of friendship when he said, "Boy, it beats hell what you can stand. I don't know about you. Stop your worry now. Isn't there something you *care* for?"

"Yes," replied Lane.

"Think of that, or it, or *her*, then to the exclusion of all else. And give nature a chance."

"Doctor, I can't control my thoughts."

"A fellow like you can do anything," snapped Bronson. "There are such men, now and then. Human nature is strange and manifold. All great men do not have statues erected in their honor. Most of them are unknown, unsung.... Lane, you could do anything—do you hear me?—*anything*."

Lane felt surprise at the force and passion of the practical little physician. But he was not greatly impressed. And he was glad when the two men went away. He felt the insidious approach of one of his states of depression—the black mood—the hopeless despair—the hell on earth. This spell had not visited him often of late, and now manifestly meant to make up for that forbearance. Lane put forth his intelligence, his courage, his spirit—all in vain. The onslaught of gloom and anguish was irresistible. Then thought of Mel Iden sustained him—held back this madness for the moment.

Every hour he lived made her dearer, yet farther away. It was the unattainableness of her, the impossibility of a fruition of love that slowly and surely removed her. On the other hand, the image of her sweet face, of her form, of her beauty, of her movements—every recall of these physical things enhanced her charm, and his love. He had cherished a delusion that it was Mel Iden's spirit alone, the wonderful soul of her, that had stormed his heart and won it. But he found to his consternation that however he revered her soul, it was the woman also who now allured him. That moment of revelation to Lane was a catastrophe. Was there no peace on earth for him? What had he done to be so tortured? He had a secret he must hide from Mel Iden. He was human, he was alone, he needed love, but this seemed madness. And at the moment of full realization Doctor Bronson's strange words of possibility returned to haunt and flay him. He might live! A fierce thrill like a flame leaped from his heart, along his veins. And a shudder, cold as ice, followed it. Love would kill his resignation. Love would add to his despair. Mel Iden could never love him. He did not want her love. And yet, to live on and on, with such love as would swell and mount from his agony, with the barrier between them growing more terrible every day, was more than he cared to face. He would rather die.

And so, at length, Lane's black demon of despair overthrew even his thoughts of Mel, and fettered him there, in darkness and strife of soul. He was an atom under the grinding, monstrous wheels of his morbid mood.

Sometime, after endless moments or hours of lying there, with crushed breast, with locked thoughts hideous and forlorn, with slow burn of pang and beat of heart, Lane heard a heavy thump on the porch outside, on the hall inside, on the stairs. Thump— thump, slow and heavy! It roused him. It drove away the drowsy, thick and thunderous atmosphere of mind. It had a familiar sound. Blair's crutch!

Presently there was a knock on the door of his room and Blair entered. Blair, as always, bright of eye, smiling of lip, erect, proud, self-sufficient, inscrutable and sure. Lane's black demon stole away. Lane saw that Blair was whiter, thinner, frailer, a little farther on that road from which there could be no turning.

"Hello, old scout," greeted Blair, as he sat down on the bed beside Lane. "I need you more than any one—but it kills me to see you."

"Same here, Blair," replied Lane, comprehendingly.

"Gosh! we oughtn't be so finicky about each other's looks," exclaimed Blair, with a smile.

But neither Lane nor Blair made further reference to the subject.

Each from the other assimilated some force, from voice and look and presence, something wanting in their contact with others. These two had measured all emotions, spanned in little time the extremes of life, plumbed the depths, and now saw each other on the heights. In the presence of Blair, Lane felt an exaltation. The more Blair seemed to fade away from life, the more luminous and beautiful the light of his countenance. For Lane the crippled and dying Blair was a deed of valor done, a wrong expiated for the sake of others, a magnificent nobility in contrast to the baseness and greed and cowardice of the self-preservation that had doomed him. Lane had only to look at Blair to feel something elevating in himself, to know beyond all doubt that the goodness, the truth, the progress of man in nature, and of God in his soul, must grow on forever.

Mel Iden had been in her home four days when Lane first saw her there.

It was a day late in June when the rich, thick, amber light of afternoon seemed to float in the air. Warm summer lay on the land. The bees were humming in the rose vines over the porch. Mrs. Iden, who evidently heard Lane's step, appeared in the path, and nodding her gladness at sight of him, she pointed to the open door.

Lane halted on the threshold. The golden light of the day seemed to have entered the room and found Mel. It warmed the pallor of her skin and the whiteness of her dress. When he had seen her before she had worn something plain and dark. Could a white gown and the golden glow of June effect such transformation? She came slowly toward him and took his hand.

"Daren, I am home," was all she could say.

Long hours before Lane had braced himself for this ordeal. It was himself he had feared, not Mel. He played the part he had created for her imagination. Behind his composure, his grave, kind earnestness, hid the subdued and scorned and unwelcome love that had come to him. He held it down, surrounded, encompassed, clamped, so that he dared look into her eyes, listen to her voice, watch the sweet and tragic tremulousness of her lips.

"Yes, Mel, where you should be," replied Lane.

"It was you—your offer to marry me—that melted father's heart."

"Mel, all he needed was to be made think," returned Lane. "And that was how I made him do it."

"Oh, Daren, I thank you, for mother's sake, for mine—I can't tell you how much."

"Mel, please don't thank me," he answered. "You understand, and that's enough. Now say you'll marry me, Mel."

Mel did not answer, but in the look of her eyes, dark, humid, with mysterious depths below the veil, Lane saw the truth; he felt it in the clasp of her hands, he divined it in all that so subtly emanated from the womanliness of her. Mel had come to love him.

And all that he had endured seemed to rise and envelop heart and soul in a strange, cold stillness.

"Mel, will you marry me?" he repeated, almost dully.

Slowly Mel withdrew her hands. The query seemed to make her mistress of herself.

"No, Daren, I cannot," she replied, and turned away to look out of a window with unseeing eyes. "Let us talk of other things.... My father says he will move away—taking me and—and—all of us—as soon as he sells the home."

"No, Mel, if you'll forgive me, we'll not talk of something else," Lane informed her. "We can argue without quarreling. Come over here and sit down."

She came slowly, as if impelled, and she stood before him. To Lane it seemed as if she were both supplicating and inexorable.

"Do you remember the last time we sat together on this couch?" she asked.

"No, Mel, I don't."

"It was four years ago—and more. I was sixteen. You tried to kiss me and were angry because I wouldn't let you."

"Well, wasn't I rude!" he exclaimed, facetiously. Then he grew serious. "Mel, do you remember it was Helen's lying that came between you and me—as boy and girl friends?"

"I never knew. Helen Wrapp! What was it?"

"It's not worth recalling and would hurt you—now," he replied. "But it served to draw me Helen's way. We were engaged when she was seventeen.... Then came the war. And the other night she laughed in my face because I was a wreck.... Mel, it's beyond understanding how things work out. Helen has chosen the fleshpots of Egypt. You have chosen a lonelier and higher path.... And here I am in your little parlor asking you to marry me."

"No, no, no! Daren, don't, I beg of you—don't talk to me this way," she besought him.

"Mel, it's a difference of opinion that makes arguments, wars and other things," he said, with a cruelty in strange antithesis to the pity and tenderness he likewise felt. He could hurt her. He had power over her. What a pang shot through his heart! There would be an irresistible delight in playing on the emotions of this woman. He could no more help it than the shame that surged over him at consciousness of his littleness. He already loved her, she was all he had left to love, he would end in a day or a week or a month by worshipping her. Through her he was going to suffer. Peace would now never abide in his soul.

"Daren, you were never like this—as a boy," she said, in wondering distress.

"Like what?"

"You're hard. You used to be so—so gentle and nice."

"Hard! I? Yes, Mel, perhaps I am—hard as war, hard as modern life, hard as my old friends, my little sister——" he broke off.

"Daren, do not mock me," she entreated. "I should not have said hard. But you're strange to me—a something terrible flashes from you. Yet it's only in glimpses.... Forgive me, Daren, I didn't mean hard."

Lane drew her down upon the couch so that she faced him, and he did not release her hand.

"Mel, I'm softer than a jelly-fish," he said. "I've no bone, no fiber, no stamina, no substance. I'm more unstable than water. I'm so soft I'm weak. I can't stand pain. I lie awake in the dead hours of night and I cry like a baby, like a fool. I weep for myself, for my mother, for Lorna, for *you*...."

"Hush!" She put a soft hand over his lips.

"Very well, I'll not be bitter," he went on, with mounting pulse, with thrill and rush of inexplicable feeling, as if at last had come the person who would not be deaf to his voice. "Mel, I'm still the boy, your schoolmate, who used to pull the bow off your braid.... I am that boy still in heart, with all the war upon my head, with the years between then and now. I'm young and old.... I've lived the whole gamut—the fresh call of war to youth, glorious, but God! as false as stairs of sand—the change of blood, hard, long, brutal, debasing labor of hands, of body, of mind to learn to kill—to survive and kill—and go on to kill.... I've seen the marching of thousands of soldiers—the long strange tramp, tramp, tramp, the beat, beat, beat, the roll of drums, the call of bugles, the boom of cannon in the dark, the lightnings of hell flaring across the midnight skies, the thunder and chaos and torture and death and pestilence and decay—the hell of war. It is not sublime. There is no glory. The sublimity is in man's acceptance of war, not for hate or gain, but love. Love of country, home, family—love of women—I fought for women—for Helen, whom I imagined my ideal, breaking her heart over me on the battlefield. Not that Helen failed *me*, but failed the ideal for which I fought!... My little sister Lorna! I fought for her, and I fought for a dream that existed only in my heart. Lorna—Alas!... I fought for other women, all women—and *you*, Mel Iden. And in you, in your sacrifice and your strength to endure, I find something healing to my sore heart. I find my ideal embodied in you. I find hope and faith for the future embodied in you. I find—"

"Oh Daren, you shame me utterly," she protested, freeing her hands in gesture of entreaty. "I am outcast."

"To a false and rotten society, yes—you are," he returned. "But Mel, that society is a mass of maggots. It is such women as you, such men as Blair, who carry the spirit onward.... So much for that. I have spoken to try to show you where I hold you. I do not call your—your trouble a blunder, or downfall, or dishonor. I call it a misfortune because—because—"

"Because there was not love," she supplemented, as he halted at fault. "Yes, that is where I wronged myself, my soul. I obeyed nature and nature is strong, raw, inevitable. She seeks only her end, which is concerned with the species. For nature the individual perishes. Nature cannot be God. For God has created a soul in woman. And through the ages woman has advanced to hold her womanhood sacred. But ever the primitive lurks in the blood, and the primitive is nature. Soul and nature are not compatible. A woman's soul sanctions only love. That is the only progress there ever was in life. Nature and war made me traitor to my soul."

"Yes, yes, Mel, it's true—and cruel, what you say," returned Lane. "All the more reason why you should do what I ask. I am home after the war. All that was vain *is* vain. I forget it when I can. I have—not a great while left. There are a few things even I can do before that time. One of them—the biggest to me—concerns you. You are in trouble. You have a boy who can be spared much unhappiness in life. If you were married—if the boy had my name—how different the future! Perhaps there can be some measure of happiness for you. For him there is every hope. You will leave Middleville. You will go far away somewhere. You are young. You have a good education. You can teach school, or help your parents while the boy is growing up. Time is kind. You will forget.... Marry me, Mel, for his sake."

She had both hands pressed to her breast as if to stay an uncontrollable feeling. Her eyes, dilated and wide, expressed a blending of emotions.

"No, no, no!" she cried.

Lane went on just the same with other words, in other vein, reiterating the same importunity. It was a tragic game, in which he divined he must lose. But the playing of it had inexplicably bitter-sweet pain. He knew now that Mel loved him. No greater proof needed he than the perception of her reaction to one word on his lips—wife. She quivered to that like a tautly strung lyre touched by a skilful hand. It fascinated her. But the temptation to accept his offer for the sake of her boy's future was counteracted by the very strength of her feeling for Lane. She would not marry him, because she loved him.

Lane read this truth, and it wrung a deeper reverence from him. And he saw, too, the one way in which he could break her spirit, make her surrender, if he could stoop to it. If he could take her in his arms, and hold her tight, and kiss her dumb and blind, and make her understand his own love for her, his need of her, she would accede with the wondrous generosity of a woman's heart. But he could not do it.

In the end, out of sheer pity that overcame the strange delight he had in torturing her, he desisted in his appeals and demands and subtle arguments. The long strain left him spent. And with the sudden let-down of his energy, the surrender to her stronger will, he fell prey at once to the sadness that more and more was encompassing him. He felt an old and broken man.

To this sudden change in Lane Mel responded with mute anxiety and fear. The alteration of his spirit stunned her. As he bade her good-bye she clung to him.

"Daren, forgive me," she implored. "You don't understand.... Oh, it's hard."

"Never mind, Mel. I guess it was just one of my dreams. Don't cry.... Good-bye."

"But you'll come again?" she entreated, almost wildly.

Lane shook his head. He did not trust himself to look at her then.

"Daren, you can't mean that," she cried. "It's too late for me. I—I—Oh! You.... To uplift me—then to cast me down! Daren, come back."

In his heart he did not deny that cry of hers. He knew he would come back, knew it with stinging shame, but he could not tell her. It had all turned out so differently from what he had dreamed. If he had not loved her he would not have felt defeat. To have made her his wife would have been to protect her, to possess her even after he was dead.

At the last she let him go. He felt her watching him, and he carried her lingering clasp away with him, to burn and to thrill and to haunt, and yet to comfort him in lonely hours.

But the next day the old spirit resurged anew, and unreconciled to defeat, he turned to what was left him. Foolish and futile hopes! To bank on the single grain of good in his wayward sister's heart! To trust the might of his spirit—to beat down the influence of an intolerant and depraved young millionaire—verily he was mad. Yet he believed. And as a final resort he held death in his hand. Richard Swann swaggered by Lane that night in the billiard room of the Bradford Inn and stared sneeringly at him.

"I've got a date," he gayly said to his sycophantic friends, in a tone that would reach Lane's ears.

The summer night came when Lane drove a hired car out the river road, keeping ever in sight a red light in front of him. He broke the law and endangered his life by traveling with darkened lamps.

There was a crescent moon, clear and exquisitely delicate in the darkening blue sky. The gleaming river shone winding away under the dusky wooded hills. The white road stretched ahead, dimming in the distance. A night for romance and love—for a maiden at a stile and a lover who hung rapt and humble upon her whispers! But that red eye before him held no romance. It leered as the luxurious sedan swayed from side to side, a diabolical thing with speed.

Lane was driving out the state highway, mile after mile. He calculated that in less than ten minutes Swann had taken a girl from a bustling corner of Middleville out into the open country. In pleasant weather, when the roads were good, cars like Swann's swerved off into the bypaths, into the edge of woods. In bad weather they parked along the highway, darkened their lights and pulled their blinds. For this, great factories turned out automobiles. And there might have pealed out to a nation, and to God, the dolorous cry of a hundred thousand ruined girls! But who would hear? And on the lips of girls of the present there was only the wild cry for excitement, for the nameless and unknown! There was a girl in Swann's car and Lane believed it was his sister. Night after night he had watched. Once he had actually seen Lorna ride off with Swann. And to-night from a vantage point under the maples, when he had a car ready to follow, he had made sure he had seen them again.

The red eye squared off at right angles to the highway, and disappeared. Lane came to a byroad, a lane lined with trees. He stopped his car and got out. It did not appear that he would have to walk far. And he was right, for presently a black object loomed against the gray obscurity. It was an automobile, without lights, in the shadow of trees.

Lane halted. He carried a flash-light in his left hand, his gun in his right. For a moment he deliberated. This being abroad in the dark on an errand fraught with peril for some one had a familiar and deadly tang. He was at home in this atmosphere. Hell itself had yawned at his feet many and many a time. He was a different man here. He deliberated because it was wise to forestall events. He did not want to kill Swann then, unless in self-defense. He waited until that peculiarly quick and tight and cold settling of his nerves told of brain control over heart. Yet he was conscious of subdued hate, of a righteous and terrible wrath held in abeyance for the sake of his sister's name. And he regretted that he had imperiously demanded of himself this assurance of Lorna's wantonness.

Then he stole forward, closer and closer. He heard a low voice of dalliance, a titter, high-pitched and sweet—sweet and wild. That was not Lorna's laugh. The car was not Swann's.

Lane swerved to the left, and in the gloom of trees, passed by noiselessly. Soon he encountered another car—an open car with shields up—as silent as if empty. But the very silence of it was potent of life. It cried out to the night and to Lane. But it was not the car he had followed.

Again he slipped by, stealthily, yet scornful of his caution. Who cared? He might have shouted his mission to the heavens. Lane passed on. All he caught from the second car was a faint fragrance of smoke, wafted on the gentle summer breeze.

Another black object loomed up—a larger car—the sedan Lane recognized. He did not bolt or hurry. His footsteps made no sound. Crouching a little he slipped round the car to one side. At the instant he reached for the handle of the door, a pang shook him. Alas, that he should be compelled to spy on Lorna! His little sister! He saw her as a curly-headed child, adoring him. Perhaps it might not be Lorna after all. But it was for her sake that he was doing this. The softer moment passed and the soldier intervened.

With one swift turn and jerk he opened the door—then flashed his light. A scream rent the air. In the glaring circle of light Lane saw red hair—green eyes transfixed in fear—white shoulders—white arms—white ringed hands suddenly flung upward. Helen! The blood left his heart in a rush. Swann blinked in the light, bewildered and startled.

"Swann, you'll have to excuse me," said Lane, coolly. "I thought you had my sister with you. I've spotted her twice with you in this car.... It may not interest you or your— your guest, but I'll add that you're damned lucky not to have Lorna here to-night."

Then he snapped off his flash-light, and slamming the car door, he wheeled away.

CHAPTER XIII

Lane left his room and went into the shady woods, where he thought the July heat would be less unendurable, where the fever in his blood might abate. But though it was cool and pleasant there he experienced no relief. Wherever he went he carried the burden of his pangs. And his grim giant of unrest trod in his shadow.

He could not stay long in the woods. He betook himself to the hills and meadows. Action was beneficial for him, though he soon exhausted himself. He would have liked to fight out his battle that day. Should he go on spending his days and nights in a slowly increasing torment? The longer he fought the less chance he had of victory. Victory! There could be none. What victory could be won over a strange ineradicable susceptibility to the sweetness, charm, mystery of a woman? He plodded the fragrant fields with bent head, in despair. Loneliness hurt him as much as anything. And a new pang, the fiercest and most insupportable, had been added to his miseries. Jealousy! Thought of the father of Mel Iden's child haunted him, flayed him, made him feel himself ignoble and base. There was no help for that. And this fiend of jealousy added fuel to his love. Only long passionate iteration of his assurance of principle and generosity subdued that frenzy and at length gave him composure. Perhaps this had some semblance to victory.

Lane returned to town weaker in one way than when he had left, yet stronger in another. Upon the outskirts of Middleville he crossed the river road and sat down upon a stone wall. The afternoon was far spent and the sun blazing red. Lane wiped his moist face and fanned himself with his hat. Behind him the shade of a wooded garden or park looked inviting. Back in the foliage he espied the vine-covered roof of an old summer house.

A fresh young voice burst upon his meditations. "Hello, Daren Lane."

Lane turned in surprise to behold a girl in white, standing in the shade of trees beyond the wall. Somewhere he had seen that beautiful golden head, the dark blue, almost purple eyes.

"Good afternoon. You startled me," said Lane.

"I called you twice."

"Indeed? I beg pardon. I didn't hear."

"Don't you remember me?" Her tone was one of pique and doubt.

Then he remembered her. "Oh, of course. Bessy Bell! You must forgive me. I've been ill and upset lately. These bad spells of mine magnify time. It seems long since the Junior Prom."

"Oh, you're ill," she returned, compassionately. "You do look pale and—won't you come in? It's dusty and hot there. Come. I'll take you where it's nice and cool."

"Thank you. I'll be glad to."

She led him to a green, fragrant nook, where a bench with cushions stood half-hidden under heavy foliage. Lane caught a glimpse of a winding flagged path, and in the distance a cottage among the trees.

"Bessy, do you live here?" he asked. "It's pretty."

"Yes, this is my home. It's too damn far from town, I'll say. I'm buried alive," she replied, passionately.

The bald speech struck Lane forcibly. All at once he remembered Bessy Bell and his former interest. She was a type of the heretofore inexplicable modern girl. Lane looked at her, seeing her suddenly with a clearer vision. Bessy Bell had a physical perfection, a loveliness that needed neither spirit nor animation. But life had given this girl so much more than beauty. A softness of light seemed to shine round her golden head; smiles played in secret behind her red lips ready to break forth, and there was a haunting hint of a dimple in her round cheek; on her lay the sweetness of youth subtly dawning into womanhood; the flashing eyes were keen with intellect, with fire, full of promise and mystic charm; and her beautiful, supple body, so plainly visible, seemed quivering with sheer, restless joy of movement and feeling. A trace of artificial color on her face and the indelicacy of her dress but slightly counteracted Lane's first impression.

"You promised to call me up and make a date," she said, and sat down close to him.

"Yes. I meant it too. But Bessy, I was ill, and then I forgot. You didn't miss much."

"Hot dog! Hear the man. Daren, I'd throw the whole bunch down to be with you," she exclaimed.

At the end of that speech she paled slightly and her breath came quickly. She looked bold, provocative, expectant, yet sincere. Child or woman, she had to be taken seriously. Here indeed was the mystery that had baffled Lane. He realized his opportunity, like a flash all his former thought and conjecture about this girl returned to him.

"You would. Well, I'm highly flattered. Why, may I ask?"

"Because I've fallen for you," she replied, leaning close to him. "That's the main reason, I guess.... But another is, I want you to tell me all about yourself—in the war, you know."

"I'd be glad to—if we get to be real friends," he said, thoughtfully. "I don't understand you."

"And I'll say I don't just get you," she retorted. "What do you want? Have you forgotten the silver platter?"

She turned away with a restless quivering. She had shown no shyness. She was bold, intense, absolutely without fear; and however stimulating or attractive the situation evidently was, it was neither new nor novel to her. Some strange leaven worked deep in her. Lane could put no other interpretation on her words and actions than that she expected him to kiss her.

"Bessy Bell, look at me," said Lane, earnestly. "You've said a mouthful, as the slang word goes. I'm sort of surprised, you remember. Bessy, you're not a girl whose head is full of excelsior. You've got brains. You can think.... Now, if you really like me—and I believe you—try to understand this. I've been away so long. All is changed. I don't know how to take girls. I'm ill—and unhappy. But if I could be your friend and could help you a little—please you—why it'd be good for me."

"Daren, they tell me you're going to die," she returned, breathlessly. Her glance was brooding, dark, pregnant with purple fire.

"Bessy, don't believe all you hear. I'm not—not so far gone yet."

"They say you're game, too."

"I hope so, Bessy."

"Oh, you make me think. You must believe me a pill. I wanted you to—to fall for me hard.... That bunch of sapheads have spoiled me, I'll say. Daren, I'm sick of them. All they want to do is mush. I like tennis, riding, golf. I want to do things. But it's too hot, or this, or that. Yet they'll break their necks to carry a girl off to some roadhouse, and dance—dance till you're melted. Then they stop along the river to go bathing. I've been twice. You see, I have to sneak away, or lie to mother and say I've gone to Gail's or somewhere."

"Bathing, at night?" queried Lane, curiously.

"Sure thing. It's spiffy, in the dark."

"Of course you took your bathing suits?"

"Hot dog! That would be telling."

Lane dropped his head and studied the dust at his feet. His heart beat thick and heavy. Through this girl the truth was going to be revealed to him. It seemed on the moment that he could not look into her eyes. She scattered his wits. He tried to erase from his mind every impression of her, so that he might begin anew to understand her. And the very first, succeeding this erasure, was a singular idea that she was the opposite of romantic.

"Bessy, can you understand that it is hard for a soldier to talk of what has happened to him?"

"I'll say I can," she replied.

"You're sorry for me?" he went on, gently.

"Sorry!... Give me a chance to prove what I am, Daren Lane."

"Very well, then. I will. We'll make a fifty-fifty bargain. Do you regard a promise sacred?"

"I think I do. Some of the girls quarrel with me because I get sore, and swear they're not square, as I try to be. I hate a liar and a quitter."

"Come then—shake hands on our bargain."

She seemed thrilled, excited. The clasp of her little hand showed force of character. She looked wonderingly up at him. Her appeal then was one of exquisite youth and beauty. Something of the baffling suggestion of an amorous expectation and response left her. This child would give what she received.

"First, then, it's for me to know a lot about you," went on Lane. "Will you tell me?"

"Sure. I'd trust you with anything," she replied, impulsively.

"How long have you been going with boys?"

"Oh, for two years, I guess. I had a passionate love affair when I was thirteen," she replied, with the nonchalance and sophistication of experience.

It was impossible for Lane to take this latter remark for anything but the glib boldness of an erotic child. But he was not making any assurances to himself that he was right. Bessy Bell was fifteen years old, according to time. But she had the physical development of eighteen, and a mental range beyond his ken. The lawlessness unleashed by the war seemed embodied in this girl.

"With an older boy?" queried Lane.

"No. He was a kid of my own age. I guess I outgrew Ted," she replied, dreamily. "But he still tries to rush me."

"With whom do you go to the secret club-rooms—above White's ice cream parlor?" asked Lane, abruptly.

Bessy never flicked an eyelash. "Hot dog! So you're wise to that? I thought it was a secret. I told Rose Clymer those fellows weren't on the level. Who told you I was there? Your sister Lorna?"

"No. No one told me. Never mind that. Who took you there? You needn't be afraid to trust *me*. I'm going to entrust my secrets to you by and bye."

"I went with Roy Vancey, the boy who was with me at Helen's the day I met you."

"Bessy, how often have you been to those club-rooms?"

"Three times."

"Were you ever there alone without any girls?"

"No. I had my chance. Dick Swann tried his damnedest to get me to go. But I've no use for him."

"Why?"

"I just don't like him, Daren," she replied, evasively. "I love to have fun. But I haven't yet been so hard up I had to go out with some one I didn't like."

"Has Swann had my sister Lorna at the club?"

Her replies had been prompt and frank. At this sudden query she seemed checked. Lane read in Bessy Bell then more of the truth of her than he had yet divined. Falsehood was naturally abhorrent to her. To lie to her parents or teachers savored of fun, and was part of the game. She did not want to lie to Lane, but in her code she could not betray another girl, especially to that girl's brother.

"Daren, I promised I'd tell you all about myself," she said.

"I shouldn't have asked you to give away one of your friends," he returned. "Some other time I'll talk to you about Lorna. Tell you what I know, and ask you to help me save her——"

"*Save* her! What do you mean, Daren?" she interrupted, with surprise.

"Bessy, I've paid you the compliment of believing you have intelligence. Hasn't it occurred to you that Lorna—or other of her friends or yours—might be going straight to ruin?"

"Ruin! No, that hadn't occurred to me. I heard Doctor Wallace make a crack like yours. Mother hauled me to church the Sunday after you broke up Fanchon Smith's dance. Doctor Wallace didn't impress me. These old people make me sick anyhow. They don't understand.... But Daren, I think I get your drift. So snow some more."

All in a moment, it seemed to Lane, this girl passed from surprise to gravity, then to contempt, and finally to humor. She was fascinating.

"To go back to the club," resumed Lane. "Bessy, what did you do there?"

"Oh, we toddled and shimmied. Cut up! Had an immense time, I'll say."

"What do you mean by cut up?"

"Why, we just ran wild, you know. Fool stunts!... Once Roy was sore because I kicked cigarettes out of Bob's mouth. But the boob was tickled stiff when I kicked for *him*. Jealous! It's all right with any one of the boys what you do for *him*. But if you do the same for *another* boy—good night!"

Bessy had no divination of the fact that her words for Lane had a clarifying significance.

"I suppose you played what we used to call kissing games?" queried Lane.

A sweet, high trill of laughter escaped Bessy's red lips.

"Daren, you are funny. Those games are as dead as Caesar.... This bunch of boys and girls paired off by themselves to spoon.... As for myself, I don't mind spooning if I like the fellow—and he hasn't been drinking. But otherwise I hate it. All the same I got what was coming to me from some of the boys of the Strong Arm Club."

"Why do they give it that name?" asked Lane, remembering Colonel Pepper's remarks.

"Why, if a girl doesn't come across she gets the strong arm.... I had to fight like the devil that last afternoon I went there."

"*Did* you fight, Bessy?"

"I'll say I did.... Roy Vancey is sore as a pup. He hasn't been near me or called me up since."

"Bessy, will you promise to stay away from that place—and not to go joy-riding with any of those boys—day or night—if I meet you, and tell you all about my experience in the war? I'll do my best to keep the time you spend with me from being tedious."

"It's another bargain," she returned deliberately, "if you just don't spend enough time with me to make me stuck on you—then throw me down. On the level, now, Daren?"

"I'll meet you as often as you want. And I'll be your friend as long as you prove to me I can be of any help, or pleasure, or good to you."

"Hot dog, but you're taking some job, Daren. Won't it be just spiffy? We'll meet here, afternoons, and evenings when mother's out. She's nutty on bridge. She makes me promise I won't leave the yard. So I'll not have to lie to meet you.... Daren, that day at Helen's, the minute I saw you I knew you were going to have something to do with my future."

"Bessy, a little while ago I made sure you had no romance in you," replied Lane, with a smile. "Now as we've gotten serious, let's think hard about the future. What do you want most? Do you care for study, for books? Have you any gift for music? Do you ever think of fitting yourself for useful work?... Or is your mind full of this jazz stuff? Do you just want to go from day to day, like a butterfly from flower to flower? Just this boy and that one—not caring much which—all this frivolity you hinted of, and worse, living this precious time of your youth all for excitement? What is it you want most?"

She responded with a thoughtfulness that inspired Lane's hope for her. This girl could be reached. She was like Lorna in many ways, but different in mentality. Bessy watched the gyrations of her shapely little foot. She could not keep still even in abstraction.

"A girl *must* have a good time," she replied presently. "I've done things I hated because I couldn't bear to be left out of the fun.... But I like most to read and dream. Music makes me strange inside, and to want to do great things. Only there *are* no great things to do. I've never been nutty about a career, like Helen is. And I always hated work.... I guess—to tell on the level—what I want most is to be loved."

With that she raised her eyes to Lane's. He tried to read her mind, and realized that if he failed it was not because she was not baring it. Dropping his own gaze, he pondered. The girl's response to his earnestness was intensely thought-provoking. No matter how immodestly she was dressed, or what she had confessed to, or whether she had really expected and desired dalliance on his part—here was the truth as to her hidden yearning. The seething and terrible Renaissance of the modern girl seemed remarkably exemplified in Bessy Bell, yet underneath it all hid the fundamental instinct of all women of all ages. Bessy wanted most to be loved. Was that the secret of her departure from the old-fashioned canons of modesty and reserve?

"Bessy," went on Lane, presently. "I've heard my sister speak of Rose Clymer. Is she a friend of yours, too?"

"You bet. And she's the square kid."

"Lorna told me she'd been expelled from school."

"Yes. She refused to tattle."

"Tattle what?"

"I wrote some verses which one of the girls copied. Miss Hill found them and raised the roof. She kept us all in after school. She let some of the girls off. But she expelled Rose and sent me home. Then she called on mama. I don't know what she said, but mama didn't let me go back. I've had a hateful old tutor for a month. In the fall I'm going to private school."

"And Rose?"

"Rose went to work. She had a hard time. I never heard from her for weeks. But she's a telephone operator at the Exchange now. She called me up one day lately and told me. I hope to see her soon."

"About those verses, Bessy. How did Miss Hill find out who wrote them?"

"I told her. Then she sent me home."

"Have you any more verses you wrote?"

"Yes, a lot of them. If you lend me your pencil, I'll write out the verse that gave Miss Hill heart disease."

Bessy took up a book that had been lying on the seat, and tearing out the fly-leaf, she began to write. Her slim, shapely hand flew. It fascinated Lane.

"There!" she said, ending with a flourish and a smile.

But Lane, foreshadowing the import of the verse, took the page with reluctance. Then he read it. Verses of this significance were new to him. Relief came to Lane in the divination that Bessy could not have had experience of what she had written. There was worldliness in the verse, but innocence in her eyes.

"Well, Bessy, my heart isn't much stronger than Miss Hill's," he said, finally.

Her merry laughter rang out.

"Bessy, what will you do for me?"

"Anything."

"Bring me every scrap of verse you have, every note you've got from boys and girls."

"Shall I get them now?"

"Yes, if it's safe. Of course, you've hidden them."

"Mama's out. I won't be a minute."

Away she flew under the trees, out through the rose bushes, a white, graceful, flitting figure. She vanished. Presently she came bounding into sight again and handed Lane a bundle of notes.

"Did you keep back any?" he asked, as he tried to find pockets enough for the collection.

"Not one."

"I'll go home and read them all. Then I'll meet you here to-night at eight o'clock."

"But—I've a date. I'll break it, though."

"With whom?"

"Gail and a couple of boys—kids."

"Does your mother know?"

"I'd tell her about Gail, but that's all. We go for ice cream—then meet the boys and take a walk."

"Bessy, you're not going to do that sort of thing any more."

Lane bent over her, took her hands. She instinctively rebelled, then slowly yielded.

"That's part of our bargain?" she asked.

"Yes, it certainly is."

"Then I won't ever again."

"Bessy, I trust you. Do you understand me?"

"I—I think so."

"Daren, will you care for me—if I'm—if I do as you want me to?"

"I do now," he replied. "And I'll care a thousand times more when you prove you're really above these things.... Bessy, I'll care for you as a friend—as a brother—as a man who has almost lost his faith and who sees in you some hope to keep his spirit alive. I'm unhappy, Bessy. Perhaps you can help me—make me a little happier.... Anyway, I trust you. Good-bye now. To-night, at eight o'clock."

Lane went home to his room and earnestly gave himself up to the perusal of the writings Bessy Bell had given him. He experienced shocks of pain and wonder, between which he had to laugh. All the fiendish wit of youthful ingenuity flashed forth from this verse. There was a parody on Tennyson's "Break, Break, Break," featuring Colonel Pepper's famous and deplorable habit. Miss Hill came in for a great share of opprobrium. One verse, if it had ever come under the eyes of the good schoolteacher, would have broken her heart.

Lane read all Bessy's verses, and then the packet of notes written by Bessy's girl friends. The truth was unbelievable. Yet here were the proofs. Over Bessy and her friends Lane saw the dim dark shape of a ghastly phantom, reaching out, enfolding, clutching. He went downstairs to the kitchen and here he burned the writings.

"It ought to be told," he muttered. "But who's going to tell it? Who'd believe me? The truth would not be comprehended by the mothers of Middleville.... And who's to blame?"

It would not do, Lane reflected, to place the blame wholly upon blind fathers and mothers, though indeed they were culpable. And in consideration of the subject, Lane excluded all except the better class of Middleville. It was no difficult task to understand lack of moral sense in children who were poor and unfortunate, who had to work, and get what pleasures they had in the streets. But how about the best families, where there were luxurious homes, books, education, amusement, kindness, love—all the supposed stimuli needed for the proper guidance of changeful vagrant minds? These good influences had failed. There was a greater moral abandonment than would ever be known.

Before the war Bessy Bell would have presented the perfect type of the beautiful, highly sensitive, delicately organized girl so peculiarly and distinctively American. She would have ripened before her time. Perhaps she would not have been greatly different in feeling from the old-fashioned girl: only different in that she had restraint, no deceit.

But after the war—now—what was Bessy Bell? What actuated her? What was the secret spring of her abnormal tendencies? Were they abnormal? Bessy was wild to abandon herself to she knew not what. Some glint of intelligence, some force of character as exceptional in her as it was wanting in Lorna, some heritage of innate sacredness of person, had kept Bessy from the abyss. She had absorbed in mind all the impurities of the day, but had miraculously escaped them in body. If her parents could have known Bessy as Lane now realized her they would have been horrified. But Lane's horror was fading. Bessy was illuminating the darkness of his mind.

To understand more clearly what the war had done to Bessy Bell, and to the millions of American girls like her, it was necessary for Lane to understand what the war had done to soldiers, to men, and to the world.

Lane could grasp some infinitesimal truth of the sublime and horrible change war had wrought in the souls of soldiers. That change was too great for any mind but the omniscient to grasp in its entirety. War had killed in some soldiers a belief in Christ: in others it had created one. War had unleashed the old hidden primitive instincts of manhood: likewise it had fired hearts to hate of hate and love of love, to the supreme ideal consciousness could conceive. War had brought out the monstrous in men and as well the godlike. Some soldiers had become cowards; others, heroes. There were thousands of soldiers who became lions to fight, hyenas to snarl, beasts to debase, hogs to wallow. There were equally as many who were forced to fight, who could not kill, whose gentleness augmented under the brutal orders of their officers. There were those who ran toward the front, heads up, singing at the top of their lungs. There were those who slunk back. Soldiers became cold, hard, materialistic, bitter, rancorous: and qualities antithetic to these developed in their comrades.

Lane exhausted his resources of memory and searched in his notes for a clipping he had torn from a magazine. He reread it, in the light of his crystallizing knowledge:

"Had I not been afraid of the scorn of my brother
officers and the scoffs of my men, I would have fled
to the rear," confesses a Wisconsin officer, writing
of a battle.

"I see war as a horrible, grasping octopus with
hundreds of poisonous, death-dealing tentacle that
squeeze out the culture and refinement of a man,"
writes a veteran.

A regimental sergeant-major: "I considered myself
hardboiled, and acted the part with everybody,
including my wife. I scoffed at religion as unworthy
of a real man and a mark of the sissy and weakling."
Before going over the top for the first time he tried
to pray, but had even forgotten the Lord's Prayer.

"If I get out of this, I will never be unhappy again,"
reflected one of the contestants under shell-fire in
the Argonne Forest. To-day he is "not afraid of dead
men any more and is not in the least afraid to die."

"I went into the army a conscientious objector, a
radical, and a recluse.... I came out of it with the
knowledge of men and the philosophy of beauty," says
another.

"My moral fiber has been coarsened. The war has
blunted my sensitiveness to human suffering. In 1914 I
wept tears of distress over a rabbit which I had shot.
I could go out now at the command of my government in
cold-blooded fashion and commit all the barbarisms of
twentieth-century legalized murder," writes a Chicago
man.

A Denver man entered the war, lost himself and God,
and found manhood. "I played poker in the box-car
which carried me to the front and read the Testament
in the hospital train which took me to the rear," he
tells us.

"To disclose it all would take the genius and the understanding of a god. I learned to talk from the side of my mouth and drink and curse with the rest of our 'noble crusaders.' Authority infuriated me and the first suspicion of an order made me sullen and dangerous.... Each man in his crudeness and lewdness nauseated me," writes a service man.

"When our boy came back," complains a mother, "we could hardly recognize for our strong, impulsive, loving son whom we had loaned to Uncle Sam this irritable, restless, nervous man with defective hearing from shells exploding all about him, and limbs aching and twitching from strain and exposure, and with that inevitable companion of all returned oversea boys, the coffin-nail, between his teeth."

"In the army I found that hard drinkers and fast livers and profane-tongued men often proved to be the kindest-hearted, squarest friends one could ever have," one mother reports.

So then the war brought to the souls of soldiers an extremity of debasement and uplift, a transformation incomprehensible to the mind of man.

Upon men outside the service the war pressed its materialism. The spiritual progress of a thousand years seemed in a day to have been destroyed. Self-preservation was the first law of nature. And all the standards of life were abased. Following the terrible fever of patriotism and sacrifice and fear came the inevitable selfishness and greed and frenzy. The primitive in man stalked forth. The world became a place of strife.

What then, reflected Lane, could have been the effect of war upon women? The mothers of the race, of men! The creatures whom emotions governed! The beings who had the sex of tigresses! "The female of the species!" What had the war done to the generation of its period—to Helen, to Mel Iden, to Lorna, to Bessy Bell? Had it made them what men wanted?

At eight o'clock that night Lane kept his tryst with Bessy. The serene, mellow light of the moon shone down upon the garden. The shade appeared spotted with patches of moonlight; the summer breeze rustled the leaves; the insects murmured their night song. Romance and beauty still lived. No war could kill them. Bessy came gliding under the trees, white and graceful like a nymph, fearless, full of her dream, ripe to be made what a man would make of her.

Lane talked to Bessy of the war. Words came like magic to his lips. He told her of the thunder and fire and blood and heroism, of fight and agony and death. He told her of himself—of his service in the hours that tried his soul. Bessy passed from fascinated intensity to rapture and terror. She clung to Lane. She kissed him. She wept.

He told her how his ideal had been to fight for Helen, for Lorna, for her, and all American girls. And then he talked about what he had come home to—of the shock— the realization—the disappointment and grief. He spoke of his sister Lorna—how he had tried so hard to make her see, and had failed. He importuned Bessy to help him as only a girl could. And lastly, he brought the conversation back to her and told her bluntly what he thought of the vile verses, how she dragged her girlhood pride in the filth and made of herself a byword for vicious boys. He told her the truth of what real men thought and felt of women. Every man had a mother. No war, no unrest, no style, no fad, no let-down of morals could change the truth. From the dark ages women had climbed on the slow realization of freedom, honor, chastity. As the future of nations depended upon women, so did their salvation. Women could never again be barbarians. All this modern license was a parody of love. It must inevitably end in the degradation and unhappiness of those of the generation who persisted on that downward path. Hard indeed it would be to encounter the ridicule of girls and the indifference of boys. But only through the intelligence and courage of one could there ever be any hope for the many.

Lane sat there under the moonlit maples and talked until he was hoarse. He could not rouse a sense of shame in Bessy, because that had been atrophied, but as he closely watched her, he realized that his victory would come through the emotion he was able to arouse in her, and the ultimate appeal to the clear logic of her mind.

When the time came for him to go she stood before him in the clear moonlight.

"I've never been so excited, so scared and sick, so miserable and thoughtful in all my life before," she said. "Daren, I know now what a soldier is. What you've seen—what you've done. Oh! it was grand!... And you're going to be my—my friend.... Daren, I thought it was great to be bad. I thought men liked a girl to be bad. The girls nicknamed me Angel Bell, but not because I was an angel, I'll tell the world.... Now I'm going to try to be the girl you want me to be."

CHAPTER XIV

The time came when Daren had to make a painful choice. His sister Lorna grew weary of his importunities and distrustful of his espionage. One night she became violent and flatly told him she would not stay in the house another day with him in it. Then she ran out, slamming the door behind her. Lane remained awake all night, in the hope that she would return. But she did not. And then he knew he must make a choice.

He made it. Lorna must not be driven from her home. Lane divided his money with his mother and packed his few effects. Mrs. Lane was distracted over the situation. She tried to convince Lane there was some kind of a law to keep a young girl home. She pleaded and begged him to remain. She dwelt on his ill health. But Lane was obdurate; and not the least of his hurts was the last one—a divination that in spite of his mother's distress there was a feeling of relief of which she was unconscious. He assured her that he would come to see her often during the afternoons and would care as best he could for his health. Then he left, saying he would send an expressman for the things he had packed.

Broodingly Lane plodded down the street. He had feared that sooner or later he would be forced to leave home, and he had shrunk from the ordeal. But now, that it was over, he felt a kind of relief, and told himself that it was of no consequence what happened to him. All that mattered was for him to achieve the few tasks he had set himself.

Then he thought of Mel Iden. She had been driven from home and would know what it meant to him. The longing to see her increased. Every disappointment left him more in need of sympathy. And now, it seemed, he would be ashamed to go to Mel Iden or Blair Maynard. Such news could not long be kept from them. Middleville was a beehive of gossips. Lane had a moment of blank despair, a feeling of utter, sick, dazed wonder at life and human nature. Then he lifted his head and went on.

Lane's first impulse was to ask Colonel Pepper if he could share his lodgings, but upon reflection he decided otherwise. He engaged a small room in a boarding house; his meals, which did not seem of much importance, he could get anywhere.

This change of residence brought Lane downtown, and naturally increased his activities. He did not husband his strength as before, nor have the leisure for bad spells. Home had been a place of rest. He could not rest in a drab little bare room he now occupied.

He became a watcher, except during the stolen hours with Bessy Bell. Then he tried to be a teacher. But he learned more than he thought. He no longer concentrated his vigilance on his sister. Having failed to force that issue, he bided his time, sensing with melancholy portent the certainty that he would soon be confronted with the stark and hateful actuality. Thus he wore somewhat away from his grim resolve to kill Swann. That adventure on the country road, when he had discovered Swann with Helen instead of Lorna, had somehow been a boon. Nevertheless he spied upon Lorna in the summer evenings when it was possible to follow her, and he dogged Swann's winding and devious path as far as possible. Apparently Swann had checked his irregularities as far as Lorna was concerned. Still Lane trusted nothing. He became an almost impassive destiny with the iron consequences in his hands.

Days passed. Every other afternoon and night he spent hours with Bessy Bell, and found a mounting happiness in the change in her, a deep and ever deeper insight into the causes that had developed her. The balance of his waking hours, which were many, he passed on the streets, in the ice cream parlors and confectionery dens, at the motion-picture theatres. He went many and odd times to Colonel Pepper's apartment, and took a peep into the club-rooms. Some of these visits were fruitful, but he did not see whom he expected to see there. At night he haunted the parks, watching and listening. Often he hired a cheap car and drove it down the river highway, where he would note the cars he passed or met. Sometimes he would stop to get out and make one of his scouting detours, or he would follow a car to some distant roadhouse, or go to the outlying summer pavilions where popular dances were given. More than once, late at night, he was an unseen and unbidden guest at one of the gay bathing parties. Strange and startling incidents seemed to gravitate toward Lane. He might have been predestined for this accumulation of facts. How vain it seethed for wild young men and women to think they hid their tracks! Some trails could not be hidden.

Toward the end of that protracted period of surveillance, Lane knew that he had become infamous in the eyes of most of that younger set. He had been seen too often, alone, watching, with no apparent excuse for his presence. And from here and there, through Bessy and Colonel Pepper, and Blair, who faithfully hunted him up, Lane learned of the unfavorable light in which he was held. Society, in the persons of the younger matrons, took exception to Lane's queer conduct and hinted of mental unbalance. The young rakes and libertines avoided him, and there was not a slacker among them who could meet his eye across cafe or billiard room.

Yet despite the peculiar species of ignominy and disgrace that Middleville gossips heaped upon Lane's head and the slow, steady decline of his speaking acquaintance with the elite, there were some who always greeted him and spoke if he gave them a chance. Helen Wrapp never failed of a green flashing glance of mockery and enticement. She smiled, she beckoned, she once called him to her car and asked him to ride with her, to come to see her. Margaret Maynard rose above dread of her mother and greeted Lane graciously when occasion offered. Dorothy Dalrymple and Elinor always evinced such unhesitating intention of friendship that Lane grew to avoid meeting them. And twice, when he had come face to face with Mel Iden, her look, her smile had been such that he had plunged away somewhere, throbbing and thrilling, to grow blind and sick and numb. It was the failure of his hopes, and the suffering he endured, and the vain longings she inspired that heightened his love. She wrote him after the last time they had passed on the street—a note that stormed Lane's heart. He did not answer. He divined that his increasing loneliness, and the sure slow decline of his health, and the heartless intolerance of the same class that had ostracized her were added burdens to Mel Iden's faithful heart. He had seen it in her face, read it in her note. And the time would come, sooner or later, when he could go to her and make her marry him.

CHAPTER XV.

To be a mystery is overpoweringly sweet to any girl and Bessy Bell was being that. Her sudden desire for solitude had worried her mother, and her distant superiority had incited the vexation of her friends. When they exerted themselves to win Bessy back to her old self she looked dreamily beyond them and became more aloof. Doctor Bronson, in reply to Mrs. Bell's appeal to him, looked the young woman over, asked her a few questions, marveled at the imperious artifice with which she evaded him, and throwing up his hands said Bessy was beyond him.

The dark fever, rising from the school yards and the playgrounds and the streets, subtly poisoning the blood of Bessy Bell, slowly lost its heat and power for the time being. Bessy lived in the full secret expression of her girlish adoration. She was worshipping a hero; she was glorifying in her sacrifice; she was faithful to a man; she was being a woman. At first she grew pale, tense, quiet, and seemed to be going into a decline. Then that stage passed; and the roseleaf flush returned to her cheeks, the purple fire deepened in her eyes, the quivering life in all her supple young body.

Night after night loneliness had no fears for her. If she heard a whistle on the avenue, the honk of a car—the familiar old signals of the boys and girls, she smiled her disdain, and curling comfortably in her great chair, bent her lovely head over her books.

In the beginning her dreams were all of Daren Lane, of the strangeness and glory of this soldier who spent so many secret hours with her. And when the time came that she did not see him so often her dreams were just as full. But gradually, as the days went by, other figures than Lane's were limned upon her fancy—vague figures of heroes, knights, soldiers. He still dominated her romances, though less personally. She built around him. Every day brought her new strange desires.

One evening in August when Bessy sat alone the telephone bell rang sharply. She ran to take down the receiver.

"Hello, hello, that you, Bessy?" came the hurried call in a girl's voice.

"Rose! Oh, how are you?"

"Fine. But say, Angel, I can't take time to talk. Something doing. Are you alone?"

"Yes, all alone, old girl."

"Listen, then, and get this.... I'm here, you know, telephone girl at the Exchange. Just heard your father on the wire. Some one has betrayed the secret of the club. There's a warrant out for the arrest of the boys. For gambling. You know there's a political vice drive on. Some time to-night they'll be raided.... But early. Bess, are you getting this?"

"Sure. Hurry—hurry," replied Bessy, in excitement.

"I tried to get Dick on the wire, but couldn't. Same with two more of the boys. But I did get wise to this. Gail and Lorna have a date at the club to-night.... Never mind how I found out. Dick has thrown me down for Gail. I'm sore as a pup. But I don't want your father to pinch those girls.... Now, Bess, I'm tied here. But you get a move on. Don't waste time. You can save them. You must. Do something. If you can't find somebody, go straight to the club. You know where the key for the outside entrance is kept. Hurry and it'll be safe. Good-bye."

Bessy stood statue-like for a moment, her big eyes glowing, changing, darkening with rapid thought, then she flew upstairs to her room, snatched a veil and a soft hat, and putting these on as she went, she flew out of the house without putting out the lights or locking the door.

It was a dark windy night, slightly cool for August, and a fine misty rain was blowing. Bessy's footsteps pattered softly as she ran block after block, and she did not slacken her pace till she reached the house where Daren Lane had his room. In answer to her ring a woman appeared, who told her Mr. Lane was out.

This was a severe disappointment to Bessy, and left her an alternative that required more than courage, but she did not vacillate. She sped swiftly on in the dark, for the electric lights were few and far between, until the black of the gloomy building, where the boys had their club, loomed up. On the corner Bessy saw a man standing with his back to a telegraph pole. This occasioned her much concern; perhaps he might be watching the building. But he had not seen her, of that she was certain. The possibility that he might be a spy made her task all the harder.

Bessy returned the way she come, crossed at the next corner, hurried round the block and up to the outside stairway that was her objective point.

By feeling along the brick wall she brought up, with a sudden bump, at the back of the stairway. Then she deliberated. If she went around to the front so as to get access to the steps, she might pass in range of the loiterer whom she mistrusted. That risk she would not incur. Examining the wall that enclosed the box-like stairway as best she could in the dark, she found it rickety, full of holes and cracks, and she decided she would climb it. A sheer perpendicular board wall, some twelve or fifteen feet high, shrouded in pitchy darkness and apparently within earshot of a police spy, did not daunt Bessy Bell. Slipping her strong fingers in crevices and her slim toes in cracks, she climbed up and up, till she got hold of the railing post on the first platform. Here she had great difficulty to keep from falling, but lifting and squirming her supple body, by a desperate effort she got her knees on the platform, and then pulled herself to safety. Once on the stairs she ran up the remaining few steps to the landing, where she rested panting and triumphant.

As she was about to go on she heard footsteps, which froze her. A man was crossing the street. He came from the direction of the corner where she had seen the supposed spy. Presently she saw him stop under one of the trees to scratch a match, and in the round glow of light she saw him puff at a cigar. Then he passed on with uncertain steps, as of one slightly under the influence of drink.

Bessy's heart warmed to life and began to beat again. Then she sought for the key. She had been told where it was, but did not remember. Slipping her hand under the railing, close to the wall, she felt a string, and, pulling at it suddenly, found the key in her hand. She glided into the dim hall, feeling along the wall for a door, until she found it. With trembling fingers she inserted the key in the lock, and the door swung inward silently. Bessy went in, leaving the key on the outside.

Dark as it had been without, it was light compared to the ebon blackness within. Bessy felt ice form in the marrow of her bones. The darkness was tangible; it seemed to envelop her in heavy folds. The sudden natural impulse to fly out of the thick creeping gloom, down the stairway to the light, strung her muscles for instant action, but checked by the swiftly following thought of her purpose, they relaxed, and she took not a backward step.

"Rose did her part and I'll do mine," she cogitated. "I've got to save them. But what to do—I may have to wait. I know—in the big room—the closet behind the curtain! I can find that even in this dark, and once in there I won't be afraid."

Bessy, fired by this inspiration, groped along the wall through the room to the large chamber, stumbled over chairs and a couch and at last got her hands on the drapery. She readily found the knob, turned it, opened the door and stepped in.

"I hope they won't be long," she thought. "I hope the girls come first. I don't want to burst into a room full of boys. Won't Daren be surprised when I tell him—maybe angry! But it's bound to come out all right, and father will never know."

CHAPTER XVI

Early one August evening Lane went out to find a cool misty rain blowing down from the hills. At the inn he encountered Colonel Pepper, who wore a most woebegone and ludicrous expression. He pounced at once upon Lane.

"Daren, what do you think?" he wailed, miserably.

"I don't think. I know. You've gone and done it—pulled that stunt of yours again," returned Lane.

"Yes—but oh, so much worse this time."

"Worse! How could it be worse, unless you mean some one punched your head."

"No. That would have been nothing.... Daren, this—this time I—it was a lady!" gasped Pepper.

"Oh, say now, Pepper—not really?" queried Lane, incredulously.

"It was. And a lady I—I admire very much."

"Who?"

"Miss Amanda Hill."

"The schoolteacher? Nice little woman like that! Pepper, why couldn't you pick on one of these Middleville gossips or society dames?"

"Lord—I didn't know who she was—until after—and I couldn't have helped it anyway," he replied, mopping his red face. "When—I saw her—and she recognized me—I nearly died.... It was at White's Confectionery Den. And I'm afraid some people saw me."

"Well. You old duffer! And you say you admire this lady very much?"

"Indeed I do. I call on her."

"Colonel, your name is Dennis," replied Lane, with merciless humor. "It serves you right."

The little man evidently found relief in his confession and in Lane's censure.

"I'm cured forever," he declared vehemently. "And say, Lane, I've been looking for you. Have you been at my rooms lately—you know—to take a peep?"

"I have not," replied Lane, turning sharply. A slight chill went over him. "I thought that club stuff was off."

"Off—nothing," whispered Colonel Pepper, drawing Lane aside. "Swann and his strong-arm gang just got foxy. They quit for a while. Now they're rushing the girls in there—say from four to five—and in the evenings a little while, not too late. Oh, they're the slick bunch, picking out the ice cream soda hour when everybody's downtown.... You run up to my rooms right now. And I'll gamble———"

"I'll go," interrupted Lane, grimly.

Not fifteen minutes before he had seen his sister Lorna and a chum, Gail Williams, go into White's place. Lane's pulse quickened. As he started to go he ran into Blair Maynard who grasped at him: "What's hurry, old scout?"

"Blair, I'm never in a hurry if you want me. But the fact is I've got rather urgent business. How about to-morrow?"

"Sure. Meet you here. I just wanted to unload on you, Dare. Looks as if my mother has hatched it up between Margie and our esteemed countryman, Richard Swann."

It was not often that Lane cursed, but he did so now.

"But Blair, didn't you *tell* your mother what this fellow is?" remonstrated Lane.

"Well, I'll say I did," replied Blair, sardonically. "Cut no ice whatever. She didn't believe. She didn't care for any proofs. All rich young men had their irregularities!... Good God! Doesn't it make you sick?"

"But how about Holt Dalrymple?"

"Holt's turned over a new leaf. He's working hard, and I think he has taken a tumble to himself. Listen to this. He met Margie with Dick Swann out at one of the lake dances—Watkins' Lake. And he cut her dead. I'm sorry for Margie. She sure is rank poison these days.... Well, speak of the devil!"

Holt Dalrymple collided with them at the entrance of the inn. The haggard, sullen, heated look that had characterized him was gone. He was sunburned, and his dark eyes were bright. He greeted his friends warmly. They chatted for a moment. Then Lane grew thoughtful, all the while gazing at Holt.

"What's the idea?" queried that worthy, presently. "Anything wrong with me?"

"Boy, you're just great. Seeing you has done me good.... You ask what's the idea. Holt, would you do me a favor?"

"Would I? Listen to the guy," returned young Dalrymple. "Daren, I'd do any old thing for you."

"Do you happen to know Bessy Bell?" went on Lane.

Dalrymple quickened with surprise. "Yes, I know her. Some little peach!... I almost ran into her down on West Street a few minutes ago. She wore a white veil. She didn't see me, or recognize me. But I sure knew her. She was almost running. I bet a million to myself she had a date at the club."

"You lose, Holt," replied Lane, shortly. "Bessy Bell is one Middleville kid who has come clean through this mess."

"Say Dare, I like to hear you talk," responded Blair, half in jest and half in earnest. "But aren't you getting a trifle unbalanced? That's how my mother apologizes for me."

"Cut the joshing, boys. Listen," returned Lane. "And don't ever tell this to a soul. I interested myself in Bessy Bell. I've met her more times than I can count. I wanted to see if it was possible to turn one of these girls around. I failed on my sister Lorna. But Bessy Bell is true blue. She had all this modern tommyrot. She had everything else too. Brains, sweetness, common sense, romance. All I tried to do was to make her forget the tommyrot. And I think I did."

"Well, I'll be darned!" ejaculated Blair. "Dare, that was ripping fine of you.... What'll you do next, I wonder."

"Come on with your favor," added Holt, with a keen bright smile.

"Would you be willing to see Bessy occasionally—and sort of be nice to her—you know?" asked Lane, earnestly. "I can't keep up my attention to her much longer. She might miss me. Take it from me, Holt, back of all this modern stuff—deep in Bessy, and in every girl who has not been debased—is the simple and good desire to be liked."

"Daren, I'll do that little thing, believe me," returned Holt, warmly.

Shaking hands with his friends, Lane left them, and went on his way. White's place was full as a beehive. As he passed, Lane found himself looking for Bessy Bell's golden head, though he knew he would not see it. He wondered if Holt had really met her, veiled and in a hurry. That had a strange look. But no shadow of distrust of Bessy came to Lane. In a few moments he reached the dark stairway leading to Colonel Pepper's apartment. Lane forgot he was weak. But at the top, with his breast laboring, he remembered well enough. He went into the Colonel's rooms and through them without making a light. And when he reached the place where he had spied upon the club he was wet with sweat and shaking with excitement. Carefully, so as not to make noise, he stole to the peep-hole and applied his eye.

He saw a gleam of light on shiny waxed floor, and then, moving to get the limit of his narrow vision, he descried Swann, evidently just arrived. With him was Gail Williams, a slip of a child not over fifteen—looking up at him as if excited and pleased. Next Lane espied his sister Lorna with a tall, well-built man. Although his back was toward Lane, he could not mistake the soldierly bearing of Captain Vane Thesel! Lorna looked perturbed and sulky, and once, turning her face toward Swann, she seemed resentful. Captain Thesel had his hand at her elbow and appeared to be talking earnestly.

Lane left his post, taking care to make no noise. But once back in the Colonel's rooms, he hurried. Feeling in the dark corner where he had kept the axe ready for just such an emergency as this, he grasped it and rushed out. Tiptoeing down the hall, he found the narrow door, stole down the black stairway and entered the main hall. Here he paused, suddenly checked in his hurry.

"This won't do," he thought, and shook his head. "Much as I'd like to kill those two dogs I can't—I can't.... I'll smash their faces, though—and if I ever catch...."

Breaking the thought off abruptly, he passed down the dim hallway to the door of the club-rooms. He raised the axe and was about to smash the lock when he espied a key in the keyhole. The door was not locked. Lane set down the axe and noiselessly turned the knob and peeped in. The first room was dark, but the door on the opposite side was ajar, and through it Lane saw the larger lighted room and the shiny floor. Moving figures crossed the space. Removing the key, Lane slipped inside the room and locked the door. Then he tip-toed to the opposite door.

Thesel and Lorna were now so close that Lane could hear them.

"But I thought I had a date with Dick," protested Lorna. Her face was red and she stamped her foot.

"See here, kiddo. If you're as thick as that I'll have to put you wise," answered Thesel, good-humoredly, as he tilted back his cigarette to blow smoke at the ceiling. "Dick is through with you."

"Oh, *is* he?" choked Lorna.

"Say, Cap, I heard a noise," suddenly called out Swann, rather nervously.

There was a moment's silence. Lane, too, had heard a noise, but could not be sure whether it was inside the building or not.

Swann hurried over to join Thesel. They looked blankly at each other. The air might have been charged. Both girls showed alarm.

Then Lane, with his hand on the gun in his pocket, strode out to confront them.

"Oh—h!" gasped Lorna, as if appalled at sight of her brother's face.

"Fellows, I'll have to break up your little party," said Lane, coolly.

Thesel turned ghastly white, while Swann grew livid with rage. He seemed to expand. His hand went back to his right hip.

When Lane got within six feet of them, Swann drew a small automatic pistol. But before he could raise it, Lane had leaped into startling activity. With terrific swing he brought his gun down on Swann's face. Then as swiftly he turned on Thesel. Swann had hardly hit the floor, a sodden heap, when Thesel, with bloody visage, reeled and fell like a log. Lane bent over them, ready to beat either back. But both were unconscious.

"Daren—for God's sake—don't murder them!" whispered Lorna, hoarsely.

Lane's humanity was in abeyance then, but his self-control did not desert him.

"You girls must hurry out of here," he ordered.

"Oh, Gail is fainting," cried Lorna.

The little Williams girl was indeed swaying and sinking down. Lane grasped her and shook her. "Brace up. If you keel over now, you'll be found out sure.... It's all right. You'll not be hurt. There——"

A heavy thumping on the door by which Lane had entered and a loud authoritative voice from the hall silenced him.

"Open up here! You're pinched!"

That voice Lane recognized as belonging to Chief of Police Bell. For a moment, fraught with suspense, Lane was at a loss to know what to do.

"Open up! We've got the place surrounded.... Open up, or we'll smash the door in!"

Lane whispered to the girls: "Is there a place to hide you?"

The Williams girl was beyond answering, but Lorna, despite her terror, had not lost her wits.

"Yes—there's a closet—hid by a curtain—here," she whispered, pointing.

Lane half carried Gail. Lorna brushed aside a heavy curtain and opened a door. Lane pushed both girls into the black void and closed the door after them.

"Once more—open up!" bellowed the officer in the hall, accompanying his demand with a thump on the door. Lane made sure some one had found his axe. He did not care how much smashing the policemen did. All that concerned Lane then was how to avert discovery from the girls. It looked hopeless. Then, as there came sudden splintering blows on the door, Lane espied Swann's cigarettes and matches on the music box. Lane seldom smoked. But while the officers were breaking in the door, Lane leisurely lighted a cigarette; and when two of them came in he faced them coolly.

The first was Chief Bell, a large handsome man, in blue uniform. The second one was a patrolman. Neither carried a weapon in sight. Bell swept the big room in one flashing blue glance—took in Lane and the prone figures on the floor.

"Well, I'll be damned," he ejaculated. "What am I up against?"

"Hello, Chief," replied Lane, coolly. "Don't get fussed up now. This is no murder case."

"Lane, what's this mean?" burst out Bell.

Lane was rather well acquainted with Chief Bell, and in a way there was friendship between them. Bell, for one, had always been sturdily loyal to the soldiers.

"Well, Chief, I was having a little friendly game with Mr. Swann and Captain Thesel," drawled Lane. "We got into an argument. And as both were such ferocious fighters I grew afraid they'd hurt me bad—so I had to soak them."

"Don't kid me," spoke up Bell, derisively. "Little game—hell! Where's the cards, chips, table?"

"Chief, I didn't say we played the game to-night."

"Lane, you're a liar," replied Bell, thoughtfully. "I'm sure of that. But you've got me buffaloed." He knelt on the floor beside the fallen men and examined each. Swann's shirt as well as face was bloody. "For a crippled soldier you've got some punch left. What'd you hit them with?"

"I'll tell you Chief. I fetched an axe with me to do the dirty job, but I decided I should use a dangerous weapon only on men. So I soaked them with a lollypop."

"Lane, are you really nutty?" demanded Bell, curiously.

"No more than you. I hit them with something hard, so it would leave a mark."

"You left one, I'll say. Thesel will lose that eye—it's gone now—and Swann is also disfigured for life. What a damned shame!"

"Chief, are you sure it's any kind of a shame?"

Lane's query appeared to provoke thought. Bell replaced the little automatic pistol he had picked up beside Swann, and rising he looked at Lane.

"Swann was a slacker. Thesel was your Captain in the war. Have these facts anything to do with your motive?"

"No, Chief," replied Lane, in sarcasm. "But when I got into action I think the facts you mentioned sort of rejuvenated a disabled soldier."

"Lane, you beat me," declared Bell, shaking his head. "Why, I had you figured as a pretty good chap.... But you've done some queer things in Middleville."

"Chief, if you're an honest officer you'll admit Middleville needs some queer things done."

Bell gazed doubtfully at Lane.

"Smith, search the rooms," he ordered, addressing his patrolman.

"We were alone here," spoke up Lane. "And I advise you to hurry those wounded veterans to a hospital in the rear."

Swann showed signs of recovering consciousness. Bell bent over him a moment. Lane had only one hope—that the patrolman would miss the door. But he brushed aside the curtain. Then he grunted.

"See here, Chief—a door—and somebody's holding it from the inside," he declared.

"Wait, Smith," ordered Bell, striding forward. But before he got half-way across the room the door opened. A girl stepped out and shut it back of her. Lane sustained a singular shock. That girl was Bessy Bell.

"Hello, Dad—it's Bessy," she said, clearly. She was pale, but did not seem frightened.

Chief Bell halted in the middle of a stride and staggered a little as his foot came down. A low curse of utter amaze escaped his lips. Suddenly he became tensely animated.

"How'd you come here?" he demanded, towering over her.

"I walked."

"What'd you come for?"

"To warn Daren Lane that you were going to raid these club-rooms to-night."

"Who told you?"

"I won't tell. I got it over the 'phone. I ran over here. I knew where the key was. I've been here before—afternoons—dancing.... I let myself in.... But when they—they came I got frightened and hid in the closet."

Chief Bell seemed about to give way to passion, but he controlled it. After that moment he changed subtly.

"Is Daren Lane your friend?" he demanded.

"Yes. The best and truest any girl ever had.... Dad, you know mother told you I had changed lately. I have. And it's through Daren."

"Where'd you see him?"

"He has been coming out to the house in the afternoons."

"Well, I'm damned," muttered the Chief, and wheeled away. Sight of his gaping patrolman seemed to galvanize him into further realization of the situation. "Smith, beat it out and draw the other men round in front. Give me time enough to get Bessy out. Send hurry call for ambulance.... And Smith, keep your mouth shut. I'll make it all right. If Mrs. Bell hears of this my life will be a hell on earth."

"Mum's the word, Chief. I'm a married man myself," he replied, and hurried out.

Lane was watching Bessy. What a wonderful girl! Modern tendencies might have corrupted the girls of the day, but for sheer nerve, wit and courage they were immeasurably superior to those of former generations. Bessy faced her father calmly, lied magnificently, gazed down at the ghastly, bloody faces with scarcely a shudder, and gave Lane a smile from her purple eyes, as if to cheer him, to assure him she could save the situation. It struck Lane that Chief Bell looked as if he might be following a similar line of thought.

"Bessy, put on your hat," ordered Bell. "And here ... tuck that veil around. There, now you beat it for home. Lane, go with her to the stairs. Take a good look in the street. Bessy, go home the back way. And Lane, you hurry back."

Lane followed Bessy out and caught up with her in the hall. She clasped his arm.

"Some adventure, I'll say!" she burst out, in breathless whisper. "It was great until I recognized your voice. Then all inside me went flooey."

"Bessy, you're the finest little girl in the world," returned Lane, stirred to emotion.

"Here, Daren, cut that. You didn't raise me on soft soap and mush. If you get to praising me I'll fall so far I'll never light.... Now, Dare, go back and fool Dad. You must save the girls. It doesn't matter about me. He's my Dad."

"I'll do my best," replied Lane.

They reached the landing of the outside stairway. Peering down, Lane did not see any one.

"I guess the coast is clear. Now, beat it, Bessy."

She lifted the white veil and raised her face. In the dim gray light Lane saw it as never before.

"Kiss me, Daren," she whispered.

Lane had never kissed her. For an instant he was confused.

"Why—little girl!" he exclaimed.

"Hurry!" she whispered, imperiously.

Some instinct beyond Lane's ken prompted him to do what she asked.

"Good-bye, my little Princess," he whispered. "Don't ever forget me."

"Never, Daren. Good-bye." She slipped down the stairway and in a moment more vanished in the gray gloom of the misty night.

Only then did Lane understand what she, with her woman's intuition, had divined—that they would never be together again. The realization gave him a pang. Bessy was his only victory.

Slowly Lane made his way back to the club-rooms. He had begun to weaken under the strain and felt the approach of something akin to collapse. When he reached the large room he found Swann half conscious and Thesel showing signs of coming to.

"Lane, come here," said the Chief, drawing Lane away from the writhing forms on the floor. "You're under arrest."

"Yes, sir. What's the charge?"

"Let's see. That's the puzzler," replied the Chief, scratching his head. "Suppose we say gambling and fighting."

"Fine!" granted Lane, with a smile.

"When the ambulance comes you get out of sight until we pack these fellows out. I'll leave the door open—so if there's any reason you want to come back—why—"

Chief Bell half averted his face, seemingly not embarrassed, but rather pondering in thought. "Thanks, Chief. You understand me perfectly," responded Lane. "I'll appear at police headquarters in half an hour."

The officer laughed, and returning to the injured men he knelt beside them. Swann sat up moaning. Blood had blinded his sight. He did not see Lane pass. Sounds of an ambulance bell had caught Lane's quick ear. Finding the washroom, he went in and, locking the door, leaned there to wait. In a very few moments the injured Swann and Thesel had been carried out. Lane waited five minutes after the sound of wheels had died away. Then he hurried out and opened the door of the closet.

Lorna almost fell over him in her eagerness. If she had been frightened, she had recovered. Gail staggered out, pale and sick looking.

"Oh, Daren, can you get us out?" whispered Lorna, breathlessly.

"Hurry, and don't talk," replied Lane.

He led them out into the hall and down to the stairway where he had taken Bessy. As before, all appeared quiet below.

"I guess it's safe.... Girls, let this be a lesson to you."

"Never any more for mine," whimpered Gail.

But Lorna was of more tempered metal.

"Believe me, Daren, I'm glad you knocked the lamps out of those swell boobs," she whispered, passionately. "Dick Swann used me like dirt. The next guy like him who tries to get gay with me will have some fall, I'll tell the world.... Me for Harry! There's nothing in this q-t stuff.... And say, what do you know about Bessy Bell? She came here to save us.... Hot dog, but she's a peach!"

Lane admonished the girls to hurry and watched them until they reached the street and turned the corner out of sight.

CHAPTER XVII

The reaction from that night landed Lane in the hospital, where, during long weeks when he did have a lucid interval, he saw that his life was despaired of and felt that he was glad of it.

But he did not die. As before, the weak places in his lungs healed over and he began to mend, and gradually his periods of rationality increased until he wholly gained his mental poise. It was, however, a long time before he was strong enough to leave the hospital.

During the worst of his illness his mother came often to see him; after he grew better she came but seldom. Blair and Colonel Pepper were the only others who visited Lane. And as soon as his memory returned and interest revived he learned much peculiarly significant to him.

The secret of the club-rooms, so far as girls were concerned, never became fully known to Middleville gossips. Strange and contrary rumors were rife for a long time, but the real truth never leaked out. There was never any warrant sworn for Lane's arrest. What the general public had heard and believed was the story concocted by Thesel and Swann, who claimed that Lane, over a gambling table, had been seized by one of the frenzied fits common to deranged soldiers, and had attacked them. Thesel lost his left eye and Swann carried a hideous red scar from brow to cheek. Neither the club-room scandal nor his disfigurement for life in any wise prevented Mrs. Maynard from announcing the engagement of her daughter Margaret to Richard Swann. The most amazing news was to hear that Helen Wrapp had married a rich young politician named Hartley, who was running for the office of magistrate. According to Blair, Daren Lane had divided Middleville into two dissenting factions, a large one who banned him in disgrace, and a small one who lifted their voices in his behalf. Of all the endless bits of news, little and big, the one that broke happily on Lane's ears was the word of a nurse, who told him that during his severe illness a girl had called on the telephone every day to inquire for him. She never gave her name. But Lane knew it was Mel and the mere thought of her made him quiver.

By the time Lane was strong enough to leave the hospital an early winter had set in. The hospital expenses had reduced his finances so materially that he could not afford the lodgings he had occupied before his illness. He realized fully that he should leave Middleville for a dry warm climate, if he wanted to live a while longer. But he was not greatly concerned about this. There would be time enough to consider the future after he had fulfilled the one hope and ambition he had left.

Rooms were at a premium. Lane was forced to apply in the sordid quarter of Middleville, and the place he eventually found was a small, bare hall bedroom, in a large, ramshackle old house, of questionable repute. But beggars could not be choosers. There was no heat in this room, and Lane decided that what time he spent in it must be in bed. He would not give any one his address.

Once installed here, Lane waited only a few days to assure himself that he was strong enough to carry out the plan upon which he had set his heart.

Late that afternoon he went to the town hall and had a marriage license made out for himself and Mel Iden. Upon returning, he found that snow had begun to fall heavily. Already the streets were white. Suddenly the thought of the nearness of Christmas shocked him. How time sped by!

That night he dressed himself carefully, wearing the service uniform he had so well preserved, and sallied forth to the most fashionable restaurant in Middleville, where in the glare and gayety he had his dinner. Lane recognized many of the dining, dancing throng, but showed no sign of it. He became aware that his presence had excited comment. How remote he seemed to feel himself from that eating, drinking, dancing crowd! So far removed that even the jazz music no longer affronted him. Rather surprised he was to find he really enjoyed his dinner. From the restaurant he engaged a taxi.

The bright lights, the falling snow, the mantle of white on everything, with their promise of the holiday season, pleased Lane with the memory of what great fun he used to have at Christmas-time.

When he arrived at Mel's home the snow was falling thickly in heavy flakes. Through the pall he caught a faint light, which grew brighter as he plodded toward the cottage. He stamped on the porch and flapped his arms to remove the generous covering of snow that had adhered to him. And as he was about to knock, the door opened, and Mel stood in the sudden brightness.

"Hello, Mel, how are you?—some snow, eh?" was his cheery greeting, and he went in and shut the door behind him.

"Why, Daren—you—you—"

"I—what! Aren't you glad to see me?"

Lane had not prepared himself for anything. He knew he could win now, and all he had allowed himself was gladness. But being face to face with Mel made it different. It had been long since he last saw her. That interval had been generous. To look at her now no one could have guessed her story. Warmth and richness of color had come back to her; and vividly they expressed her joy at sight of him.

"Glad?—I've been living—on my hopes—that you—"

Her faltering speech trailed off here, as Lane took one long stride toward her.

Lane put a firm hand to each of her cheeks, and tilting a suddenly rosy face, he kissed her full on the lips. Then he turned away without looking at her and stepped to the little open grate, where a small red fire glowed. Mel gasped there behind him and then became perfectly still.

"Nice fire, Mel," he spoke out, naturally, as if nothing unusual had happened. But the thin hands he extended to the warmth of the coals trembled like aspen leaves in the wind. How silent she was! It thrilled him. What strange sweet revel in the moment.

When he turned it seemed he saw her eyes, her lips, her whole face luminous. The next instant she came out of her spell; and Lane divined if he let her wholly recover, he would have a woman to deal with.

"Daren, what's wrong with you?" she inquired.

"Why, Mel!" he ejaculated, in feigned reproach.

"You don't look irrational, but you act so," she said, studying him more closely. The hand that had been pressed to her breast dropped down.

"Had my last crazy spell two weeks ago," he replied.

"Until to-night."

"You mean my kissing you? Well, I refuse to apologize. You see I was not prepared to find you so improved. Why, Mel, you're changed. You're just—just lovely."

Again the rich color stained her cheeks.

"Thank you, Daren," she said. "I have changed. *You* did it.... I've gotten well, and—almost happy.... But let's not talk of myself. You—there's so much—"

"Mel, I don't want to talk about myself, either," he declared. "When a man's got only a day or so longer—"

"Hush!—Or—Or—," she threatened, with a slight distension of nostrils and a paling of cheek.

"Or what?" demanded Lane.

"Or I'll do to you what you did to me."

"Oh, you'd kiss me to shut my lips?"

"Yes, I would."

"Fine, Mel. Come on. But you'd have to keep steadily busy all evening. For I've come to talk." Mel came closer to him, with a catch in her breathing, a loving radiance in her eyes. "Daren, you're strange—not like your old self. You're too gay—too happy. Oh, I'd be glad if you were sincere. But you have something on your mind."

Lane knew when to unmask a battery.

"No, it's in my pocket," he flashed, and with a quick motion he tore out the marriage license and thrust it upon her. As her dark eyes took in the meaning of the paper, and her expression changed, Lane gazed down upon her with a commingling of emotions.

"Oh, Daren—No—No!" she cried, in a wildness of amaze and pain.

Then Lane clasped her close, with a force too sudden to be gentle, and with his free hand he lifted her face.

"Look here. Look at me," he said sternly. "Every time you say no or shake your head—I'll do this."

And he kissed her twice, as he had upon his entrance.

Mel raised her head and gazed up at him, wide-eyed, open-mouthed, as if both appalled and enthralled.

"Daren. I—I don't understand you," she said, unsteadily. "You frighten me. Let me go—please, Daren. This is—so—so unlike you. You insult me."

"Mel, I can't see it that way," he replied. "I'm only asking you to come out and marry me to-night."

That galvanized her, and she tried to slip from his embrace.

"I told you no—no—no," she cried desperately.

"That's three," said Lane, and he took them mercilessly. "You will marry me," he said sternly.

"Oh, Daren, I can't—I dare not.... Ah!—"

"You will go right now—marry me to-night."

"Please be kind, Daren.... I don't know how you—"

"Mel, where're your coat, and hat, and overshoes?" he questioned, urgently.

"I told you—no!" she flashed, passionately.

Lane made good his threat, and this last onslaught left her spent and white.

"You must like my kisses, Mel Iden," he said.

"I implore you—Daren"

"I implore you to marry me."

"Dear friend, listen to reason," she begged. "You don't love me. You've just a chivalrous notion you can help me—and my boy—by giving us your name. It's noble, Daren, thank you. But—"

"Take care," warned Lane, bending low over her. "I can make good my word all night."

"Boy, you've gone crazy," she whispered, sadly.

"Well, now you may be talking sense," he laughed. "But that's neither here nor there.... Mel, I may die any day now!"

"Oh, my God!—don't say that," she cried, as if pierced by a blade.

"Yes. Mel, make me happy just for that little while."

"Happy?" she whispered.

"Yes. I've failed here in every way. I've lost all. And this thing would make the bitterness endurable."

"I'd die for you," she returned. "But marry you!—Daren—dearest—it will make you the laughing-stock of Middleville."

"Whatever it makes me, I shall be proud."

"Oh, I cannot, I dare not," she burst out.

"You seem to forget the penalty for these unflattering negatives of yours," he returned, coolly, bending to her lips.

This time she did not writhe or quiver or breathe. Lane felt surrender in her, and when he lifted his face from hers he was sure. Despite the fact that he had inflexibly clamped his will to one purpose, holding his emotion in abeyance, that brief instant seemed to be the fullest of his life.

"Mel, put your arm round my neck," he commanded.

Mel obeyed.

"Now the other."

Again she complied.

"Lift your face—look at me."

She essayed to do this also, but failed. Her head sank on his breast. He had won. Lane held her a moment closely. And then a great and overwhelming pity and tenderness, his first emotions, flooded his soul. He closed his eyes. Dimly, vaguely, they seemed to create vision of long future time; and he divined that good and happiness would come to Mel Iden some day through the pain he had given her.

"Where did you say your things are?" he asked. "It's a bad night."

"They're in—the hall," came in muffled tones from his shoulder. "I'll get them."

But she made no effort to remove her arms from round his neck or to lift her head from his breast. Lane had lost now that singular exaltation of will, and power to hold down his emotions. Her nearness stormed his heart. His test came then, when he denied utterance to the love that answered hers.

"No—Mel—you stay here," he said, freeing himself. "I'll get them."

Opening the hall door he saw the hat-rack where as a boy he had hung his cap. It now held garments over which Lane fumbled. Mel came into the hall.

"Daren, you'll not know which are mine," she said.

Lane watched her. How the shapely hands trembled. Her face shone white against her dark furs. Lane helped her put on the overshoes.

"Now—just a word to mother," she said.

Lane caught her hand and held it, following her to the end of the hall, where she opened a door and peeped into the sitting-room.

"Mother, is dad home?" she asked.

"No—he's out, and such a bad night! Who's with you, Mel?"

"Daren Lane."

"Oh, is he up again? I'm glad. Bring him in.... Why, Mel, you've your hat and coat on!"

"Yes, mother dear. We're going out for a while."

"On such a night! What for?"

"Daren and I are going to—to be married.... Good-bye. No more till we come back."

As one in a dream, Lane led Mel out in the whirling white pall of snow. It seemed to envelop them. It was mysterious and friendly, and silent.

They crossed the bridge, and Lane again listened for the river voices that always haunted here. Were they only murmurings of swift waters? Beyond the bridge lay the railroad station. A few dim lights shone through the white gloom. Lane found a taxi.

They were silent during the ride through the lonely streets. When the taxi stopped at the address given the driver, Lane whispered a word to Mel, jumped out and ran up the steps of a house and rang the bell.

"Is Doctor McCullen at home?" he inquired of the maid who answered the ring. He was informed the minister had just gone to his room.

"Will you ask him to come down upon a matter of importance?"

The maid invited him inside. In a few moments a tall, severe-looking man wearing a long dressing-coat entered the parlor.

"Doctor McCullen, I regret disturbing you, but my business is urgent. I want to be married at once. The lady is outside in a car. May I bring her in?"

"Ah! I seem to remember you. Isn't your name Lane?"

"Yes."

"Who is the woman you want to marry?"

"Miss Iden."

"Miss Iden! You mean Joshua Iden's daughter?"

"I do."

The minister showed a grave surprise. "Aren't you rather late in making amends? No, I will not marry you until I investigate the matter," he replied, coldly.

"You need not trouble yourself," replied Lane curtly, and went out.

The instant opposition stimulated Lane, and he asked the driver, "John, do you know where we can find a preacher?" "Yis, sor. Mr. Peters of the Methodist Church lives round the corner," answered the man.

"Drive on, then."

Lane got inside the taxi and slammed the door. "Mel, he refused to marry us."

Mel was silent, but the pressure of her hand answered him.

"Daren, the car has stopped," said Mel, presently.

Lane got out, walked up the steps, and pulled the bell. He was admitted. He had no better luck here. Lane felt that his lips shut tight, and his face set. Mel said nothing and sat by him, very quiet. The taxi rolled on and stopped again, and Lane had audience with another minister. He was repulsed here also.

"We're trying a magistrate," said Lane, when the car stopped again.

"But, Daren. This is where Gerald Hartley lives. Not him, Daren. Surely you wouldn't go to him?"

"Why not?" inquired Lane.

"It hasn't been two months since he married Helen Wrapp. Hadn't you heard?"

"I'd forgotten," said Lane.

"Besides, Daren, he—he once asked me to marry him—before the war."

Lane hesitated. Yes, he now remembered that in the days before the war the young lawyer had been Mel's persistent admirer. But a reckless mood had begun to manifest itself in Lane during the last hour, and it must have communicated its spirit to Mel, for she made no further protest. The world was against them. They were driving to the home of the man she had refused to marry, who had eventually married a girl who had jilted Lane. In an ordinary moment they would never have attempted such a thing. The mansion before which the car stopped was well lighted; music and laughter came faintly through the bright windows.

A maid opened the door to Lane and showed him into a drawing-room. In a library beyond he saw women and men playing cards, laughing and talking. Several old ladies were sitting close together, whispering and nodding their heads. A young fair-haired girl was playing the piano. Lane saw the maid advance and speak to a sharp-featured man whom he recognized as Hartley. Lane wanted to run out of the house. But he clenched his teeth and swore he would go through with it.

"Mr. Hartley," began Lane, as the magistrate came through the curtained doorway, "I hope you'll pardon my intrusion. My errand is important. I've come to ask you to marry me to a lady who is waiting outside."

When Hartley recognized his visitor he started back in astonishment. Then he laughed and looked more closely at Lane. It was a look that made Lane wince, for he understood it to relate to his mental condition.

"Lane! Well, by Jove!" he exclaimed. "Going to get married! You honor me. The regular fee, which in my official capacity I must charge, is one dollar. If you can pay that I will marry you."

"I can pay," replied Lane, quietly, and his level steady gaze disconcerted Hartley.

"Where's the woman?"

"She's outside in a taxi."

"Is she over eighteen?"

"Yes."

Lane expected the question as to who the woman was. It was singular that the magistrate neglected to ask this, the first query offered by every minister Lane has visited.

"Fetch her in," he said.

Lane went outside and hesitated at the car door, for he had an intuitive flash which made him doubtful. But what if Hartley did make a show of this marriage? The marriage itself was the vital thing. Lane helped Mel out of the car and led her up the icy steps. The maid again opened the door.

"Mr. Lane, walk right in," said Hartley. "Of course, it's natural for the lady to be a little shy, but then if she wants to be married at this hour she must not mind my family and guests. They can be witnesses."

He spoke in a voice in which Lane's ears detected insincerity. "Be seated, and wait until I get my book," he continued, and left the room.

Hartley had hardly glanced at Mel, and her veil had hidden her features. He had gone toward his study rubbing his hands in a peculiar manner which Lane remembered and which recalled the man as he had looked many a time in the Bradford billiard room when a good joke was going the rounds. Lane saw him hurry from his study with pleasant words of invitation to his guests, a mysterious air about him, a light upon his face. The ladies and gentlemen rose from their tables and advanced from the library to the door of the drawing-room. A girl of striking figure seized Hartley's arm and gesticulated almost wildly. It was Helen Wrapp. Her husband laughed at her and waved a hand toward the drawing-room and his guests. Turning swiftly with tigerish grace, she bent upon Lane great green eyes whose strange expression he could not fathom. What passionately curious eyes did she now fasten on his prospective bride!

Lane gripped Mel's hand. He felt the horror of what might be coming. What a blunder he had made!

"Will the lady kindly remove her veil?" Hartley's voice sounded queer. His smile had vanished.

As Mel untied and thrust back the veil her fingers trembled. The action disclosed a lovely face as white as snow.

"*Mel Iden!*" burst from the magistrate. For a moment there was an intense silence. Then, "I'll not marry you," cried Hartley vindictively.

"Why not? You said you would," demanded Lane.

"Not to save your worthless lives," Hartley returned, facing them with a dark meaning in his eyes.

Lane turned to Mel and led her from the house and down to the curb without speaking once.

Once more they went out into the blinding snow-storm. Lane threw back his head and breathed the cold air. What a relief to get out of that stifling room!

"Mel, I'm afraid it's no use," he said, finally.

"We are finding what the world thinks of us," replied Mel. "Tell the man to drive to 204 Locust Street."

Once more the driver headed his humming car into the white storm.

Once more Lane sat silent, with his heart raging. Once more Mel peered out into the white turmoil of gloom.

"Daren, we're going to Dr. Wallace, my old minister. He'll marry us," she said, presently.

"Why didn't I think of him?"

"I did," answered Mel, in a low voice. "I know he would marry us. He baptized me; he has known and loved me all my life. I used to sing in his choir and taught his Sunday School for years."

"Yet you let me go to those others. Why?"

"Because I shrank from going to him."

Once more the car lurched into the gutter, and this time they both got out and mounted the high steps. Lane knocked. They waited what appeared a long time before they heard some one fumbling with the lock. Just then the bell in the church tower nearby began chiming the midnight hour. The door opened, and Doctor Wallace himself admitted them.

"Well! Who's this?... Why, if it's not Mel Iden! What a night to be out in!" he exclaimed. He led them into a room, evidently his study, where a cheerful wood fire blazed. There he took both her hands and looked from her to Lane. "You look so white and distressed. This late hour—this young man whom I know. What has happened? Why do you come to me—the first time in so many months?"

"To ask you to marry us," answered Mel.

"To *marry* you?... Is this the soldier who wronged you?"

"No. This is Daren Lane.... He wants to marry me to give my boy a name.... Somehow he finally made me consent."

"Well, well, here is a story. Come, take off this snowy cloak and get nearer the fire. Your hands are like ice." His voice was very calm and kind. It soothed Lane's strained nerves. With what eagerness did he scrutinize the old minister's face. He knew the penetrating eye, the lofty brow and white hair, the serious lined face, sad in a noble austerity. But the lips were kind with that softness and sweetness which comes from gentle words and frequent smiles. Lane's aroused antagonism vanished in the old man's presence.

"Doctor Wallace," went on Mel. "We have been to several ministers, and to Mr. Hartley, the magistrate. All refused to marry us. So I came to my old friend. You've known me all my life. Daren has at last convinced me—broke down my resistance. So—I ask—will you marry us?"

Doctor Wallace was silent for many moments while he gazed into the fire and stroked her hand. Suddenly a smile broke over his fine face.

"You say you asked Hartley to marry you?"

"Yes, we went to him. It was a reckless thing to do. I'm sorry."

"To say the least, it was original." The old minister seemed to have difficulty in restraining a laugh. Then for a moment he pondered.

"My friends, I am very old," he said at length, "but you have taught me something. I will marry you."

It was a strange marriage. Behind Mel and Daren stood the red-faced, grinning driver, his coarse long coat covered with snow, and the simpering housemaid, respectful, yet glorifying in her share in this midnight romance. The old minister with his striking face and white hair, gravely turned the leaves of his book. No bridegroom ever wore such a stern, haggard countenance. The bride's face might have been a happier one, but it could not have been more beautiful.

Doctor Wallace's voice was low and grave; it quavered here and there in passages. Lane's was hardly audible. Mel's rang deep and full.

The witnesses signed their names; husband and wife wrote theirs; the minister filled out the license, and the ceremony was over.

Then Doctor Wallace took a hand of each.

"Mel and Daren," he said. "No human can read the secret ways of God. But it seems there is divinity in you both. You have been sacrificed to the war. You are builders, not destroyers. You are Christians, not pagans. You have a vision limned against the mystery of the future. Mammon seems now to rule. Civilization rocks on its foundations. But the world will go on growing better. Peace on earth, good will to men! That is the ultimate. It was Christ's teaching.... You two give me greater faith.... Go now and face the world with heads erect—whatever you do, Mel—and however long you live, Daren. Who can tell what will happen? But time proves all things, and the blindness of people does not last forever.... You both belong to the Kingdom of God."

But few words were spoken by Lane or Mel on the ride home. Mel seemed lost in a trance. She had one hand slipped under Lane's arm, the other clasped over it. As for Lane, he had overestimated his strength. A deadly numbness attacked his nerves, and he had almost lost the sense of touch. When they arrived at Mel's home the snow-storm had abated somewhat, and the lighted windows of the cottage shone brightly.

Lane helped Mel wade through the deep snow, or he pretended to help her, for in reality he needed her support more than she needed his. They entered the warm little parlor. Some one had replenished the fire. The clock pointed to the hour of one. Lane laid the marriage certificate on the open book Mel had been reading. Mel threw off hat, coat, overshoes and gloves. Her hair was wet with melted snow.

"Now, Daren Lane," she said softly. "Now that you have made me your wife—!"

Up until then Lane had been master of the situation. He had thought no farther than this moment. And now he weakened. Was this beautiful woman, with head uplifted and eyes full of fire, the Mel Iden of his school days? Now that he had made her his wife—.

"Mel, there's no *now* for me," he replied, with a sad finality. "From this moment, I'll live in the past. I have no future.... Thank God, you let me do what I could. I'll try to come again soon. But I must go now. I'm afraid—I overtaxed my strength."

"Oh, you look so—so," she faltered. "Stay, Daren—and let me nurse you.... We have a little spare room, warm, cozy. I'll wait on you, Daren. Oh, it would mean so much to me—now I am your wife."

The look of her, the tones of her voice, made him weak. Then he thought of his cold, sordid lodgings, and he realized that one more moment here alone with Mel Iden would make him a coward in his own eyes. He thanked her, and told her how impossible it was for him to stay, and bidding her good night he reeled out into the white gloom. At the gate he was already tired; at the bridge he needed rest. Once more, then, he heard the imagined voices of the waters calling to him.

CHAPTER XVIII

Seldom did Blair Maynard ever trust himself any more in the presence of his mother's guests. Since Mrs. Maynard had announced the engagement of his sister Margaret to Richard Swann, she had changed remarkably. Blair did not love her any the better for the change. All his life, as long as he could remember, he and Margaret had hated pretension, and the littleness of living beyond their means. But now, with this one *coup d'etat*, his mother had regained her position as the leader of Middleville society. Haughty, proud, forever absorbed in the material side of everything, she moved in a self-created atmosphere Blair could not abide. He went hungry many a time rather than sit at table with guests such as Mrs. Maynard delighted to honor.

Blair and Margaret had become estranged, and Blair spent most of his time alone, reading or dreaming, but mostly sleeping. He knew he grew weaker every day and his weakness appeared to induce slumber.

On New Year's day, after dinner, he fell asleep in a big chair, across the hall from the drawing-room. And when he awoke the drawing-room was full of people making New Year's calls. If there was anything Blair hated it was to thump on his crutch past curious, cold-eyed persons. So he remained where he was, hoping not to be seen. But unfortunately for him, he had exceedingly keen ears and exceedingly sensitive feelings.

Some of the guests he knew very well without having to see them. The Swanns, and Fanchon Smith, with her brother and mother, Gerald Hartley and his bride, Helen Wrapp, and a number of others prominent as Middleville's elect were recognizable by their voices. While he was sitting there, trying not to hear what he could not help hearing, a number more arrived.

They talked. It gradually dawned on Blair that some gossip was rife anent a midnight marriage between his friend Daren Lane and Mel Iden. Blair was deeply shocked. Then his emotions, never calm, grew poignant. He listened. What he heard spoken of Daren and Mel made his blood boil. Sweet voices, low-pitched, well-modulated, with the intonation of culture, made witty and scarcely veiled remarks of a suggestiveness that gave rise to laughter. Voices of men, bland, blase, deriding Daren Lane! Blair listened, and slowly his passion mounted to a white heat. And then it seemed, fate fully, in a lull of the conversation, some one remarked graciously to Mrs. Maynard that it was a pity that Blair had lost a leg in the war.

Blair thumped up on his crutch, and thumped across the hall to confront this assembly.

"Ladies and gentlemen, pray pardon me," he said, in his high-pitched tenor, cold now, and under perfect control. "I could not help hearing your conversation. And I cannot help illuminating your minds. It seems exceedingly strange to me that people of intelligence should make the blunders they do. So strange that in the future I intend to take such as you have made as nothing but the plain cold fact of perversion of human nature! Daren Lane is so far above your comprehension that it seems useless to defend him. I have never done it before. He would not thank me. But this once I will speak.... In our group of service men—so few of whom came home—he was a hero. We all loved him. And for soldiers at war that tribute is the greatest. If there was a dirty job to be done, Daren Lane volunteered for it. If there was a comrade to be helped, Daren Lane was the first to see it. He never thought of himself. The dregs of war did not engulf him as they did so many of us. He was true to his ideal. He would have been advanced for honors many a time but for the enmity of our captain. He won the *Croix de Guerre* by as splendid a feat as I saw during the war.... Thank God, we had some officers who treated us like men—who were men themselves. But for the majority we common soldiers were merely beasts of burden, dogs to drive. This captain of whom I speak was a padded shape—shirker from the front line—a parader of his uniform before women. And he is that to-day—a chaser of women—girls—*girls* of fifteen.... Yet he has the adulation of Middleville while Daren Lane is an outcast.... My God, is there no justice? At home here Daren Lane has not done one thing that was not right. Some of the gossip about him is as false as hell. He has tried to do noble things. If he married Mel Iden, as you say, it was in some exalted mood to help her, or to give his name to her poor little nameless boy."

Blair paused a moment in a deliberate speech that toward the end had grown breathless. The faces before him seemed swaying in a mist.

"As for myself," he continued in passionate hurry, "I did not *lose* my leg!... I *sacrificed* it. I *gave* my career, my youth, my health, my body—and I will soon have given my life— for my country and my people. I was proud to do it. Never for a moment have I regretted it.... What I lost—Ah! what I *lost* was respect for"—Blair choked—"for the institution that had deluded me. What I *lost* was not my leg but my faith in God, in my country, in the gratitude of men left at home, in the honor of women."

Friday, the tenth of January, dawned cold, dark, dreary, and all day a dull clouded sky promised rain or snow. From a bride's point of view it was not a propitious day for a wedding. A half hour before five o'clock a stream of carriages began to flow toward St. Marks and promptly at five the door of the church shut upon a large and fashionable assembly.

The swelling music of the wedding march pealed out. The bridal party filed into the church. The organ peals hushed. The resonant voice of a minister, with sing-song solemnity, began the marriage service.

Margaret Maynard knew she stood there in the flesh, yet the shimmering white satin, the flowing veil, covered some one who was a stranger to her.

And this other, this strange being who dominated her movements, stood passively and willingly by, while her despairing and truer self saw the shame and truth. She was a lie. The guests, friends, attendants, bridesmaids, the minister, the father, mother, groom—all were lies. They expressed nothing of their true feelings.

The unwelcomed curious, who had crowded into the back of the church, were the sincerest, for in their eyes, covetousness was openly unveiled. The guests and friends wore the conventional shallow smiles of guests and friends. They whispered to one another—a beautiful wedding—a gorgeous gown—a perfect bride—a handsome groom; and exclaimed in their hearts: How sad the father! How lofty, proud, exultant the mother! How like her to move heaven and earth to make this marriage! The attendants posed awkwardly, a personification of the uselessness of their situation, and they pitied the bride while they envied him for whose friendship they stood. The bridesmaids graced their position and gloried in it, and serenely smiled, and thought that to be launched in life in such dazzling manner might be compensation for the loss of much. He of the flowing robe, of the saintly expression, of the trained earnestness, the minister who had power to unite these lives, saw nothing behind that white veil, saw only his fashionable audience, while his resonant voice rolled down the aisles of the church: "Who gives this woman to be wedded to this man?" The father answered and straightway the years rolled back to his youth, to hope, to himself as he stood at the altar with love and trust, and then again to the present, to the failure of health and love and life, to the unalterable destiny accorded him, to the one shame of an honest if unsuccessful life—the countenancing of this marriage. The worldly mother had, for once, a full and swelling heart. For her this was the crowning moment. In one sense this fashionable crowd had been pitted against her and she had won. What to her had been the pleading of a daughter, the importunity of a father, the reasoning of a few old-fashioned friends? The groom, who represented so much and so little in this ceremony, had entered the church with head held high, had faced his bride with gratified smile and the altar with serene unconsciousness.

Margaret Maynard saw all this; saw even the bride, with her splendidly regular loveliness; and then, out of heaven, it seemed there thundered an awful command, rolling the dream away, striking terror to her heart.

"If any man can show just cause why they may not lawfully be joined together, let him now speak, or else hereafter for ever hold his peace!"

One long, silent, terrible moment! Would not an angel appear, with flaming sword, to smite her dead? But the sing-song voice went on, like flowing silk.

The last guest at Mrs. Maynard's reception had gone, reluctantly, out into the snow, and the hostess sat in her drawing-room, amid the ruins of flowers and palms. She was alone with her triumph. Mr. Maynard and Mr. Swann were smoking in the library. Owing to the storm and delicate health of the bride the wedding journey had been postponed.

Margaret was left alone, at length, in the little blue-and-white room which had known her as a child and maiden, where she now sat as wife. For weeks past she had been emotionless. To-night, with that trenchant command, unanswered except in her heart, a spasm of pain had broken the serenity of her calm, and had left her quivering.

"It is done," she whispered.

The endless stream of congratulations, meaningless and abhorrent to her, the elaborate refreshments, the warm embraces of old friends had greatly fatigued her. But she could not rest. She paced the little room; she passed the beautiful white bridal finery, so neatly folded by the bridesmaids, and she averted her eyes. She seemed not to hate her mother, nor love her father; she had no interest in her husband. She was slipping back again into that creature apart from her real self.

The house became very quiet; the snow brushed softly against the windows.

A step in the hall made Margaret pause like a listening deer; a tap sounded lightly on her door; a voice awoke her at last to life and to torture.

"Margaret, may I come in?"

It was Swann's voice, a little softer than usual, with a subtle eagerness.

"No" answered Margaret, involuntarily.

"I beg your pardon. I'll wait." Swann's footsteps died away in the direction of the library.

The spring of a panther was in Margaret's action as she began to repace the room. All her blood quickened to the thought suggested by her husband's soft voice. In the mirror she saw a crimsoned face and shamed eyes from which she turned away.

All the pain and repression, the fight and bitter resignation and trained indifference of the past months were as if they had never been. This was her hour of real agony; now was the time to pay the price. Pride, honor, love never smothered, reserve rooted in the very core of a sensitive woman's heart, availed nothing. Once again catching sight of her reflection in the mirror she stopped before it, and crossing her hands on her heaving breast, she regarded herself with scorn. She was false to her love, she was false to herself, false to the man to whom she had sold herself. "Oh! Why did I yield!" she cried. She was a coward; she belonged to the luxurious class that would suffer anything rather than lose position. Fallen had she as low as any of them; gold had been the price of her soul. To keep her position she must marry one man when she loved another. She cried out in her wretchedness; she felt in her whole being a bitter humiliation; she felt stir in her a terrible tumult.

Margaret wondered how many thousands of girls had been similarly placed, and pitied them. She thought of the atmosphere in which she lived, where it seemed to her every mother was possessed singularly and entirely of one aim, to marry her daughter as soon as possible to a man as rich as possible. Marrying well simply meant marrying money. Only a few days before her mother had come to her and said: "Mrs. Fisher called and she was telling me about her daughter Alice. It seems Alice is growing very pretty and very popular. She said she was afraid Alice had taken, a liking to that Brandeth fellow, who's only a clerk. So Mrs. Fisher intends taking Alice to the seashore this summer, to an exclusive resort, of course, but one where there will be excitement and plenty of young gentlemen."

At the remembrance Margaret gave a little contemptuous laugh. A year ago she would not have divined the real purport of her mother's words. How easy that was now! Mrs. Fisher had decided that as Alice was eighteen it was time a suitable husband was found for her. Poor Alice! Balls, parties, receptions there would be, and trips to the seashore and all the other society manoeuvers, made ostensibly to introduce Alice to the world; but if the truth were told in cold blood all this was simply a parading of the girl before a number of rich and marriageable men. Poor Harry Brandeth!

She recalled many marriages of friends and acquaintances. With strange intensity of purpose she brought each one to mind, and thought separately and earnestly over her. What melancholy facts this exercise revealed! She could not recall one girl who was happy, perfectly happy, unless it was Jane Silvey who ran off with and married a telegraph operator. Jane was still bright-eyed and fresh, happy no doubt in her little house with her work and her baby, even though her people passed her by as if she were a stranger. Then Margaret remembered with a little shock there was another friend, a bride who had been found on her wedding night wandering in the fields. There had been some talk, quickly hushed, of a drunken husband, but it had never definitely transpired what had made her run out into the dark night. Margaret recollected the time she had seen this girl's husband, when he was drunk, beat his dog brutally. Then Margaret reflected on the gossip she never wanted to hear, yet could not avoid hearing, over her mother's tea-table; on the intimations and implications. Many things she would not otherwise have thought of again, but they now recurred and added their significance to her awakening mind. She was not keen nor analytical; she possessed only an ordinary intelligence; she could not trace her way through a labyrinth of perplexing problems; still, suffering had opened her eyes and she saw something terribly wrong in her mother's world.

Once more she stopped pacing her room, for a step in the hall arrested her, and made her stand quivering, as if under the lash.

"I won't!" she breathed intensely. Swiftly and lightly she sped across her room, opened a door leading to the balcony and went out, closing the door behind her softly.

Mr. Maynard sat before the library fire with a neglected cigar between his fingers. The events of the day had stirred him deeply. The cold shock he had felt when he touched his daughter's cheek in the accustomed good-night kiss remained with him, still chilled his lips. For an hour he sat there motionless, with his eyes fixed on the dying fire, and in his mind hope, doubt and remorse strangely mingled. Hope persuaded him that Margaret was only a girl, still sentimental and unpoised. Unquestionably she had made a good marriage. Her girlish notions about romance and love must give way to sane acceptance of real human life. After all money meant a great deal. She would come around to a sensible view, and get that strange look out of her eyes, that strained blighted look which hurt him. Then he writhed in his self-contempt; doubt routed all his hope, and remorse made him miserable.

A hurried step on the stairs aroused Mr. Maynard. Swann came running into the library. He was white; his sharp featured face wore a combination of expressions; alarm, incredulity, wonder were all visible there, but the most striking was mortification.

"Mr. Maynard, Margaret has left her room. I can't find her anywhere."

The father stared blankly at his son-in-law.

Swann repeated his statement.

"What!" All at once Mr. Maynard sank helplessly into his chair. In that moment certainty made him an old broken man.

"She's gone!" said Swann, in a shaken voice. "She has run off from me. I knew she would; I knew she'd do something. I've never been able to kiss her—only last night we quarreled about it. I tell you it's—"

"Pray do not get excited," interrupted Mr. Maynard, bracing up. "I'm sure you exaggerate. Tell me what you know."

"I went to her room an hour, two hours ago, and knocked. She was there but refused me admittance. She spoke sharply—as if—as if she was afraid. I went and knocked again long after. She didn't answer. I knocked again and again. Then I tried her door. It was not locked. I opened it. She was not in the room. I waited, but she didn't come. I—I am afraid something is—wrong."

"She might be with her mother," faltered Mr. Maynard.

"No, I'm sure not," asserted Swann. "Not to-night of all nights. Margaret has grown—somewhat cold toward her mother. Besides Mrs. Maynard retired hours ago."

The father and the husband stole noiselessly up the stairs and entered Margaret's room. The light was turned on full. The room was somewhat disordered; bridal finery lay littered about; a rug was crumpled; a wicker basket overturned. The father's instinct was true. His first move was to open the door leading out upon the balcony. In the thin snow drifted upon this porch were the imprints of little feet.

Something gleamed pale blue in the light of the open door. Mr. Maynard picked it up, and with a sigh that was a groan held it out to Swann. It was a blue satin slipper.

"Heavens!" exclaimed Swann. "She's run out in the snow—she might as well be barefooted."

"S-sh-h!" warned Mr. Maynard. Unhappy and excited as he was he did not forget Mrs. Maynard. "Let us not alarm any one."

"There! See, her footsteps down the stairs," whispered Swann. "I can see them clear to the ground."

"You stay here, Swann, so in case Mrs. Maynard or the servants awake you can prevent alarm. We must think of that. I'll bring her back."

Mr. Maynard descended the narrow stairway to the lower porch and went out into the yard. The storm had ceased. A few inches of snow had fallen and in places was deeper in drifts. The moon was out and shone down on a white world. It was cold and quiet. When Mr. Maynard had trailed the footsteps across his wide lawn and saw them lead out into the street toward the park, he fell against a tree, unable, for a moment, to command himself. Hope he had none left, nor a doubt. On the other side of the park, hardly a quarter of a mile away, was the river. Margaret had gone straight toward it.

Outside in the middle of the street he found her other slipper. She had not even stockings on now; he could tell by the impressions of her feet in the snow. He remembered quite mournfully how small Margaret's feet were, how perfectly shaped. He hurried into the park, but was careful to obliterate every vestige of her trail by walking in the soft snow directly over her footprints. A hope that she might have fainted before she could carry out her determination arose in him and gave him strength. He kept on. Her trail led straight across the park, in the short cut she had learned and run over hundreds of times when a little girl. It was hastening her now to her death.

At first her footsteps were clear-cut, distinct and wide apart. Soon they began to show evidences of weariness; the stride shortened; the imprints dragged. Here a great crushing in a snow drift showed where she had fallen.

Mr. Maynard's hope revived; he redoubled his efforts. She could not be far. How she dragged along! Then with a leap of his heart, and a sob of thankfulness he found her, with disheveled hair, and face white as the snow where it rested, sad and still in the moonlight.

CHAPTER XIX

Middleville was noted for its severe winters, but this year the zero weather held off until late in January. Lane was peculiarly susceptible to the cold and he found himself facing a discomfort he knew he could not long endure. Every day he felt more and more that he should go to a warm and dry climate; and yet he could not determine to leave Middleville. Something held him.

The warmth of bright hotel lobbies and theatres and restaurants uptown was no longer available for Lane. His money had dwindled beyond the possibility of luxury, and besides he shrank now from meeting any one who knew him. His life was empty, dreary and comfortless.

One wintry afternoon Lane did not wander round as long as usual, for the reason that his endurance was lessening. He returned early to his new quarters, and in the dim hallway he passed a slight pale girl who looked at him. She seemed familiar, but Lane could not place her. Evidently she had a room in the building. Lane hated the big barn-like house, and especially the bare cold room where he had to seek rest. Of late he had not eaten any dinner. He usually remained in bed as long as he could, and made a midday meal answer all requirements. Appetite, like many other things, was failing him. This day he sat upon his bed, in the abstraction of the lonely and unhappy, until the cold forced him to get under the covers.

His weary eyelids had just closed when he was awakened. The confused sense of being torn from slumber gave way to a perception of a voice in the room next to his. It was a man's voice, rough with the huskiness Lane recognized as peculiar to drunkards. And the reply to it seemed to be a low-toned appeal from a woman.

"Playin' off sick, eh? You don't want to work. But you'll get me some money, girl, d'ye hear?"

A door slammed, rattling the thin partition between the two rooms, and heavy footsteps dragged in the hall and on the stairway.

Sleep refused to come back to Lane. As he lay there he was surprised at the many sounds he heard. The ramshackle old structure, which he had supposed almost vacant, was busy with life. Stealthy footfalls in the hallways passed and repassed; a piano drummed somewhere; a man's loud voice rang out, and a woman's laugh faint, hollow and far away, like the ghost of laughter, returned in echo. The musical clinking of glasses, the ring of a cash register, the rattling click of pool balls, came up from below.

Presently Lane remembered the nature of the place. It was a house of night. In daylight it was silent; its inmates were asleep. But as the darkness unfolded a cloak over it, all the hidden springs of its obscure humanity began to flow. Lying there with the woman's appeal haunting him and all those sounds in his ears he thought of their meaning. The drunkard with his lust for money; his moaning victim; the discordant piano; the man with the vacant laugh; the lost hope and youth in the woman's that echoed it; the stealing, slipping feet of those who must tread softly—all conveyed to Lane that he had awakened in another world, a world which shunned sunlight.

Toward morning he dozed off into a fitful sleep which lasted until ten o'clock when he arose and dressed. As he was about to go out a knock on the door of the room next to his recalled the incident of the night. He listened. Another knock followed, somewhat louder, but no response came from within.

"Say, you in there," cried a voice Lane recognized as the landlady's. She rattled the door-knob.

A girl's voice answered weakly: "Come in."

Lane heard the door open.

"I wants my room rent. I can't get a dollar out of your drunken father. Will you pay? It's four weeks overdue."

"I have no money."

"Then get out an' leave me the room." The landlady spoke angrily.

"I'm ill. I can't get up." The answer was faint.

Lane opened his door quickly, and confronted the broad person of the landlady.

"How much does the woman owe?" he asked, quietly.

"Ah-huh!" the exclamation was trenchant with meaning. "Twenty dollars, if it's anything to you."

"I'll pay it. I think I heard the woman say she was ill."

"She says she is."

"May I be of any assistance?"

"Ask her."

Lane glanced into the little room, a counterpart of his. But it was so dark he could see nothing distinctly.

"May I come in? Let me raise the blind. There, the sun is fine this morning. Now, may I not—"

He looked down at a curly head and a sweet pretty face that he knew.

"I know you," he said, groping among past associations.

"I am Rose Clymer," she whispered, and a momentary color came into her wan cheeks.

"Rose Clymer! Bessy Bell's friend!"

"Yes, Mr. Lane. I'm not so surprised as you. I recognized you last night."

"Then it was you who passed me in the hall?"

"Yes."

"Well! And you're ill? What is the matter? Ah! Last night—it was your—your father—I heard?"

"Yes," she answered. "I've not been well since—for a long time, and I gave out last night."

"Here I am talking when I might be of some use," said Lane, and he hurried out of the room. The landlady had discreetly retired to the other end of the hall. He thrust some money into her hands.

"She seems pretty sick. Do all you can for her, be kind to her. I'll pay. I'm going for a doctor."

He telephoned for Doctor Bronson.

An hour later Lane, coming upstairs from his meal, met the physician at Rose's door. He looked strangely at Lane and shook his head.

"Daren, how is it I find you here in this place?"

"Beggars can't be choosers," answered Lane, with his old frank smile.

"Humph!" exclaimed the doctor, gruffly.

"How about the girl?" asked Lane.

"She's in bad shape," replied Bronson.... "Lane, are you aware of her condition?"

"Why, she's ill—that's all I know," replied Lane, slowly. "Rose didn't tell me what ailed her. I just found out she was here."

Doctor Bronson looked at Lane. "Too bad you didn't find out sooner. I'll call again to-day and see her.... And say, Daren, you look all in yourself."

"Never mind me, Doctor. It's mighty good of you to look after Rose. I know you've more patients than you can take care of. Rose has nothing and her father's a poor devil. But I'll pay you."

"Never mind about money," rejoined Bronson, turning to go.

Lane could learn little from Rose. Questions seemed to make her shrink, so Lane refrained from them and tried to cheer her. The landlady had taken a sudden liking to Lane which evinced itself in her change of attitude toward Rose, and she was communicative. She informed Lane that the girl had been there about two months; that her father had made her work till she dropped. Old Clymer had often brought men to the hotel to drink and gamble, and to the girl's credit she had avoided them.

For several days Doctor Bronson came twice daily to see Rose. He made little comment upon her condition, except to state that she had developed peritonitis, and he was not hopeful. Soon Rose took a turn for the worse. The doctor came to Lane's room and told him the girl would not have the strength to go through with her ordeal. Lane was so shocked he could not speak. Dr. Bronson's shoulders sagged a little, an unusual thing for him. "I'm sorry, Daren," he said. "I know you wanted to help the poor girl out of this. But too late. I can ease her pain, and that's all."

Strangely shaken and frightened Lane lay down in the dark. The partition between his room and Rose's might as well have been paper for all the sound it deadened. He could have escaped that, but he wanted to be near her.... And he listened to Rose's moans in the darkness. Lane shuddered there, helpless, suffering, realizing. Then the foreboding silence became more dreadful than any sound.... It was terrible for Lane. That strange cold knot in his breast, that coil of panic, seemed to spring and tear, quivering through all his body. What had he known of torture, of sacrifice, of divine selflessness? He understood now how the loved and guarded woman went down into the Valley of the Shadow for the sake of a man. Likewise, he knew the infinite tragedy of a ruined girl who lay in agony, gripped by relentless nature.

Lane was called into the hall by Mrs. O'Brien. She was weeping. Bronson met him at the door.

"She's dying," he whispered. "You'd better come in. I've 'phoned to Doctor Wallace."

Lane went in, almost blinded. The light seemed dim. Yet he saw Rose with a luminous glow radiating from her white face.

"I feel—so light," she said, with a wan smile.

Lane sat by the bed, but he could not speak. The moments dragged. He had a feeling of their slow but remorseless certainty.

Then there were soft steps outside—Mrs. O'Brien opened the door—and Doctor Wallace entered the room.

"My child," he gravely began, bending over her.

Rose's big eyes with their strained questioning gaze sought his face and Doctor Bronson's and Lane's.

"Rose—are you—in pain?"

"The burning's gone," she said.

"My child," began Doctor Wallace, again. "Your pain is almost over. Will you not pray with me?"

"No. I never was two-faced," replied Rose, with a weary shake of the tangled curls. "I won't show yellow now."

Lane turned away blindly. It was terrible to think of her dying bitter, unrepentant.

"Oh! if I could hope!" murmured Rose. "To see my mother!"

Then there were shuffling steps outside and voices. The door was opened by Mrs. O'Brien. Old Clymer crossed the threshold. He was sober, haggard, grieved. He had been told. No one spoke as he approached Rose's bedside.

"Lass—lass—" he began, brokenly.

Then he sought from the men confirmation of a fear borne by a glance into Rose's white still face. And silence answered him.

"Lass, if you're goin'—tell me—who was to blame?"

"No one—but myself—father," she replied.

"Tell me, who was to blame?" demanded Clymer, harshly.

Her pale lips curled a little bitterly, and suddenly, as a change seemed to come over her, they set that way. She looked up at Lane with a different light in her eyes. Then she turned her face to the wall.

Lane left the room, to pace up and down the hall outside. His thoughts seemed deadlocked. By and bye, Doctor Bronson came out with Doctor Wallace, who was evidently leaving.

"She is unconscious and dying," said Doctor Bronson to Lane, and then bade the minister good-bye and returned to the room.

"How strangely bitter she was!" exclaimed Doctor Wallace to Lane. "Yet she seemed such a frank honest girl. Her attitude was an acknowledgment of sin. But she did not believe it herself. She seemed to have a terrible resentment. Not against one man, or many persons, but perhaps life itself! She was beyond me. A modern girl—a pagan! But such a brave, loyal, generous little soul. What a pity! I find my religion at fault because it can accomplish nothing these days."

CHAPTER XX

Lane took Rose's death to heart as if she had been his sister or sweetheart. The exhaustion and exposure he was subjected to during these days dragged him farther down.

One bitter February day he took refuge in the railroad station. The old negro porter who had known Lane since he was a boy evidently read the truth of Lane's condition, for he contrived to lead him back into a corner of the irregular room. It was an obscure corner, rather hidden by a supporting pillar and the projecting end of a news counter. This seat was directly over the furnace in the cellar. Several pipes, too hot to touch, came up through the floor. It was the warmest place Lane had found, and he sat there for hours. He could see the people passing to and fro through the station, arriving and leaving on trains, without himself being seen. That afternoon was good for him, and he went back next day.

But before he could get to the coveted seat he was accosted by Blair Maynard. Lane winced under Blair's piercing gaze; and the haggard face of his friend renewed Lane's deadened pangs. Lane led Blair to the warm corner, and they sat down. It had been many weeks since they had seen each other. Blair talked in one uninterrupted flow for an hour, and so the life of the people Lane had given up was once again open to him. It was like the scoring of an old wound. Then Lane told what little there was to tell about himself. And the things he omitted Blair divined. After that they sat silent for a while.

"Of course you knew Mel's boy died," said Blair, presently.

"Oh—No!" exclaimed Lane.

"Hadn't you heard? I thought—of course you—.... Yes, he died some time ago. Croup or flu, I forget."

"Dead!" whispered Lane, and he leaned forward to cover his face with his hands. He had seemed so numb to feeling. But now a storm shook him.

"Dare, it's better for him—and Mel too," said Blair, with a hand going to his friend's shoulder. "That idea never occurred to me until day before yesterday when I ran into Mel. She looked—Oh, I can't tell you how. But I got that strange impression."

"Did—did she ask about me?" queried Lane, hoarsely, as he uncovered his face, and sat back.

"She certainly did," replied Blair, warmly. "And I lied like a trooper. I didn't know where you were or how you were, but I pretended you were O.K."

"And then—" asked Lane, breathlessly.

"She said, 'Tell Daren I must see him.' I promised and set out to find you. I was pretty lucky to run into you.... And now, old sport, let me get personal, will you?"

"Go as far as you like," replied Lane, in muffled voice.

"Well, I think Mel loves you," went on Blair, in hurried softness. "I always thought so—even when we were kids. And now I know it.... And Lord! Dare you just ought to see her now. She's lovely. And she's your wife."

"What if she is—both lovely—and my wife?" queried Lane, bitterly.

"If I were you I'd go to her. I'd sure let her take care of me.... Dare, the way you're living is horrible. I have a home, such as it is. My room is warm and clean, and I can stay in it. But you—Dare, it hurts me to see you—as you are——"

"No!" interrupted Lane, passionately. The temptation Blair suggested was not to be borne.

Lane met Blair the next afternoon at the station, and again on the next. That established a habit in which both found much comfort and some happiness. Thereafter they met every day at the same hour. Often for long they sat silent, each occupied with his own thoughts. Occasionally Blair would bring a package which contained food he had ransacked from the larder at home. Together they would fall upon it like two schoolboys. But what Lane was most grateful for was just Blair's presence.

It was distressing then, after these meetings had extended over a period of two weeks, to be confronted one afternoon by a new station agent who called Blair and Lane bums and ordered them out of the place.

Blair raised his crutch to knock the man down. But Lane intercepted it, and got his friend out of the station. It was late afternoon with the sun going down over the hill across the railroad yards. Blair stood a moment bare-headed, with the light on his handsome haggard face. How frail he seemed—too frail of body for the magnificent spirit so flashing in his eyes, so scathing on his bitter lips. Lane bade him good-bye and turned away, with a strange intimation that this was the last time he would ever see Blair alive.

Wretched and desperate, Lane bought drink and took it to his room with him. On that dark winter night he sat by the window of his room. Insensible now to the cold, to the wind moaning outside, to the snow whirling against the pane, he lived with phantoms. To and fro, to and fro glided the wraith-forms, vanishing and appearing. The soft rustling sound of the snow was the rustle of their movements. Across the gleam of light, streaking coldly through the pane, flickering fitfully on the wall, floated shadows and faces.

He did not know when he succumbed to drowsy weakness. But he awoke at daylight, lying on the floor, stiff with cold. Drink helped him to drag through that day. Then something happened to him, and time meant nothing. Night and day were the same. He did not eat. When he lay back upon his bed he became irrational, yet seemed to be conscious of it. When he sat up his senses slowly righted. But he preferred the spells of aberration. Sometimes he was possessed by hideous nightmares, out of which he awoke with the terror of a child. Then he would have to sit up in the dark, in a cold sweat, and wait, and wait, until he dared to lie back again.

In the daytime delusions grew upon him. One was that he was always hearing the strange voices of the river, and another that he was being pursued by an old woman clad in a flowing black mantle, with a hood on her head and a crooked staff in her hand. The voices and apparition came to him, now in his waking hours; they came suddenly without any prelude or warning. He explained them as odd fancies resulting from strong drink; they grew on him until his harsh laugh could not shake them off. He managed occasionally to drag himself out of the house. In the streets he felt this old black hag following him; but later she came to him in the lonely silence of his room. He never noticed her unless he glanced behind him, and he was powerless to resist that impulse. At length the dreary old woman, who seemed to grow more gaunt and ghostly every day, took the form in Lane's disordered fancy of the misfortune that war had put upon him.

Lane dreamed once that it was a gray winter afternoon; dark lowering clouds hung over the drab-colored hills, and a chill north wind scurried over the bare meadows, sending the dead leaves rustling over the heath and moaning through the leafless oaks. What a sad day it was, he thought, as he faced the biting wind: sad as was his life and a fitting one for the deed on which he had determined! Long since he had left the city and was on the country road. He ascended a steep hill. From its highest point he looked back toward the city he was leaving forever. Faint it lay in the distance, only a few of its white spires shining out dimly from the purple haze.

What was that dark shadow? Far down the winding road he discerned an object moving slowly up the hill. Closer he looked, and trembled. An old woman with flowing black robes was laboriously climbing the hill. Whirling, he placed his hand on his breast, firmly grasped something there, and then strode onward. Soon he glanced over his shoulder. Yes, there she came, hobbling over the crest, her bent form and long crooked staff clearly silhouetted against the gray background. She raised the long staff and pointed it at him.

Now it seemed the day was waning; deep shadows lay in the valleys, and night already enveloped the forest. Through rents in the broken clouds a few pale stars twinkled fitfully. Soon dark cloud curtains scurried across these spaces shutting out the light.

He plunged into the forest. His footsteps made no sound on the soft moss as he glided through wooded aisles and under giant trees. Once well into the deep woods, he turned to look behind him. He saw a shadow, blacker than the forest-gloom, stealthily slipping from tree to tree. He looked no more. For hours he traveled on and on, never stopping, never looking backward, never listening, intent only on placing a great distance between him and his pursuer.

He came upon a swamp where his feet sank in the soft earth, and through all the night, with tireless strength and fateful resolve, he toiled into this dreamy waste of woods and waters, until at length a huge black rock loomed up in his way. He ascended to its summit and looked beyond.

It seemed now that he had reached his destination. Wood spirits and phantoms of night would mourn over him, but they would keep his secret. He peered across a shining lake, and tried to pierce the gloom. No living thing moved before his vision. Silver rippling waves shimmered under that starlit sky; tall weird pines waved gently in the night breeze; slender cedars, resembling spectres, reared their heads toward the blue-black vault of heaven. He listened intently. There was a faint rustling of the few leaves left upon the oaks. The strange voices that had always haunted him, the murmuring of river waters, or whispering of maidens, or muttering of women were now clear.

Suddenly two white forms came gliding across the waters. The face of one was that of a young girl. Golden hair clustered round the face and over the fair brow. The lips smiled with mournful sweetness. The other form seemed instinct with life. The face was that of a living, breathing girl, soulful, passionate, her arms outstretched, her eyes shining with a strange hopeful light.

Down, down, down he fell and sank through chill depths, falling slowly, falling softly. The cool waters passed; he floated through misty, shadowy space. An infinitude of silence enclosed him. Then a dim and sullen roar of waters came to his ears, borne faintly, then stronger, on a breeze that was not of earth. Anguish and despair tinged that sodden wind. Weird and terrible came a cry. Steaming, boiling, burning, rumbling chaos—a fearful rushing sullen water! Then a flash of light like a falling star sped out of the dark clouds.

Lane found himself sitting up in bed, wet and shaking. The room was dark. Some one was pounding on the door.

"Hello, Lane, are you there?" called a man's deep voice.

"Yes. What's wanted?" answered Lane.

The door opened wide, impelled by a powerful arm. Light from the hallway streamed in over the burly form of a man in a heavy coat. He stood in the doorway evidently trying to see.

"Sick in bed, hey?" he queried, with gruff kind voice.

"I guess I am. Who're you?"

"I'm Joshua Iden and I've come to pack you out of here," he said.

"No!" protested Lane, faintly.

"Your wife is downstairs in a taxi waiting," went on his strange visitor.

"My wife!" whispered Lane.

"Yes. Mel Iden, my daughter. You've forgotten maybe, but she hasn't. She learned to-day from Doctor Bronson how ill you were. And so she's come to take you home."

Mel Iden! The name seemed a part of the past. This was only another dream, thought Lane, and slowly fell back upon his bed.

"Say, aren't you able to sit up?" queried this visitor Lane took for the spectre of a dream. He advanced into the room. He grasped Lane with firm hand. And then Lane realized this was no nightmare. He began to shake.

"Sit up?" he echoed, vaguely. "Sure I can.... You're Mel's father?"

"Yes," replied the other. "Come, get out of this.... Well, you haven't much dressing to do. And that's good.... Steady there."

As he rose, Lane would have fallen but for a quick move of Iden's.

"Only shoes and coat," said Lane, fumbling around. "They're somewhere."

"Here you are.... Let me help.... There. Have you an overcoat?"

"No," replied Lane.

"Well, there's a robe in the taxi. Come on now. I'll come back and pack your belongings."

He put an arm under Lane's and led him out into the hall and down the dim stairway to the street. Under the yellow light Lane saw a cab, toward which Iden urged him. Lane knew that he moved, but he seemed not to have any feeling in his legs. The cabman put a hand back to open the door.

"Mel, here he is," called out Iden, cheerfully.

Lane felt himself being pushed into the cab. His knees failed and he sank forward, even as he saw Mel's face.

"Daren!" she cried, and caught him.

Then all went black.

CHAPTER XXI

Lane's return to consciousness was an awakening into what seemed as unreal and unbelievable as any of his morbid dreams.

But he knew that his mind was clear. It did not take him a moment to realize from the feel of his body and the fact that he could not lift his hand that he had been prostrate a long time.

The room he lay in was strange to him. It had a neatness and cleanliness that spoke of a woman's care. It had two small windows, one of which was open. Sunshine flooded in, and the twitter of swallows and hum of bees filled the air outside. Lane could scarcely believe his senses. A warm fragrance floated in. Spring! What struck Lane then most singularly was the fact of the silence. There were no city sounds. This was not the Iden home. Presently he heard soft footfalls downstairs, and a low voice, as of some one humming a tune. What then had happened?

As if in answer to his query there came from below a sound of heavy footfalls on a porch, the opening and closing of a door, a man's cheery voice, and then steps on the stairs. The door opened and Doctor Bronson entered.

"Hello, Doc," said Lane, in a very faint voice.

"Well, you son of a gun!" ejaculated the doctor, in delight. Then he called down the stairs. "Mel, come up here quick."

Then came a low cry and a flying patter of light feet. Mel ran past the doctor into the room. To Lane she seemed to have grown along with the enchantments his old memories had invoked. With parted lips, eager-eyed, she flashed a look from Lane to Doctor Bronson and back again. Then she fell upon her knees by the bed.

"Do you know me?" she asked, her voice tremulous.

"Sure. You're the wife—of a poor sick soldier—Daren Lane."

"Oh, Doctor, he has come to," cried Mel, in rapture.

"Fine. I've been expecting it every day," said Doctor Bronson, rubbing his hands. "Now, Daren, you can listen all you want. But don't try to talk. You've really been improving ever since we got you out here to the country. For a while I was worried about your mind. Lately, though, you showed signs of rationality. And now all's O.K. In a few days we'll have you sitting up."

Doctor Bronson's prophecy was more than fulfilled. From the hour of Lane's return to consciousness, he made rapid improvement. Most of the time he slept and, upon awakening, he seemed to feel stronger. Lane had been ill often during the last eighteen months, but after this illness there was a difference, inasmuch as he began to make surprising strides toward recovery. Doctor Bronson was nonplussed, and elated. Mel seemed mute in her gratitude. Lane could have told them the reason for his improvement, but it was a secret he hid in his heart.

In less than a week he was up, walking round his little room, peering out of the windows.

Mel had told Lane the circumstances attending his illness. It had been late in February when she and her father had called for him at his lodgings. He had collapsed in the cab. They took him to the Iden home where he was severely ill during March. In April he began to improve, although he did not come to his senses. One day Mr. Iden brought Jacob Lane, an uncle of Lane's, to see him. Lane's uncle had been at odds with the family for many years. There had been a time when he had cared much for his nephew Daren. The visit had evidently revived the old man's affection, for the result was that Jacob Lane offered Daren the use of a cottage and several acres of land on

Sycamore River, just out of town. Joshua Iden had seen to the overhauling of the cottage; and as soon as the weather got warm, Doctor Bronson had consented to Lane's removal to the country. And in a few days after his arrival at the cottage, Lane recovered consciousness.

"Well, this beats me," said Lane, for the hundredth time. "Uncle Jake letting us have this farm. I thought he hated us all."

"Daren, it was your going to war—and coming back—that you were ill and fell to so sad a plight. I think if your uncle had known, he'd have helped you."

"Mel, I couldn't ask anybody for help," said Lane. "Don't you understand that?"

"You were a stubborn fellow," mused Mel.

"Me? Never. I'm the meekest of mortals.... Mel, I know every rock along the river here. This is just above where at flood time the Sycamore cuts across that rocky flat below, and makes a bad rapid. There's a creek above and a big woods. I used to fish and hunt there a good deal."

Two weeks passed by and Daren felt himself slowly but surely getting stronger. Every morning when he came down to breakfast he felt a little better, had a little more color in his pale cheeks. At first he could not eat, but as the days went by he regained an appetite which, to Mel's delight, manifestly grew stronger. No woman could have been brighter and merrier. She laughed at the expression on his face when he saw her hands red from hot dish-water, and she would not allow him to help her. The boast she had made to him of her housekeeping abilities had not been an idle one. She prepared the meals and kept the cottage tidy, and went about other duties in a manner that showed she was thoroughly conversant with them.

The way in which she had absolutely put aside the past, her witty sallies and her innocent humor, her habit of singing while at work, the depth of her earnest conversation; in all, the sweet wholesome strength and beauty of her nature had a remarkable effect on Lane. He began to live again. It was simply impossible to be morbid in her presence. While he was with her he escaped from himself.

The day came when he felt strong enough to take a walk. He labored up the hillside toward a wood. Thereafter he went every day and walked farther every time.

With his returning strength there crept into his mind the dawning of a hope that he might get well. At first he denied it, denied even the conviction that he wished to live. But not long. The hope grew, and soon he found himself deliberately trying to build up his health. Every day he put a greater test upon himself, and as summer drew on he felt his strength gradually increasing. Against Doctor Bronson's advice, he got an axe and set to work on the wood pile, very cautiously at first.

Every day he wielded the axe until from sheer exhaustion he could not lift it. Then he would sit on a log and pant and scorn his weakness. What a poor man it was who could not chop wood for ten minutes without getting out of breath! This pile of logs became to him a serious and meaning obstacle. Every morning he went at it doggedly. His back grew lame, his arms sore, his hands raw and blistered. But he did not give up.

Mel seemed happy to see him so occupied, and was loath to call him even when it was necessary. After lunch it was his habit to walk in the woods. Unmindful of weather, every day he climbed the hill, plunged into the woods, and tramped until late in the afternoon. Returning, he usually slept until Mel called him to dinner. Afterward they spent the evening in the little library. The past seemed buried. Lane's curiosity as to family and friends had not reawakened.

Mel possessed a rich contralto voice which had been carefully cultivated. Every evening in the twilight, with only the flickering of the wood fire in the room, she would sit at the piano and sing. Lane would close his eyes and let the mellow voice charm his every sense. It called up his highest feelings; it lingered in his soul, thrilled along his heart and played on the chords of love and hope. It dispelled the heavy gloom that so often pressed down upon him; it vanquished the depression that was the forerunner of his old terrible black mood.

It came about that Lane spent most of his time outdoors, in the fields, along the river, on the wooded hills. The morbid brooding lost its hold on his mind, and in its place came memories, dreams, imaginations. He walked those hills with phantoms of the past and phantoms of his fancy.

The birds sang, the leaves fluttered, the wind rustled through the branches. White clouds sailed across the blue sky, a crow cawed from a hilltop, a hawk screeched from above, the roar of the river rapids came faintly upward. And Lane saw eyes gazing dreamily downward, thoughtful at a word, looking into life, trying to pierce the veil. It was all so beautiful—so terrible.

The peeping of frogs roused in Lane sensations thrilling and strange. The quick sharp notes were suggestive of cool nights, of flooded streams and marshy places. How often Lane wandered in the dusk along the shore to listen to this chorus!

At that hour twilight stole down; the dark hills rose to the pale blue sky; there was a fair star and a wisp of purple cloud; and the shadowy waters gleamed. Breaking into the trill of the frogs came the song of a lonely whippoorwill.

Lane felt a better spirit resurging. He felt the silence, the beauty, the mystery, the eternal that was there. All that was small and frail was passing from him. There came a regurgitation of physical strength—a change of blood.

The following morning while Lane was laboring over his wood pile, he thought he heard voices in the front yard, and presently Mel came around the walk accompanied by Doctor Wallace and Doctor Bronson.

"Well, Lane, glad to see you," said Doctor Bronson, in his hearty tones. "Doctor Wallace and I are on our way to the Grange and thought we'd stop off a minute."

"How are you, Mr. Lane? I see you're taking work seriously," put in Doctor Wallace, in his kindly way.

"Oh, I'm coming round all right," replied Lane.

He stood there with his shirt sleeves rolled up, his face bronzed a little and now warm and moist from the exercise, with something proven about him, with a suggestion of a new force which made him different.

There was an unmistakable kindliness in the regard of both men and a scarcely veiled fear Lane was quick to read. Both men were afraid they would not find him as they had hoped to.

"Mel, you've chosen a charming location for a home," observed Doctor Wallace.

When Mel was showing her old teacher and friend the garden and flowerbeds the practical Doctor Bronson asked Lane: "Did you chop all that wood?"

The doctor pointed to three long piles of wood, composed of short pieces regularly stacked one upon another.

"I did."

"How long did it take you?"

"I've been weeks at it. That's a long time, but you know, Doctor, I was in pretty poor condition. I had to go slow."

"Well, you've done wonders. I want to tell you that. I hardly knew you. You're still thin, but you're gaining. I won't say now what I think. Be careful of sudden or violent exertion. That's all. You've done more than doctors can do."

CHAPTER XXII

"Mel, come here," called Lane from the back porch, "who the deuce are those people coming down the hill?"

Mel shaded her eyes from the glare of the bright morning sun. "The lady is Miss Hill, my old schoolteacher. I'd know her as far as I could see her. Look how she carries her left arm. This is Saturday, for she has neither a lunch basket nor a prayer book in that outstretched hand. If you see Miss Hill without either you can be certain it's Saturday. As to the gentleman—Daren, can it possibly be Colonel Pepper?"

"That's the Colonel, sure as you're alive," declared Lane, with alacrity. "They must be coming here. Where else could they be making for? But Mel, for them to be together! Why, the Colonel's an old sport, and she—Mel—you know Miss Hill!"

Whereupon Mel acquainted Daren with the circumstances of a romance between Miss Hill and the gallant Colonel.

"Well—of all things!" gasped Lane, and straightway became speechless.

"You're right, Daren; they are coming in. Isn't that nice of them? Now, don't you dare show I told you anything. Miss Hill is so easily embarrassed. She's the most sensitive woman I ever knew."

Lane recovered in time to go through the cottage to the front porch and to hear Miss Hill greet Mel affectionately, and announce with the tone of a society woman that she had encountered Colonel Pepper on the way and had brought him along. Lane had met the little schoolteacher, but did not remember her as she appeared now, for she was no longer plain, and there was life and color in her face. And as for embarrassment, not a trace of it was evident in her bearing. According to Mel, the mere sight of man, much less of one of such repute as Colonel Pepper, would once have been sufficient to reduce Miss Hill to a trembling shadow.

But the Colonel! None of his courage manifested an appearance now. To Lane's hearty welcome he mumbled some incoherent reply and mopped his moist red face. He was wonderfully and gorgeously arrayed in a new suit of light check, patent leather shoes, a tie almost as bright as his complexion, and he had a carnation in his buttonhole. This last proof of the Colonel's mental condition was such an overwhelming shock to Lane that all he could do for a moment was stare. The Colonel saw the stare and it rendered him helpless.

Miss Hill came to the rescue with pleasant chat and most interesting news to the exiles. She had intended coming out to the cottage for ever so long, but the weather and one thing or another falling on a Saturday, had prevented until to-day. How pretty the little home! Did not the Colonel agree with her that it was so sweet, so cosy, and picturesquely situated? Did they have chickens? What pleasure to have chickens, and flowers, too! Of course they had heard about Mr. Harry White and the widow, about the dissension in Doctor Wallace's church. And Margaret Maynard was far from well, and Helen Wrapp had gone back home to her mother, and Bessy Bell had grown into a tall ravishingly beautiful girl and had distracted her mother by refusing a millionaire, and seemed very much in love with young Dalrymple.

"And I've the worst class of girls I ever had," went on Miss Hill. "The one I had last year was a class of angels compared to what I have now. I reproved one girl whose mother wrote me that as long as Middleville had preachers like Doctor Wallace and teachers like myself there wasn't much chance of a girl being good. So I'm going to give up teaching."

The little schoolmistress straightened up in her chair and looked severe. Colonel Pepper shifted uneasily, bent his glance for the hundredth time on his shiny shoes and once more had recourse to his huge handkerchief and heated brow.

"Well, Colonel, it seems good to see you once more," put in Lane. "Tell me about yourself. How do you pass the time?"

"Same old story, Daren, same old way, a game of billiards now and then, and a little game of cards. But I'm more lonely than I used to be."

"Why, you never were lonely!" exclaimed Lane.

"Oh, yes indeed I was, always," protested the Colonel.

"A little game of cards," mused Lane. "How well I remember! You used to have some pretty big games, too."

"Er—yes—you see—once in a while, very seldom, just for fun," he replied.

"How about your old weakness? Hope you've conquered that," went on Lane, mercilessly.

The Colonel was thrown into utter confusion. And when Miss Hill turned terrible eyes upon him, poor Pepper looked as if he wanted to sink through the porch.

Lane took pity on him and carried him off to the garden and the river bank, where he became himself again.

They talked for a while, but neither mentioned the subject that had once drawn them together. For both of them a different life had begun.

A little while afterward Mel and Lane watched the bright figure and the slight dark one go up the hillside cityward.

"What do you know about that!" ejaculated Lane for the tenth time.

"Hush!" said Mel, and she touched his lips with a soft exquisite gesture.

At three o'clock one June afternoon Mel and Daren were lounging on a mossy bank that lined the shady side of a clear rapid-running brook. A canoe was pulled up on the grass below them. With an expression of utter content, Lane was leaning over the brook absorbed in the contemplation of a piece of thread which was tied to a crooked stick he held in his hand. He had gone back to his boyhood days. Just then the greatest happiness on earth was the outwitting of bright-sided minnows and golden flecked sunfish. Mel sat nearby with her lap full of flowers which she had gathered in the long grass and was now arranging. She was dressed in blue; a sunbonnet slipped back from her head; her glossy hair waved in the breeze. She looked as fresh as a violet.

"Well, Daren, we have spent four delightful, happy hours. How time flies! But it's growing late and we must go," said Mel.

"Wait a minute or two," replied Lane. "I'll catch this fellow. See him bite! He's cunning. He's taken my bait time and again, but I'll get him. There! See him run with the line. It's a big sunfish!"

"How do you know? You haven't seen him."

"I can tell by the way he bites. Ha! I've got him now," cried Lane, giving a quick jerk. There was a splash and he pulled out a squirming eel.

"Ugh! The nasty thing!" cried Mel, jumping up. Lane had flung the eel back on the bank and it just missed falling into Mel's lap. She screamed, and then when safely out of the way she laughed at the disgust in his face.

"So it was a big sunfish? My! What a disillusion! So much for a man's boastful knowledge."

"Well, if it isn't a slimy old eel. There! be off with you; go back into the water," said Lane, as he shook the eel free from the hook.

"Come, we must be starting."

He pushed the canoe into the brook, helped Mel to a seat in the bow and shoved off. In some places the stream was only a few feet wide, but there was enough room and water for the light craft and it went skimming along. The brook turned through the woods and twisted through the meadows, sometimes lying cool and dark in the shade and again shining in the sunlight. Often Lane would have to duck his head to get under the alders and willows. Here in an overshadowed bend of the stream a heron rose lumbering from his weedy retreat and winged his slow flight away out of sight; a water wagtail, that cunning sentinel of the brooks, gave a startled *tweet! tweet!* and went flitting like a gray streak of light round the bend.

"Daren, please don't be so energetic," said Mel, nervously.

"I'm strong as a horse now. I'm—hello! What's that?"

"I didn't hear anything."

"I imagined I heard a laugh or shout."

The stream was widening now as it neared its mouth. Lane was sending the canoe along swiftly with vigorous strokes. It passed under a water-gate, round a quick turn in the stream, where a bridge spanned it, and before Lane had a suspicion of anything unusual he was right upon a merry picnic party. There were young men and girls resting on the banks and several sitting on the bridge. Automobiles were parked back on the bank.

Lane swore under his breath. He recognized Margaret, Dick Swann and several other old-time acquaintances and friends of Mel's.

"Who is it?" asked Mel. Her back was turned. She did not look round, though she heard voices.

"It doesn't matter," said Lane, calmly.

He would have given the world to spare Mel the ordeal before her, but that was impossible. He put more power into his stroke and the canoe shot ahead.

It passed under the bridge, not twenty feet from Margaret Swann. There was a strange, eager, wondering look in Margaret's clear eyes as she recognized Mel. Then she seemed to be swallowed up by the green willows.

"That was damned annoying," muttered Lane to himself. He could have met them all face to face without being affected, but he realized how painful this meeting must be to Mel. These were Mel's old friends. He had caught Margaret's glance. Old memories came surging back. His gaze returned to Mel. Her face was grave and sad; her eyes had darkened, and there was a shadow in them. His glance sought the green-lined channel ahead. The canoe cut the placid water, turned the last bend, and glided into the swift river. Soon Lane saw the little cottage shining white in the light of the setting sun.

One afternoon, as Lane was returning from the woods, he met a car coming out of the grassy road that led down to his cottage. As he was about to step aside, a gay voice hailed him. He waited. The car came on. It contained Holt Dalrymple and Bessy Bell.

"Say, don't you dodge us," called Holt.

"Daren Lane!" screamed Bessy.

Then the car halted, and with two strides Lane found himself face to face with the young friends he had not seen for months. Holt appeared a man now. And Bessy—no longer with bobbed hair—older, taller, changed incalculably, struck him as having fulfilled her girlish promise of character and beauty. "Well, it's good to see you youngsters", said Lane, as he shook hands with them.

Holt seemed trying to hide emotion. But Bessy, after that first scream, sat staring at Lane with a growing comprehending light in her purple eyes.

Suddenly she burst out. "Daren—you're *well*.... Oh, how glad I am! Holt, just look at him."

"I'm looking, Bess. And if he's really Daren Lane, I'll eat him," responded Holt.

"This is all I needed to make to-day the happiest day of my life," said Bessy, with serious sweetness.

"This? Do you mean meeting me? I'm greatly flattered, Bessy," said Lane, with a smile.

Then both a blush and a glow made her radiant.

"Daren, I'm sixteen to-day. Holt and I are—we're engaged I told mother, and expected a row. She was really pleased.... And then seeing you well again. Why, Daren, you've actually got color. Then Holt has been given a splendid business opportunity.... And—Oh! it's all too good to be true."

"Well, of all things!" cried Lane, when he had a chance to speak. "You two engaged! I—I could never tell you how glad I am." Lane felt that he could have hugged them both. "I congratulate you with all my heart. Now Holt—Bessy, make a go of it. You're the luckiest kids in the world."

"Daren, we've both had our fling and we've both been hurt," said Bessy, seriously. "And you bet *we* know how lucky we are—and what we owe Daren Lane for our happiness to-day."

"Bessy, that means a great deal to me," replied Lane, earnestly. "I know you'll be happy. You have everything to live for. Just be true to yourself."

So the moment of feeling passed.

"We went down to your place," said Holt, "and stayed a while waiting for you."

"Daren, I think Mel is lovely. May I not come often to see you both?" added Bessy.

"You know how pleased we'll be.... Bessy, do you ever see my sister Lorna?" asked Lane, hesitantly.

"Yes, I see her now and then. Only the other day I met her in a store. Daren, she's getting some sense. She has a better position now. And she said she was not going with any fellow but Harry."

"And my mother?" Lane went on.

"She is quite well, Lorna said. And they are getting along well now. Lorna hinted that a relative—an uncle, I think, was helping them."

Lane was silent a moment, too stirred to trust his voice. Presently he said: "Bessy, your birthday has brought happiness to some one besides yourself."

He bade them good-bye and strode on down the hill toward the cottage. How strangely meetings changed the future! Holt's pride of possession in Bessy brought poignantly back to Lane his own hidden love for Mel. And Bessy's rapture of amaze at his improvement in health put Lane face to face with a possibility he had dreamed of but had never believed in—that he might live.

That night was for Lane a sleepless one. He seemed to have traveled in a dreamy circle, and was now returning to memories and pangs from which he had long been free.

Next morning, without any hint to Mel of his intentions, he left the cottage and made his way into town. Almost he felt as he had upon his return from France. He dropped in to see his mother and was happy to find her condition of mind and health improved. She was overjoyed to see Lane. Her surprise was pitiful. She told him she was sure that he had recovered.

It was this matter of his physical condition that had brought Lane into Middleville. For many months he had resigned himself to death. And now he could not deny even his morbid fancy that he felt stronger than at any time since he left France. He had worked hard to try to get well, but he had never, in his heart, believed that possible.

Lane called upon Doctor Bronson and asked to be thoroughly examined. The doctor manifestly found the examination a task of mounting gratification. At length he concluded.

"Daren, I told you over a year ago I didn't know of anything that could save your life," he said. "I didn't. But something *has* saved your life. You are thirty pounds heavier and gaining fast. That hole in your back is healed. Your lungs are nearly normal. You have only to be careful of a very violent physical strain. That weak place in your back seems gone.... You're going to *live*, my boy.... There has been some magic at work. I'm very happy about it. How little doctors know!"

Dazed and stunned by this intelligence, Lane left the doctor's residence and turned through town on his way homeward. As he plodded on, he began to realize the marvelous truth. What would Blair say? He hurried to a telephone exchange to acquaint his friend with the strange thing that had happened. But Blair had been taken to a sanitarium in the mountains. Lane hurried out of town into the country, down the river road, to the cottage, there to burst in upon Mel.

"Daren!" she cried, in alarm. "What's happened?"

She rose unsteadily, her eyes dilating.

"Doctor Bronson said—I was—well," panted Lane.

"Oh!... Daren, is *that* it?" she replied, with a wonderful light coming to her face. "I've known that for weeks."

"After all—I'm not going—to die!... My God!"

Lane rushed out and strode along the river, and followed the creek into the woods. Once hidden in the leafy recesses he abandoned himself to a frenzy of rapture. What he had given up had come back to him. Life! And he lay on his back with his senses magnified to an intense degree.

The day was late in June, and a rich, thick amber light floated through the glades of the forest. Majestic white clouds sailed in the deep blue sky. The sun shone hot down into the glades. Under the pines and maples there was a cool sweet shade. Wild flowers bloomed. A fragrance of the woods came on the gentle breeze. The leaves rustled. The melancholy song of a hermit thrush pierced the stillness. A crow cawed from a high oak. The murmur of shallow water running over rocks came faintly to Lane's ears.

Lane surrendered utterly to the sheer primitive exultation of life. The supreme ecstasy of that hour could never have been experienced but for the long hopeless months which had preceded it. For a long time he lay there in a transport of the senses, without thinking. As soon as thought regained dominance over his feelings there came a subtle change in his reaction to this situation.

He had forgotten much. He had lived in a dream. He had unconsciously grown well. He had been strangely, unbelievably happy. Why? Mel Iden had nursed him, loved him, inspired him back to health. Her very presence near him, even unseen, had been a profound happiness. He made the astonishing discovery that for months he had thought of little else besides his wife. He had lived a lonely life, in his room, and in the open, but all of it had been dominated by his dreams and fancies and emotions about her. He had roused from his last illness with the past apparently dead. There was no future. So he lived in the moment, the hour. While he lay awake in the silence of night, or toiled over his wood pile, or wandered by the brook under the trees, his dreamy thoughts centered about her. And now the truth burst upon him. His love for her had been stronger than his ruined health and blasted life, stronger than misfortune, stronger than death. It had made him well. He had not now to face death, but life. And the revelation brought on shuddering dread.

Lane lingered in the woods until late afternoon. Then he felt forced to return to the cottage. The look of the whole world seemed changed. All was actual, vivid, striking. Mel's loveliness burst upon him as new and strange and terrible as the fact of his recovery. He had hidden his secret from her. He had been like a brother, kind, thoughtful, gay at times, always helpful. But he had remained aloof. He had basked in the sunshine of her presence, dreamily reveling in the consciousness of what she was to him. That hour had passed forever.

He saw her now as his wife, a girl still, one who had been cruelly wronged by life, who had turned her back upon the past and who lived for him alone. She had beauty and brains, a wonderful voice, and personality that might have fitted her for any career or station in life. She thought only of him. She had found content in ministering to him. She was noble and good.

In the light of these truths coming to him, Lane took stock of his love for Mel. It had come to be too mighty a thing to understand in a moment. He lived with it in the darkness of midnight and in the loneliness of the hills. He had never loved Helen. Always he had loved Mel Iden—all his life. Clear as a crystal he saw the truth. The war with its ruin for both of them had only augmented the powers to love. Lane's year of agony in Middleville had been the mere cradling of a mounting and passionate love. He must face it now, no longer in dreamy lulled unconsciousness, but in all its insidious and complex meaning. The spiritual side of it had not changed. This girl with the bloom of woman's loveliness upon her, with her grace and sweetness and fire, with the love that comes only once in life, belonged to him, was his wife. She did not try to hide anything. She was unconscious of appeal. Her wistfulness came from her lonely soul.

The longer Lane dwelt on this matter of his love for Mel the deeper he found it, the more inexplicable and alluring. And when at last it stood out appallingly, master of him, so beautiful and strange and bitter, he realized that between him and Mel was an insurmountable and indestructible barrier.

Then came storm and strife of soul. Night and day the conflict went on. Outwardly he did not show much sign of his trouble, though he often caught Mel's dark eyes upon him, sadly conjecturing. He worked in the garden; he fished the creek, and rowed miles on the river; he wandered in the woods. And the only change that seemed to rise out of his tumult was increasing love for this girl with whom his fate had been linked.

So once more Lane became a sufferer, burdened by pangs, a wanderer along the naked and lonely shore of grief. His passion and his ideal were at odds. Unless he changed his nature, his reverence for womanhood, he could never realize the happiness that might become his. All that he had sacrificed had indeed been in vain. But he had been true to himself. His pity for Mel was supreme. It was only by the most desperate self-control that he could resist taking her in his arms, confessing his love, swearing with lying lips he had forgotten the wrong done her and asking her to face the future as his loving wife. The thought was maddening. It needed no pity for Mel to strengthen it. He needed love. He needed to fulfill his life.

But Lane did not yield, though he knew that if he continued to live with Mel, in time the sweetness and enchantment of her would be too great for him. This he confessed.

More and more he had to fight his jealousy and the treacherous imagination that would create for him scenes of torment. He cursed himself as base and ignoble. Yet the truth was always there. If Mel had only loved the father of her child—if she had only loved blindly and passionately as a woman—it would have been different. But her sacrifice had not been one of love. It had been one of war. It had the nobility of woman's sacrifice to the race. But as an individual she had perished.

CHAPTER XXIII

Summer waned. The long hot days dragged by. The fading rushes along the river drooped wearily over their dry beds. The yellowing leaves of the trees hung dejected; they were mute petitioners for cool breezes and rain. The grasshoppers chirped monotonously, the locusts screeched shrilly, both being products of the long hot summer, and survivors of the heat, inclined to voice their exultation far into the fall season.

September yielded them full sway, and burned away day by day, week by week, dusty and scorching, without even a promise of rain. October, however, dawned, misty and dark; the clouds crept up reluctantly at first and then, as if to make amends for neglect, trooped black and threatening toward the zenith. Storm followed storm, and at evening, after the violent crashing thunder and vivid lightning and driving torrents of rain had ceased, a soft, steady downpour persisted all night and all the next day.

The drought was broken. A rainy fall season was prophesied. The old danger of the river rising in flood was feared.

After the sear and lifeless color of the fields and forests, what a welcome relief to Daren Lane were the freshened green, the dawning red, the tinging gold! The forest on the hill was soft and warm, and but for the gleams of autumn, would have showed some of the tenderness of spring. Down in the lowlands a sea of color waved under a blue, smoky, melancholy haze.

Lane climbed high that Sunday afternoon and penetrated deep into the woods.

There was rest here. The forest was rich, warm with the scent of pine, of arbor vitae. There was the haunting promise of more brilliant hues. Thoughts swept through Lane's mind. The great striving world was out of sight. Here in the gold-flecked shade, under the murmuring pines and pattering poplars, there was a world full of joy, wise in its teaching, significant of the glory that was fading but which would come again.

Lane loved the low hills, the deep, colorful woods in autumn. There he lost himself. He learned. Silence and solitude taught him. From there he had vision of the horde of men righting down the false impossible trails of the world. He felt the sweetness, the frailty, the dependence, the glory and the doom of women battling with life. He realized the hopeless traits of human nature. Like dead scales his egotism dropped from him. He divined the weaving of chances, the unknown and unnamed, the pondering fates in store. The dominance of pain over all—the wraith of the past—the importunity of a future never to be gained—the insistence of nature, ever-pressing closer its ruthless claims—all these which became intelligible to Lane, could not keep life from looming sweet, hopeful, wonderful, worthy man's best fight.

And sometimes the old haunting voices whispered to him out of the river shadows—deeper, different, strangely more unintelligible than ever before, calling more to his soul.

Next morning Lane got up at the usual hour and went outdoors, but returned almost immediately.

"The river is rising fast. Listen. Hear that roar. There's a regular old Niagara just below."

"I imagined that roar was the wind."

"The water has come up three feet since daylight. I guess I'll go down now and pull in some driftwood."

"Oh, Daren! Don't be so adventurous. When the river is high there's a dangerous rapid below."

"You're right about that. But I won't take any risks. I can easily manage the boat, and I'll be careful."

The following three days it rained incessantly. Outside, on the gravel walks, there was a ceaseless drip, drip, drip.

Friday evening the rain ceased, the murky clouds cleared away and for a few moments a rainbow mingled its changing hues with the ruddy glow of the setting sun. The next day dawned bright and dear.

Lane was indeed grateful for a change. Mel had been unaccountably depressed during those gloomy days. And it worried him that this morning she did not appear her usual self.

"Mel, are you well?" he asked.

"Yes, I am perfectly well," she replied. "I couldn't sleep much last night on account of that roar."

"Don't wonder. This flood will be the greatest ever known in Middleville."

"Yes, and that makes more suffering for the poor."

"There are already many homeless. It's fortunate our cottage is situated on this high bank. Just look! I declare, jostling logs and whirling drifts! There's a pen of some kind with an object upon it."

"It's a pig. Oh! poor piggy!" said Mel, compassionately.

A hundred yards out in the rushing yellow current a small house or shed drifted swiftly down stream. Upon it stood a pig. The animal seemed to be stolidly contemplating the turbid flood as if unaware of its danger.

Here the river was half a mile wide, and full of trees, stumps, fences, bridges, sheds—all kinds of drifts. Just below the cottage the river narrowed between two rocky cliffs and roared madly over reefs and rocks which at a low stage of water furnished a playground for children. But now that space was terrible to look upon and the dull roar, with a hollow boom at intervals, was dreadful to hear.

"Daren—I—I've kept something from you," said Mel, nervously. "I should have told you yesterday."

"What?" interrupted Lane, sharply.

"It's this. It's about poor Blair.... He—he's dead!"

Lane stared at her white face as if it were that of a ghost.

"Blair! You should have told me. I must go to see him."

It was not a long ride from the terminus of the car line to where the Maynards lived, yet measured by Lane's growing distress of mind it seemed a never-ending journey.

He breathed a deep breath of relief when he got off the car, and when the Maynard homestead loomed up dark and silent, he hung back slightly. A maid admitted Lane, and informed him that Mr. Maynard was ill and Mrs. Maynard would not see any one. Margaret was not at home. The maid led Lane across the hall into the drawing-room and left him alone.

In the middle of the room stood a long black cloth-covered box. Lane stepped forward. Upon the dark background, in striking contrast, lay a white, stern face, marble-like in its stone-cold rigidity. Blair, his comrade!

The moment Lane saw the face, his strange fear and old gloomy bitterness returned. Something shot through him which trembled in his soul. To him the story of Blair's sacrifice was there to read in his quiet face, and with it was an expression he had never seen, a faint wonder of relief, which suggested peace.

How strange to look upon Blair and find him no longer responsive! Something splendid, loyal, generous, loving had passed away. Gone was the vital spark that had quickened and glowed to noble thoughts; gone was the strength that had been weakness; gone the quick, nervous, high-strung spirit; gone the love that had no recompense. The drawn face told of physical suffering. Hard Blair had found the world, bitter the reward of the soldier, wretched the unholy worship of money and luxury, vain and hollow mockery the home of his boyhood.

Lane went down the path and out of the gate. He had faint perceptions of the dark trees along the road. He came to a little pine grove. It was very quiet. There was a hum of insects, and the familiar, sad, ever-present swishing of the wind through the trees. He listened to its soft moan, and it eased the intensity of his feelings. This emotion was new to him. Death, however, had touched him more than once. Well he remembered his stunned faculties, the unintelligible mystery, the awe and the grief consequent on the death of his first soldier comrade in France. But this was different; it was a strange disturbance of his heart. Oppression began to weight him down, and a nameless fear.

He had to cross the river on his way home to the cottage. In the middle of the bridge he halted to watch the sliding flood go over the dam, to see the yellow turgid threshing of waves below. The mystic voices that had always assailed his ears were now roaring. They had a message for him. It was death. Had he not just looked upon the tragic face of his comrade? Out over the tumbling waters Lane's strained gaze swept, up and down, to and fro, while the agony in his heart reached its height. The tumult of the flood resembled his soul. He spent an hour there, then turned slowly homeward.

He stopped at the cottage gate. It was now almost dark. The evening star, lonely and radiant, peeped over the black hill. With some strange working at his heart, with some strange presence felt, Lane gazed at the brilliant star. How often had he watched it! Out there in the gloom somewhere, perhaps near at hand, had lurked the grim enemy waiting for Blair, that now might be waiting for him. He trembled. The old morbidness knocked at his heart. He shivered again and fought against something intangible. The old conviction thrust itself upon him. He had been marked by fate, life, war, death! He knew it; he had only forgotten.

"Daren! Daren!"

Mel's voice broke the spell. Lane made a savage gesture, as if he were in the act of striking. Thought of Mel recalled the stingingly sweet and bitter fact of his love, and of life that called so imperiously.

CHAPTER XXIV

"If Amanda would only marry me!" sighed Colonel A Pepper, as he stacked the few dishes on the cupboard shelf and surveyed his untidy little kitchen with disparaging eyes.

The once-contented Colonel was being consumed by two great fires—remorse and love. For more years than he could remember he had been a victim of a deplorable habit. Then two soft eyes shone into his life, and in their light he saw things differently, and he tried to redeem himself.

Even good fortune, in the shape of some half-forgotten meadow property suddenly becoming valuable, had not revived his once genial spirits. Remorse was with him because Miss Hill refused to marry him till he overcame the habit which had earned him undesirable fame.

So day by day poor Colonel Pepper grew sicker of his lonely rooms, his lonely life, and of himself.

"If Amanda only would," he murmured for the thousandth time, and taking his hat he went out. The sunshine was bright, but did not give him the old pleasure. He walked and walked, taking no interest in anything. Presently he found himself on the outskirts of Middleville within sound of the muffled roar of the flooded river, and he wandered in its direction. At sight of the old wooden bridge he remembered he had read that it was expected to give way to the pressure of the rushing water. On the levee, which protected the low-lying country above the city, were crowds of people watching the river.

"Ye've no rivers loike thot in Garminy," observed a half-drunken Irishman. He and several more of his kind evidently were teasing a little German.

Colonel Pepper had not stood there long before he heard a number of witticisms from these red-faced men.

After the manner of his kind the German had stolidly swallowed the remarks about his big head, and its shock of stubby hair, and his checked buff trousers; but at reference to his native country his little blue eyes snapped, and he made a remark that this river was extremely like one in Germany.

At this the characteristic contrary spirit of the Irishman burst forth.

"Dutchy, I'd loike ye to know ye're exaggeratin'," he said. "Garminy ain't big enough for a river the loike o' this. An' I'll leave it to me intilligint-lookin' fri'nd here."

Colonel Pepper, thus appealed to, blushed, looked embarrassed, coughed, and then replied that he thought Germany was quite large enough for such a river.

"Did ye study gographie?" questioned the Irishman with fine scorn.

Colonel Pepper retired within himself.

The unsteady and excitable fellow had been crowded to the rear by his comrades, who evidently wished to lessen, in some degree, the possibilities of a fight.

"Phwat's in thim rivers ye're spoutin' about?" asked one.

"Vater, ov course."

"Me wooden-shoed fri'nd, ye mane beer—beer."

"You insolt me, you red-headed——"

"Was that Dutchman addressin' of me?" demanded the half-drunken Irishman, trying to push by his friends.

"It'd be a foiner river if it wasn't yaller," said a peacemaker, holding his comrade.

In the slight scuffle which ensued one of the men unintentionally jostled the German. His pipe fell to the ground. He bent to recover it.

Through Colonel Pepper's whole being shot the lightning of his strange impulse, a tingling tremor ran over him; a thousand giants lifted and swung his arm. He fought to check it, but in vain. With his blood bursting, with his strength expending itself in one irresistible effort, with his soul expanding in fiendish, unholy glee he brought his powerful hand down upon the bending German.

There was a great shout of laughter.

The German fell forward at length and knocked a man off the levee wall. Then the laughter changed to excited shouts.

The wall was steep but not perfectly perpendicular. Several men made frantic grabs at the sliding figure; they failed, however, to catch it. Then the man turned over and rolled into the river with a great splash. Cries of horror followed his disappearance in the muddy water, and when, an instant later, his head bobbed up yells filled the air.

No one had time to help him. He tried ineffectually to reach the levee; then the current whirled him away. The crowd caught a glimpse of a white despairing face, which rose on the crest of a muddy wave, and then was lost.

In the excitement of the moment the Colonel hurried from the spot. Horror possessed him; he felt no less than a murderer. Again he walked and walked. Retribution had overtaken him. The accursed habit that had disgraced him for twenty years had wrought its punishment. Plunged into despair he plodded along the streets, till at length, out of his stupefaction, came the question—what would Amanda say?

With that an overwhelming truth awakened him. He was free. He might have killed a man, but he certainly had killed his habit. He felt the thing dead within him. Wildly he gazed around to see where he was, and thought it a deed of fate that he had unconsciously traveled toward the home of his love. For there before his eyes was Amanda's cottage with the red geranium in her window. He ran to the window and tapped mysteriously and peered within. Then he ran to the door and knocked. It opened with a vigorous swing.

"Mr. Pepper, what do you mean—tapping on my window in such clandestine manner, and in broad daylight, too?" demanded Miss Hill with a stern voice none of her scholars had ever heard.

"Amanda, dear, I am a murderer!" cried Pepper, in tones of unmistakable joy. "I am a murderer, but I'll never do *it* again."

"Laws!" exclaimed Miss Hill

He pushed her aside and closed the door, and got possession of her hands, all the time pouring out incoherent speech, in which only *it* was distinguishable.

"Man alive! Are you crazy?" asked Miss Hill, getting away from him into a corner. But it happened to be a corner with a couch, and when her trembling legs touched it she sat down.

"Never, never again will I do it!" cried the Colonel, with a grand gesture.

"Can you talk sense?" faltered the schoolmistress.

Colonel Pepper flung himself down beside her, and with many breathless stops and repetitions and eloquent glances and applications of his bandana to his heated face, he finally got his tragic story told.

"Is that all?" inquired Miss Hill, with a touch of sarcasm. "Why, you're not a murderer, even if the man drowns, which isn't at all likely. You've only fallen again."

"Fallen. But I never fell so terribly. This was the worst."

"Stuff! Where's the chivalry you tried to make me think you were full of? Didn't you humiliate me, a poor helpless woman? Wasn't that worse? Didn't you humiliate me before a crowd of people in a candy-store? Could anything be more monstrous? You did *it*, you remember?"

"Amanda! Never! Never!" gasped the Colonel.

"You did, and I let you think I believed your lies."

"Amanda! I'll never do it again, never to any one, so long as I live. It's dead, same as the card tricks. Forgive me, Amanda, and marry me. I'm so fond of you, and I'm so lonely, and those meadow lots of mine, they'll make me rich. Amanda, would you marry me? Would you love an old duffer like me? Would you like a nice little home, and an occasional silk dress, and no more teaching, and some one to love you—always? Would you, Amanda, would you?"

"Yes, I would," replied Amanda.

CHAPTER XXV

Lane was returning from a restless wandering in the woods. As he neared the flooded river he thought he heard a shout for help. He hurried down to the bank, and looked around him, but saw no living thing. Then he was brought up sharply by a cry, the unmistakable scream of a human being in distress. It seemed to come from behind a boathouse. Running as far round the building as the water would permit he peered up and down the river in both directions.

At first he saw only the half-submerged float, the sunken hull of a launch, the fast-running river, and across the wide expanse of muddy water the outline of the levee. Suddenly he spied out in the river a piece of driftwood to which a man was clinging.

"Help! Help!" came faintly over the water.

Lane glanced quickly about him. Several boats were pulled up on the shore, one of which evidently had been used by a boatman collecting driftwood that morning, for it contained oars and a long pike-pole. The boat was long, wide of beam, and flat of bottom, with a sharp bow and a blunt stern, a craft such as experienced rivermen used for heavy work. Without a moment's hesitation Lane shoved it into the water and sprang aboard.

Meanwhile, short though the time had been, the log with its human freight had disappeared beyond the open space in the willows.

Although Lane pulled a powerful stroke, when he got out of the slack water into the current, so swift was it that the boat sheered abruptly and went down stream with a sweep. Marking the piece of driftwood and aided by the swiftly running stream Lane soon overhauled it.

The log which the man appeared to be clutching was a square piece of timber, probably a beam of a bridge, for it was long and full of spikes. When near enough Lane saw that the fellow was not holding on but was helpless and fast on the spikes. His head and arms were above water.

Lane steered the boat alongside and shouted to the man. As he made no outcry or movement, Lane, after shipping the oars, reached over and grasped his collar. Steadying himself, so as not to overturn the boat, Lane pulled him half-way over the gunwale, and then with a second effort, he dragged him into the boat.

The man evidently had fainted after his last outcry. His body slipped off the seat and flopped to the bottom of the boat where it lay with the white face fully exposed to the glare of the sun. A broad scar, now doubly sinister in the pallid face, disfigured the brow.

Lane recoiled from the well-remembered features of Richard Swann.

"God Almighty!" he cried. And his caustic laughter rolled out over the whirling waters. The boat, now disengaged from the driftwood, floated swiftly down the river.

Lane stared in bewilderment at Swann's pale features. His amazement at being brought so strangely face to face with this man made him deaf to the increasing roar of the waters and blind to the greater momentum of the boat.

A heavy thump, a grating sound and splintering of wood, followed by a lurch of the boat and a splashing of cold water in his face brought Lane back to a realization of the situation.

He looked up from the white face of the unconscious man. The boat had turned round. He saw a huge stone that poked its ugly nose above the water. He turned his face down stream. A sea of irregular waves, twisting currents, dark, dangerous rocks and patches of swirling foam met his gaze.

When Lane stood up, with a boatman's instinct, to see the water far ahead, the spectacle thrilled him. A yellow flood, in changeful yet consistent action, rolled and whirled down the wide incline between the stony banks, and lost itself a mile below in a smoky veil of mist. Visions of past scenes whipped in and out his mind, and he saw an ocean careening and frothing under a golden moon; a tide sweeping down, curdled with sand, a grim stream of silt, rushing on with the sullen sweep of doom and the wildfire of the prairie, leaping, cavorting, reaching out, turning and shooting, irresistibly borne under the lash of the wind. He saw in the current a live thing freeing itself in terror.

A roar, like the blending of a thousand storms among the pines, filled his ears and muffled his sense of hearing and appalled him. He sat down with his cheeks blanching, his skin tightening, his heart sinking, for in that roar he heard death. Escape was impossible. The end he had always expected was now at hand. But he was not to meet it alone. The man who had ruined his sister and so many others must go to render his accounting, and in this justice of fate Lane felt a wretched gratification.

The boat glanced with a hard grind on a rock and shot down a long yellow incline; a great curling wave whirled back on Lane; a heavy shock sent him flying from his seat; a gurgling demoniacal roar deafened his ears and a cold eager flood engulfed him. He was drawn under, as the whirlpool sucks a feather; he was tossed up, as the wind throws a straw. The boat bobbed upright near him. He grasped the gunwale and held on.

It bounced on the buffeting waves and rode the long swells like a cork; it careened on the brink of falls and glided over them; it thumped on hidden stones and floating logs; it sped by black-nosed rocks; it drifted through fogs of yellow mist; it ran on piles of driftwood; it trembled with the shock of beating waves and twisted with the swirling current.

Still Lane held on with a vise-like clutch.

Suddenly he seemed to feel some mighty propelling force under him; he rose high with the stern of the boat. Then the bow pitched down into a yawning hole. A long instant he and the boat slid down a glancing fall—then thunderous roar—furious contending wrestle—cold, yellow, flying spray—icy, immersing, enveloping blackness!

A giant tore his hands from the boat. He whirled round and round as he sank. A languid softness stole over him. He saw the smile of his mother, the schoolmate of his boyhood, the old attic where he played on rainy days, and the spotted cows in the pasture and the running brook. He saw himself a tall young man, favorite of all, winning his way in life that was bright.

Then terrible blows of his heart hammered at his ribs, throbs of mighty pain burst his brain; great constrictions of his throat choked him. He began fighting the encompassing waters with frenzied strength. Up and up he fought his way to see at last the light, to gasp at the air. But the flood sucked at him, a weight pulled at his feet. As he went down again something hard struck him. With the last instinctive desperate love of life in his action he flung out his hand and grasped the saving thing. It was the boat. He hooked his elbow over the gunwale. Then darkness filmed over his eyes and he seemed to feel himself whirling round and round, round and round. A long time, seemingly, he whirled, while the darkness before his eyes gave way to smoky light, his dead ears awoke to confused blur of sound. But the weight on his numb legs did not lessen.

All at once the boat grated on a rock, and his knees struck. He lay there holding on while life and sense seemed to return. Something black and awful retreated. Then the rush and roar of the rapids was again about him. He saw that he had drifted into a back eddy behind the ledge of rock, and had whirled slowly round and round with a miscellaneous collection of driftwood.

Lane steadied himself on the slippery ledge and got to his feet. The boat was half full of water, out of which Swarm's ghastly face protruded. By dint of great effort Lane pulled it sideways on the ledge, and turned most of the water out.

Swann lay limp and sodden. But for his eyes he would have appeared dead, and they shone with a conscious light of terror, of passionate appeal and hope, the look with which a man prayed for his life. Presently his lips moved imperceptibly. "Save me! for God's sake, save me!"

Shuddering emotion that had the shock of electricity shook Lane. In his ears again rang the sullen, hollow, reverberating boom of the flood. Here was the man who had done most to harm him, begging to be saved. Swann, poor wretch, was afraid to die; he feared the unknown; he had a terror of that seething turmoil of waters; he could not face the end of that cold ride. Why?

"Fool!" Lane cried, glaring wildly about him. Was it another dream? Unreality swayed him again. He heard the roar, he saw the splitting white-crested waves, the clouds of yellow vapor. He beat his numb legs and shook himself like a savage dog. Then he made a discovery—in some way he could not account for, the oars had remained in the boat. They had been loose in their oar-locks.

Questions formed in Lane's mind, questions that seemed put by a dawning significance. Why had he heard the cry for help? Why had he found the boat? Why had the drowning man proved to be one of two men on earth he hated, one of the two men whom he wanted to kill? Why had he drifted into the rapids? Why had he come safely through a vortex of death? Why had Swann's lips formed that prayer? Why had the oars remained in the boat?

Far below over the choppy sea of waves he saw a bridge. It was his old familiar resting place. Through the white enveloping glow he seemed to see himself standing on that bridge. Then came to him a strange revelation. Yesterday he had stood on that bridge, after seeing Blair for the last time. He had stood there while he lived through an hour of the keenest anguish that had come to him; and in that agony he had watched the plunging river. He had watched it with eyes that could never forget. His mind, exquisitely alive, with the sensibility of a plexus of racked and broken nerves, had taken up every line, every channel and stone and rapid of that flood, and had engraved them in ineffaceable characters. With the unintelligible vagary of thought, while his breast seemed crushed, his heart broken, he had imagined himself adrift on that surging river, and he had planned his escape through the rapids.

As Lane stood on the ledge, knee-deep in the water, with the certainty that he had a perfect photograph of the field of tumbling waters below in his mind's eye, a strange voice seemed to whisper in his ear.

"This is your great trial!"

Without further hesitation he shoved the boat off the ledge.

Round and round the back eddy he floated. At the outlet on the down-stream side, where the gleaming line of foam marked the escape of water into the on-rushing current, he whirled his boat, stern ahead. Down he shot with a plunge and then up with a rise. Racing on over the uneven swells he felt the hissing spray, and the malignant tips of the waves that broke their fury on the boat and expended it in a shower of stinging drops. The wind cut his face. He rode a sea of foam, then turgid rolling mounds of water that heaved him up and up, and down long planes that laughed with hollow boom, then into channels of smooth current, where the torrent wreathed the black stones in yellowish white.

Lane saw the golden sun, the blue sky, the fleecy clouds, the red and purple of the colored hills; and felt his chest expand with the mounting glory of great effort. The muscles of his back and arms, strengthened by the long toil with his heavy axe, rippled and swelled and burned, and stretched like rubber cords, and strung tight like steel bands. The boat was a toy.

He rodes the waves, and threaded a labyrinth of ugly stones, and shot an unobstructed channel, and evaded a menacing drift. The current carried him irresistibly onward. When his keen eye caught danger ahead he sunk the oars deep and pulled back. A powerful stroke made the boat pause, another turned her bow to the right or left, then the swift water hitting her obliquely sheered her in the safe direction. So Lane kept afloat through the spray that smelled fresh and dank, through the crash and surge and roar and boom, through the boiling caldron.

The descent quickened. On! On! he was borne with increasing velocity. The yellow demons rose in fury. Boo—oom! Boo—oom! The old river god voiced his remorseless roar. The shrill screaming shriek of splitting water on sharp stones cut into the boom. On! On! Into the yellow mist that might have been smoke from hell streaked the boat, out upon a curving billow, then down! down! upon an upheaving curl of frothy water. The river, like a huge yellow mound, hurled its mass at Lane. All was fog and steam and whistling spray and rumble.

At length the boat swept out into the open with a long plunge over the last bit of roughened water. Here the current set in a curve to the left, running off the rocky embankment into the natural channel of the river. The dam was now only a couple of hundred yards distant. The water was smooth and the drift had settled to a slow, ponderous, sliding movement.

Lane pulled powerfully against the current and toward the right-hand shore. That was closest. Besides, he remembered a long sluice at the end of the dam where the water ran down as on a mill-race. If he could row into that!

In front of Lane, extending some distance, was a broad unbroken expanse of water leading to the dam. A tremendous roar issued from that fall. The muddy spray and mist rose high. To drift over there would be fatal. Logs and pieces of debris were kept rolling there for hours before some vagary of current caught them and released them.

Lane calculated the distance with cunning eye. He had been an expert boatman all his boyhood days. By the expenditure of his last bit of reserve strength he could make the sluice. And he redoubled his efforts to such an extent that the boat scarcely went down stream at all, yet edged closer to the right hand shore. Lane saw a crowd of people on the bridge below the dam. They were waving encouragement. He saw men run down the steep river bank below the mill; and he knew they were going to be ready to assist him if he were fortunate enough to ride down the sluice into the shallow backwater on that side.

Rowing now with the most powerful of strokes, Lane kept the bow of the boat upstream and a little to the right. Thus he gained more toward the shore. But he must time the moment when it would be necessary to turn sharply.

"I can—make—it," muttered Lane. He felt no excitement. The thing had been given him to do. His strokes were swift, but there was no hurry.

Suddenly he felt a strange catching of breath in his lungs. He coughed. Blood, warm and salt, welled up from his throat. Then his bitter, strangled cry went out over the waters. At last he understood the voices of the river.

Lane quickened his strokes. He swung the bow in. He pointed it shoreward. Straight for the opening of the sluice! His last strokes were prodigious. The boat swung the right way and shot into the channel. Lane dropped his oars. He saw men below wading knee-deep in the water. The boat rode the incline, down to the long swell and curled yellow billows below, where it was checked with violent shock. Lane felt himself propelled as if into darkness.

When Lane opened his eyes he recognized as through a veil the little parlor of the Idens. All about him seemed dim and far away. Faces and voices were there, indistinguishable. A dark cloud settled over his eyes. He dreamed but could not understand the dreams. The black veil came and went.

What was the meaning of the numbness of his body? The immense weight upon his breast! Then it seemed he saw better, though he could not move. Sunlight streamed in at the window. Outside were maple leaves, gold and red and purple, swaying gently. Then a great roaring sound seemed to engulf him. The rapids? The voice of the river.

Then Mel was there kneeling beside him. All save her face grew vague.

"Swann?" he whispered.

"You saved his life," said Mel.

"Ah!" And straightway he forgot. "Mel—what's—wrong—with me?"

Mel's face was like white marble and her hands on his trembled violently. She could not answer. But he knew. There seemed to be a growing shadow in the room. Her eyes held a terrible darkness.

"Mel, I—never told—you," he whispered. "I married you—because I loved you.... But I was—jealous.... I hated.... I couldn't forgive. I couldn't understand.... Now I know. There's a law no woman—can transgress. Soul and love are the same—in a woman. They must be inviolable.... If I could have lived—I'd have surrendered to you. For I loved you—beyond words to tell. It was love that made me well.... But we could not have been happy. Never, with that spectre between us.... And, so—it must be—always.... In spite of war—and wealth—in spite of men—women must rise...."

His voice failed, and again the strange rush and roar enveloped him. But it seemed internal, dimmer and farther away. Mel's face was fading. She spoke. And her words were sweet, without meaning. Then the fading grayness merged into night.

THE END

Printed in the United States
81799LV00003B/178